Black Moon

Black Moon

KENNETH CALHOUN

HOGARTH
LONDON · NEW YORK

Published by Hogarth 2014

2 4 6 8 10 9 7 5 3 1

First published in Great Britain in 2014 by Hogarth,
an imprint of Chatto & Windus
Random House, 20 Vauxhall Bridge Road,
London SW1V 2SA
www.randomhouse.co.uk

Addresses for companies within The Random House Group Limited can be
found at: www.randomhouse.co.uk/offices.htm

The Random House Group Limited Reg. No. 954009

A CIP catalogue record for this book
is available from the British Library

ISBN 9781781090145

The Random House Group Limited supports the Forest Stewardship Council®
(FSC®), the leading international forest-certification organisation. Our books
carrying the FSC label are printed on FSC®-certified paper. FSC is the only
forest-certification scheme supported by the leading environmental organisations,
including Greenpeace. Our paper procurement policy can be found at
www.randomhouse.co.uk/environment

Typeset in Nexus Serif by Palimpsest Book Production Ltd, Falkirk, Stirlingshire
Printed and bound in Great Britain by Clays Ltd, St Ives plc

For Anya and Sophie

Through the suburbs sleepless people stagger,
as though just delivered from a shipwreck of blood.

—Federico García Lorca, 'The Dawn'

Are you awake now too?

—Wilco, 'Black Moon'

Black Moon

One

Biggs ran in bursts down the street, wanting to move quickly but without attracting attention. These dark blocks between their building and the ransacked drugstore were sketchy. He moved through the cold corridor of shade, relieved to find the streets empty, except for a few figures, stumbling in the distance like drunks. At the intersection, abandoned cars were stalled in a mad jumble and he had to squeeze through the gaps, pressed against the cool barriers of automotive gloss.

Shops were shuttered. Many had been looted – windows smashed, the shelves inside empty. The sidewalk was gritty with glass shards and spotted with ancient stains of chewing gum. A great splatter of DNA, blackened with urban grime.

He could hear distant wailing and the occasional shout or scream from the offices and apartments above. Protruding from one window five floors up, he saw an elderly man leaning far out over the street, teetering on the brink, his thin arms extended toward the sky. Beyond him, a few floors higher, someone was throwing fistfuls of paper from an open window. The sheets drifted and turned like leaves in the air funneling between the buildings.

Biggs crossed to the other side to avoid a stoop where, earlier, he had seen dogs tearing at an unidentifiable carcass – white bone shining through the marbled meat. He ducked down an alley. At the far end, a large woman in a Lakers jersey paced while shouting into her cell phone. 'A lawsuit isn't wanted by you at all believe me very fucking much,' she warned, jowls quivering.

When Biggs neared, he could see that she wasn't holding a phone. Even if she had one in hand, a phone call was an impossible feat. The sky was now without signals, the web of fibers dead in the earth. Networks expiring without sound human minds needed to maintain them.

The woman tracked Biggs with her bleary eyes as he shuffled past. 'Wait one,' she said into her palm. 'Some asshole here like a rat.'

Half a block ahead, a flat-screen TV exploded on the pavement – tossed from several stories up. It fell like an obsidian slate, a tile of nighttime sky. He felt the impact in his teeth, the shatter in his chest.

A storm was gathering behind dark windows and closed doors. It could spill out into the streets at any moment. He jogged two blocks, keeping to the middle of the street, before slowing to a walk.

He could see the ruins of the drugstore now, on the other side of the park.

His wife, Carolyn, was in bad shape. What was it now, six days? Almost a week without even a nod, her head always pedaling in place. She radiated exhaustion: a dying star. Soon what – a black hole?

Biggs had to take some kind of action but, before he did anything, he needed to clear his own head. In the effort to convince her that he too had succumbed to sleeplessness, he had deprived himself of any significant downtime. He had a plan that involved pills and some showmanship, but first some quick sleep out of view was necessary. He went into the park and looked around before pushing into the shrubbery. They used to picnic here, blanket spread on the lawn. Carolyn rolling up her sleeves to get some sun on her shoulders. In the thicket, he found the place where, only two days earlier, he had created a nest of twigs and grass. Curling up inside, it wasn't long before his thoughts took on the lawlessness of sleep. Images and ideas now drifted, unmoored by reason. A heavier sleep soon fell over him like a rug and he saw nothing.

Two hours later, he had a dream: Carolyn shining light into his eyes from clusters of crystalline fractals she cradled in her hands. He returned to the slowly imploding world, blinking at shards of the sun through the weave of saplings.

He sat up, both astonished and relieved. Something inside him continued to hold firm. I *still* sleep. And dream.

Biggs believed that Carolyn, and perhaps millions of others, were responding to the epidemic psychosomatically. He held a desperate hope to cure her with a good story and nothing more than some aspirin, or maybe even some kind of generic-looking vitamin. Whatever. As long as Carolyn couldn't identify it. The pill had to be an empty vessel that she could fill with the medicine of her mind.

He was banking on the climate of heightened susceptibility. The sleepless, in their total exhaustion, quickly lost their ability to distinguish fact from fiction. The unguarded gate in their heads was now propped wide open to suggestion and persuasion. It was a great time for storytellers, he thought, for magicians and, of course, advertisers – his abandoned trade. It was the ideal era for placebos: well-intended, white lies that produce truth in spite of themselves.

He made his way into the pharmacy. Only ten days earlier, a mob had formed in front of it demanding sleeping pills.

They broke in, heaving a motorcycle through the window, and overpowered the few unfortunate employees that had reported for duty. They looted until the police arrived, some naked and others bristling with guns and knives. They chased off the mob. Then it was this tribe of cops themselves who shot out the surveillance cameras and aisle mirrors before snorting crushed pills off the floor and chugging cough syrups.

Biggs stepped through the jagged window frame into the dim cavern of ransacked space. The hall, stripped of its commercial order, was chilling in its silence and disarray. Pills and glass crunched underfoot. There were others there in the poor lighting, picking through the shelves, throwing unwanted items on the floor. He could hear them mumbling, an occasional cough. He avoided them, negotiating the aisles like a maze. In the darkness, he almost tripped over an elderly woman crawling on the cluttered tiles. She grabbed at his pants suddenly, startling him.

He swore and jerked himself free.

'I'm looking and needing for tea,' she said from the floor. 'Can you point me to the tea in the packets?'

'It's all gone,' Biggs said, annoyed.

'They threw it in the harbor is that what they did to gone it?'

'Yeah, that's what they did to gone it,' Biggs said, stepping around her like a snake in the path.

He continued toward the back of the store. He had been here many times before, for the usual items and, at least five times, for pregnancy tests. The shelves were empty but the floor was littered with capsules and tablets. He picked through the empty plastic jars and smashed boxes. The ground was fluffy with the cotton stuffing, remnants of snowfall in the dimness. He knelt and picked out a handful of pills. They sat in his palm like baby teeth. He carried them outside and quickly crossed to the sunny side of the street, like a kid who just made a grab in a candy store. Opening his fist, he saw that the pills were a variety of shapes and colors.

Some say this is what started it, he noted. All these drugs we take. These could be the seeds to our apocalypse. In his agency days, he had worked on a few pharmaceutical accounts, where the notions of truth and fact were never more elastic. Studies show. Ha.

God only knows what's in this stuff.

He picked out five simple white pills – generic aspirin with no discernible branding – and put them in his left pocket. He shoved the rest into his right, thinking they could come in handy. You never know.

Coming home with five magic beans.

He started for the loft, but circled back to the drugstore. He went inside and was able to find two bags of tea, which he gave to the old woman on the floor.

Biggs took the stairs up to the sixth floor. The elevator still worked, but he was wary of being trapped, knowing that no one would come to his rescue. Because he didn't want to encounter any of his afflicted neighbors, he took off his shoes and silently passed down the hall. He listened at his door before putting the key to the lock. Inside, the loft was dim, with the exception of a soft square of light on the floor cast from the open skylight. It was a tiny, book-filled space: table and chairs, a stylish leather sofa. The windows on the far wall hung over a narrow alley and opened to a building identical to theirs, a converted wool warehouse now crammed with dimly lit, book-filled lofts. There was no sign of Carolyn in the main room.

He went to her studio, where she had, until about a year ago, made painstakingly detailed stop-motion films. Along with a small alcove that they used as a bedroom, the studio was the only closed-off space in the otherwise open plan. The walls were padded with sound blankets. The small room was crammed with tripods and lighting stands, racks filled with props, and outfitted with heavy blinds so she could control the light. She was there standing with her back to him, staring out the window.

'Carolyn?'

She turned and, at first, seemed unable to recognize him. She was ancient around the eyes, stooped with weariness and holding one of the articulated dolls from an early film. Her hair curtained her face. She was wearing a promotional T-shirt from a former client of his. It was far too large and hung off her thin frame like a shapeless dress. She had managed to find a slipper for one foot. The other – nails flecked with remnants of red polish – was bare against the wood floor. It gutted him to see her this way: even worse than when he left her, just hours earlier. He still entertained the hope that this thing destroying them would simply play itself out and stop, that he would come home to find her sleeping. He would press his lips against her closed eyes. He would feel her eyes moving as dreams unfurled before them, a churning kaleidoscope of stories.

'Where did you what?' she asked, her face now full of sorrow. 'You don't go for so long all around and around if you're who you said you are.'

He assumed a smile, though it took a beat for his eyes to catch up with the curve of his mouth. With that, the show had begun.

'It's over,' he said, taking her by the shoulders. 'They've done it with a cure!'

He hugged her and felt her stiffen against him.

'Do you understand this that I say?'

It was important to keep the pose of his sleeplessness going, to perform the lazy scramble of diction, the hint of slur.

She looked up at him suddenly and asked, 'Where's my mother is she?'

'Your mother?'

'Mom was here earlier,' Carolyn said matter-of-factly. Her mother had been dead for almost nine years. Yet he was not surprised that she would make an appearance since she was a fixture of Carolyn's dreams. Whatever lived there was now here, it seemed.

'She told me that you should up the floor,' Carolyn said, 'if you think this is ever going to work so you can kill the scorpions there.'

What was this – some echo of old resentments, filtered and mutated as it passed through the sieve of hallucinations?

He led her to the couch and sat her down. The way she said thank you was distant and professional, as if he were a waiter seating her at a decent table. It got to him, but he pushed back on it and stayed focused. She was changing, slipping away with every hour. No one knew where all this was heading, but he didn't want her going there. They had been together for nearly a decade, weathering his career change, her creative block and the resulting depression, not to mention the cosmic denial of their medically ritualized, vaguely carnal request for a child of their own. A project they had both abandoned. But all of that was preferable to what they lived with now.

'Listen,' he said, 'everything's going to be okay now because it's over.'

'Over?' She looked up at him through her hair. She brought up her hand and traced the lines on his face with her fingers. He reached out to her other hand to remove the doll – an elaborate model of a moon goddess. She surrendered it without a word, allowing him to place it on the drawing desk.

'Baby, look,' he said. 'This is what will fix us all.'

Now for the reveal. He showed her the pills in his hand,

slowly peeling his fingers away. They looked pitifully inadequate in his palm, but smaller things have brought down beasts or ended empires. The smallest of things are the plot points of history.

'Hey,' she brightened, 'what are those for doing?' She looked at them with sweet wonder. The temporary absence of exhaustion made her suddenly so familiar – the real her surfacing from under the swamp of sleeplessness. He needed to hug her.

'Big squeeze,' she said in his ear.

He saw an opening and told the story he had been working on in his head, like a campaign for a new client. He had always been good in a pitch and he tapped those skills now as he set up the backstory, explaining that the government hadn't completely disappeared, as everyone believed.

'Representatives are in the city distributing experimental pills. They're wearing such soothing blue suits, like they were cut right out of the sky. I mean, just seeing them makes you want to sleep. You should see the lines,' he told her. 'They wind all around the park – old people, families, everyone. And the pills work. They had people in a glass bus, sleeping in bunks. Just people off the street who volunteered to take the pills, neighbors even. Mrs Mineo from the third floor. Matt Rovogin, Marcy LeBreau. Bunch of other people from the building. You can see them sleeping in there, snoring away. Slobbering on those government-issue pillows. Someone has figured this thing out. Science is going to beat this thing. That's what happens when we get our back to the wall, right? The answers come.'

He had ventured into wishful speculation now. Somehow, perhaps because he had yet to succumb, he had come to believe that the epidemic was merely a sticky little story of demise that moved like spores in the breeze and attached itself to the sides of people's minds. His intention, with Carolyn at least, was to replace that story with another.

Carolyn listened, wincing as she stared at the pills in his hand. She managed to frown and smile at the same time, pained but believing. 'I want to want to sleep so terribly, terribly bad,' she told him, adding: 'Those birds are circling way up but they never come down for the take.'

She was no stranger to insomnia, struggling with it her entire life, especially over the last year. Early in the crisis, they had joked that she was sleepless before it was cool. Now she stared out at him from inside the catastrophe, hoping he could tug her out of the maelstrom. He grabbed her, pulled her close, adoring her. She squeezed his arm with both hands, as if wanting to wring answers out of his flesh.

'You will sleep. You take one of these pills and you will. We both will.'

'I want to take one of those pills,' she said, awestruck by what it offered.

She was buying it. The story itself might prove to be enough. Yet he was prepared to play his ace, if needed. To provide a testimonial that she could believe in. It was risky – dangerous for both of them – but it was the ultimate argument. He would show her that the pills worked.

He would sleep for her.

They swallowed their pills and sat looking at each other. Biggs watched Carolyn's eyes dart around, as if she expected the cure to descend upon her, dropping like a net from above. He had made a big show of dressing in pajamas and coaxing Carolyn into her nightgown – items they rarely wore. Everything should be enlisted to urge along the suggestion. The stage was set for a theater of sleep.

In bed, Biggs lay on his side, next to Carolyn, watching her face. His plan was to see if she would drift off, then follow her up into the clouds. His demonstration would be held as a last resort. He also wanted to make sure she didn't leave the bed and start pacing around. This was how she would pass the night lately: walking about the loft or standing in corners mumbling a litany of regrets to one of her doll actors.

He would get out of bed too, and sit at the table in the middle of their studio, urging her to at least lie down on the couch. Early in the crisis, they watched TV, but now only the words 'no signal found' appeared on the screen.

He wanted very badly to sleep on those nights, but fought it off for the sake of convincing Carolyn that he was also afflicted. He had no idea why he had been spared, at least so far. In fact, he was constantly wondering if he had somehow succumbed and had taken to sneaking off for power naps to test his fears. It was rest he sought, but also proof that the capability persisted, sitting like leaden silt in his veins.

Unlike Carolyn, he had never had trouble sleeping. Early in their relationship, his ability to drop off anytime, and anywhere, had been a point of occasional contention. It offended her not only in that she felt he was using sleep as a means of avoidance, but also because she held sleep so precariously. The slightest noise or change in the light could wake her. Her mind, roaring in the chassis of her skull, pounced on painful memories and worries about the future or the challenges of her studio work, batting them around for hours as she tossed and turned. Meanwhile, he snored at her side. They had decided that sleep was his super-power, just as causing computers to crash or pens to run dry were hers. And not getting pregnant, she sometimes added.

Sleep, or rather dreams, had played an important role in their story, he often felt compelled to remind her, especially when she was critical of his afternoon naps. Soon after they first met, at a forty-eight-hour film festival at school in which writers and filmmakers were randomly paired, Biggs had what they now called The Dream. It wasn't as though they had taken special notice of each other. They weren't even teamed up for the festival. So the fact that Carolyn had been the subject of a particularly intense dream seemed significant to Biggs and, later, to both of them.

In the dream, Biggs was standing on the shore of a vast lake or sea. A dark storm hung low over the water, dragging along curtains of rain and stirring up the waves. A young woman – that film nerd Carolyn from school, he recognized – ran past him, into the water. She leaned her small wiry frame into the current. Her black hair, wildly animated by the wind, was slicked down, tamed, as a wave crashed over her.

She was calling out, but her words were garbled by the wind. Biggs noticed a small boat, a rowboat, drifting out to sea. The riptides pulled it out into the waves as Carolyn struggled to make her way toward it, waist-deep in the churning water. He could see her struggling to stand. The current was tugging at her legs beneath the surface.

He could see, as the rowboat tilted up the side of a wave, that there was someone in the boat. Someone dead. A body lying lengthwise, wrapped tightly in white cloth. The boat rose up the face of the waves, hanging nearly vertical – the shrouded body practically standing on the water – for an instant before flopping over the crest. Carolyn, however, struggled through the wash before her as it rumbled whitely up the shore, knocking her off her feet and pushing her back, then dragging her out in green-black churn.

She screamed after the boat and fought on, but it was clear to Biggs that she would drown. She was already beginning to panic. Then he was in the water reaching out to her, telling her to stop flailing. Lie down in the water, he yelled over the crash of waves. Pretend to sleep on the water facing up at the sky. She followed his instructions and leaned back until her toes surfaced. She drifted within reach as the rowboat continued to travel beyond the waves. He saw it in glimpses as the horizon shifted, now small and close to forever gone.

He was able to grab a fistful of her black hair and draw her into his arms. She clung to him as he carried her back to shore and held her, restrained her, until the rowboat dipped behind the horizon.

Later that week he sought her out on campus, eventually finding her in the dark cave of editing suites. She was cutting together an animation she had made with an origami dove. He watched through the sliding glass door as she composited the dove over a still of an unidentifiable city. Its wings flapped as the city slid slowly by. He had to knock several times to cut through the noise in her bulky, ancient headphones. She turned, frowning. Even as a student, she was capable of a furious degree of focus and hated interruptions when in the zone.

He slid open the door. 'Do you mind if I come in?' he asked.

It was clear that she did mind, but manners overrode her impulse to say no. It was pretty, he thought, how her mouth and eyes weren't in agreement.

He entered and sat on the console table as she pushed the headphones down and wore them at her throat. 'What's up?' she asked, even as her fingers hit the keyboard shortcut for saving her file to the hard drive.

'Hey, it's Carolyn, right?'

'Right.'

'I'm Matt. Matt Biggs? We were introduced at the festival? That forty-eight-hour thing?'

'Oh, yeah. Yeah, I remember. You're a writer.'

'Well.' He smiled sheepishly. 'Not really.'

She looked him over, waiting. Her eyes eager to return to the screen.

'Okay, look,' he said. 'I know this is going to sound really weird, and I've tried not to bother you with this, but it's been a few days now and I can't shake it.'

She smiled and shook her head. 'I have no idea what you are talking about.'

'Okay, well, yeah. Basically,' he said, 'I had a dream. A dream about you.'

She couldn't help wincing. He saw her brace herself for something inconvenient and potentially embarrassing for both of them.

'Not that kind of dream,' he reassured her. Then he told her about the waves, the rowboat and its cargo, how she almost drowned.

Her expression went from a thinly veiled impatience, to skepticism, to a long gaze into the nowhere that hung between them. Tears came to her eyes and he stopped talking.

'Oh, hey,' he said. 'God, I'm sorry. I didn't mean to upset you.'

She covered her face and cried hard into her hands.

'I should go,' he said. He stood and was reaching for the door when she said, 'It's my mother. She's dying and won't admit it.'

He stood, staring down at the pale part in her hair, then sat back down.

Now in bed, trying to feel the pill working, she sighed, a hint of frustration already present in this wordless utterance. He wanted to use The Dream, to reference it as a source of authority. He wanted to say, I had a dream that these pills would cure you, just like when I had a dream that your mother was going to die and you would need to be rescued from your despair. But he had never used The Dream that way. It was a sacred text in their own domestic religion.

She mumbled to herself.

'Shh,' he said softly, as though she were a restless child. Imagine what it must be like, he thought, feeling a dull crushing in his chest. He almost said out loud, It's a blessing that we never brought a little someone into all this. His thoughts flashed quickly to his brother and his wife, together with their newborn in their suburban home. A kind of hell had happened, even out among those quiet streets.

She looked at him.

'Close your eyes,' he told her.

She let her heavy lids drop and pressed her cheek into the pillow.

He felt her rubbing her small feet together – a kinetic mantra, a physical focal point that she sometimes employed. She was trying and he loved her for it. He wanted to tell her to quiet her mind, to let the pill do its job, but he knew that would only cause her to think too much about it. The best thing to do was keep still and quiet. No touching, no singing, no counting of sheep. Just let the story do its job. Let it work its way in.

Minutes passed and she fell still, even her feet coming to rest. Could it have worked already? He studied her face, allowing some hope to spark. But it was immediately snuffed when she clapped her hand over her mouth. She squeezed her eyes tightly shut, crushing out tears.

'Baby,' he said softly. 'Carolyn.'

She shook her head, refusing to open her eyes.

'Come on, don't quit now. I can feel it working in me, that pill in my blood.'

She covered her eyes with her hand, concealing her mounting skepticism.

Now it was time, he recognized. Time for the stain to magically disappear, the hair to grow back on the barren scalp. Time for the blind to suddenly see, the dead to emerge from the cave. Show her.

'Look,' he said, providing an introduction, as if a new actor had arrived on stage.

He yawned loudly. Hearing it – that ancient intake of air – her eyes snapped open between her parted fingers. She stared into his mouth as his body put itself in that obsolete mode. Eyes glazing over, blinking slowed.

She watched, her eyes now wide and intense, her mouth gaping. Was she trying to mimic his yawn? He wasn't sure that this was the reaction he hoped for – this expression of astonishment she now wore.

'See what's happening?' he said, knowing she hadn't seen him yawn in days. Hadn't yawned herself in almost a week. He shut his eyes, let his head sink into the pillow, and spoke to her in whispers: 'It's working. It will with you too but just might take a little longer since you've been without for more.'

Sleep was tugging at him now, pulling him toward the edge, away from her. He let it happen, tumbling off the summit of consciousness in mere minutes. A black honey spread warmly in his mind, smoothing over any cautionary murmurs from the reptilian part of his brain: vague warnings about Carolyn's sudden focus, the clenching of her fists.

He had only slept for what seemed like seconds when his skull exploded.

A lamp had come apart in her hands, but she continued to swing it at his head. His arms came up instinctively, covering himself briefly, then striking out to bat away her blows. He yelled for her to stop, but nothing seemed to get past her animal grunts. He threw himself at her, wrestling down her arms, shaking her. It was as though she was the one asleep, attacking him in a trancelike state. He pinned her to the mattress and she screamed.

She spat out a stream of words from underneath him. She tried to buck him off a few times, but he held fast, pinning her arms behind her head. Eventually she went limp and only the words came at him. The jolt of adrenaline seemed to have provided a window of clear diction, of proper syntax. He listened, pressing the gash on his brow against the sheets and printing a scarlet wound there. He tried to distinguish those utterances that were true attempts to communicate with him from those that seemed to be received from some far-off transmission.

The yawn, she told him, was like a paper lantern or a bag that had opened in front of his face, forming a pink tunnel through his head and revealing his contents. There was shiny stuff in there, and ignorance like charcoal.

When she was a child, she told him, she had seen a man suffering a heart attack on the street. He was a clerk in a liquor store and his co-workers had sat him against a telephone pole on the sidewalk as they waited for paramedics. The man clutched at his chest, doubled over with pain. Carolyn never told her mother this, but she had seen a large spiderlike creature on the chest of the man. Instead of claws, it had drills and it was boring through the man's sternum. No one had ever said anything about this detail, though she was sure everyone, her mother included, had seen it.

I tried to make dreams that would change real dreams, replace them, she told him, adding that this was a great sin, like bringing back the dead.

I'm like the bottom of the ocean inside, she told him, crushing submarines.

Then she broke down, sobbing, 'I'm so tired of animals and their fucking secrets. Who gives them their orders?'

He rolled off her, releasing her hands.

She cried into them and he was moved to gently squeeze the back of her thin neck. 'Baby,' he said. 'I'm right here.'

'What do you know about it?' she mumbled. 'Nothing has ever died inside you.'

She talked into the night, her logic and language gradually falling apart, reverting to a scrambled state. His story, with all its props and stagecraft, had failed to save her.

The next morning he started tying her to a chair.

Two

As planned, Chase drove up to the cinderblock dumpster corral behind the Sunrise Pharmacy and put the car in park, but left the engine running. The white trash bag was slouched in the corner as Jordan said it would be, soft from the heat. Chase scooped it up, backhanding flies, and was quickly back in the car, the bag riding shotgun like some kind of prop for a companion. He drove off, glancing once in the rearview mirror down the strip mall service road. There was no sign of anyone anywhere, just some litter twirling in his wake. He hadn't been seen, he was pretty sure. Great. Now he too – just like that – was stealing drugs from the pharmacy with Jordan.

He took the most direct route home even though that brought him past Felicia's cul-de-sac. He couldn't help glancing up at her parents' house. She wouldn't be there until her birthday visit later in the month. What if he did catch a glimpse of her car in the driveway as he shot by? I'd probably freak out and crash, he thought. Get found dead with a stolen bag of trash in my lap.

He noticed he was speeding past the tract houses, the residential rhythm of manicured yards, driveways, and personalized mailboxes ticking by. Whoa, slow down! He was giddy from the heist, and paranoid, constantly checking the rearview. Yet he made it home without incident, pulling into his parents' garage. The automatic door closed slowly behind him, lowered by the creaking winch overhead. The space going dark. He grabbed the bag and went inside the quiet empty house.

They hadn't discussed what he was to do once home. Just sit and wait for Jordan to get off work, he supposed. But meanwhile, here was all this incriminating evidence sitting on the low shag of the family room. Chase stared at the bag. Jordan had packed it earlier, mixing stolen drugs with trash, then setting it in the corral for Chase to pick up. Jordan had been doing this alone all spring. This was Chase's first run. Maybe he should fish out the pills and burn the rest of it.

Probably better to just wait. Try to be cool for once, he told himself.

Still feeling the jangle of nerves, he went to the living room window and peered out at the quiet street. All was in order. Summer had only started and the world was still weeks away from an irreversible transformation. There was no hint of crisis in this suburban scene: the neighbors' low houses, the pale sky. The sun poured down on the neighborhood, baking the tongue-colored Spanish tiles of the rooftops, yellowing the grass. Dusty leaves hung limply in the parkway trees. It was too hot for anyone to be out. Kids would emerge in the evening and couples walking their dogs. Someone would wash their car, sending suds down the gutter. He studied the sky for a hint of the mountains that loomed over the valley, but they were concealed by the dirty gauze of smog. He had been away for a year, studying at a university on the coast. Yet it felt as though he had never left, despite the fact that the house was completely empty, his family gone.

It had only taken him ten minutes to move in a few nights ago, reclaiming the house from the renters. His parents wouldn't return from Boston – where Chase's dad had accepted a visiting faculty position – until the end of summer. They weren't thrilled about Chase moving in early, hoping he would find a summer job near the university instead. 'But there's no furniture!' his mother had tried. He assured them that wasn't a problem. He'd bring his own.

As soon as classes ended, he packed up his meager belongings, tossing most of it into the massive move-out bins set up in front of the dorms. He was looking forward to putting some distance between himself and the campus, not to mention his roommates. The experience had been a hollow one. Next year, he would try living alone, off campus. It was one of the things he needed to discuss with his parents. He hadn't told them about breaking up with Felicia and they would assume he intended to live with her. The thought of having to explain himself made him queasy. Maybe he wouldn't even go back, he thought. Just work at the music store again.

His first night home, he had explored the rooms in the darkness, feeling very detached from the space, uneasy about the emptiness. He didn't like being alone, not here. There were no curtains and a yellowy light seeped in from the street, casting skewed squares on the floors. Without furniture, the modest ranch-style home felt weirdly vast. In the bathroom his sneeze rang out as he studied his face in the mirror. How had he changed? He had gained some weight in college and now wore his hair cropped close to his head. His dark eyes looked wet in the glass, peering out from under his hooded brow, and his beard scruff framed his narrow face with shadow. This same glass had witnessed his pale youth, his scrawny chest and thin arms; his white, clenched ass and hairless groin. How did it recognize him now? What remained?

Something in the eyes, he knew. An uncertainty that he had thought would be gone by now. A childish worry, too, about being alone in the house – directly tied to his old anxieties about random violence and home invasion. An escaped prisoner, maybe, breaking in during the night, like what happened to that family in Chino years back.

He found that his own room had been transformed almost beyond recognition by the absence of his childhood possessions. The walls had long been stripped of his concert posters and gig flyers, but most absent was the mural he had painted on the room's only unpaneled wall. The renters had requested it be papered over, since they had intended to use the room as a nursery. The imagery, featuring a life-sized tiger and the jungle-infested ruins of a post-nuclear city, was too disturbing for an infant. Now the wall was covered with a pattern of cartoonish butterflies.

That first night, he had set up his small, archaic TV and unfolded two beach chairs that sat lightly atop the low, sand-colored carpet. He slid an old microwave, flecked inside with the remnants of exploded burritos, onto the kitchen counter. The renters had canceled the alarm service and he wished they hadn't. He chained the front door and fell into his old habit of touring the house, making sure all the windows and doors were locked. He rolled out his sleeping bag in his room, threw a black trash bag of clothes in the closet, then called it a day. From the floor, the familiar ceiling looked impossibly high. He was exhausted, so it wasn't long before he started to drift off with hopes of seeing Felicia in his dreams. But the sound of a soft fire crackling in the closet caused him to sit up abruptly.

It was only the trash bag, decompressing in the dark, slowly blooming like a monstrous black rose.

Now, three days later, a white trash bag sat in the family room, smelling of bandages. Chase was standing at the kitchen counter, staring at the bag, when he heard Jordan's car pull up to the curb. He waited for the sound of the door and, after minutes passed, he went to the window. Jordan was still sitting there, frozen behind the wheel of his weathered Tercel. By the time Chase opened the garage, Jordan was walking down the driveway in his blue Sunrise Pharmacy smock and nametag. He was leaner than he had been in high school, with sinewy arms and a face going prematurely gaunt. He had always worn his hair short and spiky, and sometime during the last year he had pierced his ears. The holes in his lobes now held thick black cylinders.

'What were you doing?' Chase asked.

'Working.'

'No, I mean now. Sitting in the car.'

'Oh, yeah, that.' Jordan nodded as Chase slapped the switch and the door descended behind them. 'That was one of the few mainstream media stories I've heard about the crisis. I had to hear the end.'

'On the radio?'

'Yeah. NPR.'

Chase studied Jordan as he walked past, stepping into the house. He didn't believe there had been a story about insomnia on the radio, nor did he believe in the so-called sleep crisis that was Jordan's apparent obsession. Yet, for reasons he was reluctant to reveal, he was helping Jordan steal sleeping pills from the Sunrise Pharmacy. The end of sleep was near, Jordan had explained two nights ago. The human species will die in a fit of hallucinations and devastating physical and mental exhaustion. The drugs, he believed, would not only ensure that he would continue to sleep when no one else could, but they would be a powerful bartering tool when cash, even gold, would mean nothing. He speculated that pills would be the new currency.

'It's coming,' Jordan said. 'Even the clueless are picking up on it.'

He followed Chase into the family room and they stood looking at the white plastic trash bag. Jordan greeted it. 'Hello, little dude.'

'What did they say?' Chase asked, testing.

'Who?'

'The story on the radio. Did they say what's causing it?'

Jordan reached into the loose pocket of his smock and produced a box cutter. He snapped it open and shook his head. 'They're not there yet. They can't afford that kind of honesty. They still have to disguise it as a story about the stock market.'

Chase smiled and nodded. He could see that this annoyed Jordan.

'Don't believe,' Jordan said with a shrug. 'Hang with the sheeple.' He had a dead eye that was fogged and streaked with a jagged scar, the result of a childhood accident when a defective hammer shattered in his face. When he glared, which he did now at Chase, the wound amped up the menace.

Jordan dropped to his knee and grabbed the bag. He bleated like a lamb, then punched in the blade and slashed out a long stroke, revealing the contents inside.

Chase wasn't ready to let it go. 'I bet they didn't even say the word "sleep."'

'When they talk about Big Pharma still raking it in, they're talking about sleep,' Jordan said as he sorted through the trash. 'This is what they're selling. I've seen it in the store with my own eyes. Shit's flying off the shelves.'

He arranged a number of sleep aid products on the floor – boxes that held plastic bottles stuffed with cotton and pills, foil-backed sheets bubbled with capsules. This was his evidence of apocalypse: the anecdotally observed spike in sleeping pill sales combined with online rants of conspiracy sites. He had shown Chase a few, which Chase wrote off as typical Web-based hysteria.

'They say anything about Bigfoot plotting to kill the president?' he had joked.

Jordan, as far as Chase was concerned, had become some kind of conspiracy geek. He watched Jordan stuff the litter back in the bag, then stand, looking down at their take. Not bad. He nodded and raised his hand for a fist bump. Chase obliged.

'Hold on a second. Be right back,' Jordan said, grinning. He slapped Chase on the back as he headed for the front door, moving like a man with a plan.

It was the first time he had seen Jordan smile since he had serendipitously reconnected with his old high school friend three days earlier. Chase had gone to the Sunrise Music Store, hoping to talk his old boss Sam into giving him his job back, if only for the summer. After learning that Sam had been out sick for a week, Chase exited the back way, through the service road, wanting to avoid the coffee shop where Felicia used to work. They would ask about her. They would hope to hear that she had left him. All those assholes were in love with her. Walking along the back of the stores, past the dumpster corrals, he was happy to encounter Jordan on the pharmacy loading dock, slicing up boxes.

That first conversation was pretty one-sided, with Chase explaining that he was only back for the summer. He was sure Jordan would ask about Felicia. After all, he had known her longer than Chase had. But he didn't. He was aloof, remote, eyeing Chase as he continued to hack up the cardboard. Strange, because they had been close once, before Chase ditched everyone to be with Felicia.

Maybe this coolness was about college, Chase had thought. Maybe he still resents that we went off to school and he's here, working his high school job. Jordan had had the grades to go. In fact, he had been accepted to several good schools. It came down to money. His mother, Chase knew, had squandered whatever they had won in the lawsuit over Jordan's eye injury. She lived like a movie star for a few years, driving an expensive car and dating an army of men, before landing her and her impaired son back in a shady apartment complex. Everyone had known this at school. It was always under the surface, especially when the topic of college became central to their conversations.

Fuck college. You're not missing much, Chase wanted to tell him. His freshman year had been a disaster, as far as he was concerned. With Felicia dumping him and making new friends while he shut himself alone in the dorm room and struggled to pass his classes. She blossomed in every school setting – in the classroom, intramural sports, at the parties – and was offered a coveted lab assistant job for the summer. He found himself with nowhere to go but back home. Now he was finding that even connecting with an old friend was a challenge.

Jordan eventually did look up from slashing boxes and engage, but only after Chase mentioned that he was living at his parents' empty house alone until they moved back from Boston.

'Maybe I'll swing by tonight,' Jordan had said, snapping his blade shut. 'There's a lot you should know.'

That was three nights ago.

Now here he was, returning from his car with two more large plastic bags on his back, like some kind of junkyard Santa. It was a matching set to the two already on the premises: one black, one white. Jordan untied the white bag to reveal his entire stash of stolen sleeping pills.

'Check it out,' he said. 'That's a month's worth.'

'A month's worth of sleep, or you've been doing this for a month?' Chase asked as Jordan scooped up the day's score and added it to the mix.

'Doing it for a month. It's an eternity's worth of sleep if you take them all at once.'

'What's in the other bag?'

Jordan retied the white bag and looked over at the black Hefty, staring at it for a beat. 'That's my stuff, man. Clothes and shit. I was hoping I could crash here for a while. I can't take my mom's new boyfriend. Guy's a major dickhole.'

He looked up at Chase, eyebrows raised.

Chase was quiet, weighing things out. In truth, he liked the idea of having someone else in the house at night. He never felt this way at school, always seeking out privacy and hoping his roommates would go away for the weekend. But nights in the suburbs had always unsettled him. As a kid, he had read too many police reports and followed too many serial killer cases, looking for details that put him outside the victim profile. He had a handle on it most of the time. But if left alone, he knew it could color his thoughts in a dangerous way. Jordan's presence would prevent this, he was sure.

'Well,' he finally said, 'we do have the same taste in luggage.'

That night the housemates climbed up on the roof and got drunk with their backs against the chimney. The TV aerial, an artifact from another era, rattled in the wind. A breeze had picked up with the setting of the sun, which had dropped like a warped copper plate through the low, grainy belt of valley haze. They threw the empties onto the lawn below, where the weedy mix of grass silently caught each can. Cricketsong flared up and Jordan silenced it, for a moment, with a belch that rattled the Spanish tile shingles.

'That's talent,' Chase said, but Jordan didn't laugh. He was different now, humorless, and the transformation was a little unnerving. After all, Jordan had been the class clown. He had always loved pranks, like the *Sunrise Guyz* calendar he had threatened to make. An ironic beefcake calendar, he liked to call it, featuring the nonhunky dudes of the dilapidated strip mall where they both had worked their high school jobs. He had walked the idea around, taking imaginary orders and signing up the most unlikely models from the mall's ailing shops: sad-faced Sandy, the cook from the Pizza Palace; the obese Jerry Tift from the auto body shop; the mustachioed Mr Sato at the nursery, who would add an element of Oriental elegance, Jordan insisted. It was a fantasy artifact that people now talked about as if it had really existed. This pleased Jordan. That's so much better than if we had really made it, he liked to say, grinning.

But there was no sign of that whimsy now, as they watched bats swoop at the insects swarming the streetlights and listened to coyotes yapping in the chaparral foothills. Jordan stared intently into his surroundings, speculating aloud about the number of insomniacs sitting behind the glowing windows in the nearby houses. He said, 'Look, we're going to have to step it up. Over-the-counter stuff isn't going to cut it in the long run. We need to get at the stuff that's like a hammer to the head. Schedule two stuff that you see all those commercials about.'

'Can you do that?' Chase asked.

'*We* can,' Jordan said.

Chase could feel him staring at the back of his head, waiting for a reaction. He sensed that Jordan was asking him to do more than merely swing by to pick up the stash. His impulse was to back out now, tell him he wanted no part of it. He was too paranoid, too fearful. But the fact was that he did want a part of it. It had occurred to him soon after encountering Jordan at the pharmacy. Jordan could help him. Knowing this had made Chase both tolerant – of Jordan's new weirdness and delusions – and bold. But in two days of wrestling with it, he had yet to come up with a way to tell Jordan what he wanted without revealing his failure with Felicia. He thought he could get it across disguised as a joke – Hey, while you're in there, grab me some of those man pills. Jordan would see into that. At least the old Jordan would, and he wouldn't let it go until he knew the whole story. Maybe the new Jordan wouldn't give it a thought. Maybe it's time to say something, get it over with. The alcohol helped.

But when he turned to face Jordan, his friend's piercing gaze shut him down. There was something tightly coiled, a lacerating energy, behind Jordan's eyes. The guy really did appear to believe that the world was about to end, and the weird thing was, he seemed to be looking forward to it. He looked determined not only to survive it, but to rule whatever was left. It was spooky, but also potentially useful. At least for now.

'What do you need me to do?'

The plan was simple, but not without risk. They discussed it while tripping along the winding horse trails between the houses, peering through wood-slatted fences or chain-link at the black glossy surfaces of swimming pools and into the TV-lit dioramas of identical homes. Wind chimes stirred, clinking musically in the late night breeze, and heat lightning flashed beyond the mountains, lashing at the warm banks of air over the desert. They kept knocking shoulders and drunkenly lurching off course as they passed a bottle of inky wine between them.

Jordan had done his homework, watching for gaps to exploit while cutting up boxes and stocking shelves. Only pharmacists and techs could get into the cage, which is what they called the elevated and secure area behind the pharmacy counter where the bins were lined with serious drugs. Jordan wasn't a tech. He was only a cashier, which meant he did everything from ringing up purchases to dry-mopping the aisles. The only time he was let into the cage was for cleanup, but he was never alone. A pharmacist had to be present. Even the store managers couldn't get back there alone. There were spare keys, but they were kept in a safe, inside sealed envelopes. The only vulnerability, Jordan had determined, was Mel, the aging owner whose every waking hour was spent aiming anger vibes at the large pharmaceutical chains that were popping up all over town. He claimed they were driving him out of business, despite the fact that sales were up for everyone.

Jordan put his arm out in front of Chase, stopping him, and nodded toward a high window. A silhouette – man or woman, they couldn't tell – appeared behind the blinds, pacing relentlessly. 'See that?'

'Yeah, but so what?' Chase went right up to the fence and peered through the chain-link, swaying from the alcohol. He gripped the fence to steady himself.

'What time is it?' Jordan asked.

Chase checked his watch, squinting as he tried to lock in on the numbers. He saw some ones. 'It's either eleven eleven or one eleventeen.'

'Yeah, late,' Jordan said. 'Past bedtime.'

'That doesn't prove jack,' Chase said, nodding up at the person in the window. He pushed off the fence like a swimmer from the side of the pool. 'People pace,' he said.

They stumbled on, with Jordan rambling about dreams and how insistent they are, how they have to happen. 'Because if you stay awake long enough, you have them whether you're sleeping or not. Hallucinations, man. Don't you see what that means? It means that it's where we really live, and when we're awake, we're just coming up for air.'

'Whoa, dude, you're blowing my mind,' Chase said sarcastically. 'Just tell me how you're going to get into the cage.'

'What cage?'

'The cage at the fucking pharmacy.'

'Yeah, the cage.' Jordan leaned against a eucalyptus trunk and tried to focus. 'Here's the thing. The security gap is Mel. Why? I'll tell you why. Because he's a serious, big-time napper.'

A dog pounced at them from the other side of the fence, snarling and barking in frothy rage. They ran, startled, crossing a street and pushing into another dark neighborhood. The dog's threats receded behind them. When they were in the clear, Chase said, 'Ha-ha. The gap is the nap. That's just perfect.'

'Isn't it?' Jordan slurred. 'His nap is our way in. Every day, he falls asleep at his desk in his office. Head back, mouth all open. I've seen it. If you listen you can hear his fucking snores on the floor. Just talk to him around two and his eyes are drooping shut. He says it's because he's borderline diabetic and something about low blood sugar. The point is I'm going to snag his keys and you'll come in and take them and copy them and then bring them back and I'll have them back on his belt loop before he wakes up again.'

'Great plan,' Chase said, teetering then tipping into irony. 'But what if he can't sleep? What if he gets the insomintis! Oh no! *The whole plan will be foiled! It's the end of the world!*'

'Jesus, keep it down!'

Chase ran down the trail in a pantomime of panicked citizenry. Arms flailing, screaming in silence. He quickly lost steam, stopped, and smiled crookedly, head lolling, as Jordan caught up.

'You think I haven't thought about that?' Jordan said, still serious. 'That's exactly why we have to do it soon.'

'Dude,' Chase said, nearly falling backward. 'Speaking of pills, take a chill pill.'

But Jordan didn't seem to hear him. Instead, he was focused

on something over Chase's shoulder. 'Hey,' he said, 'isn't this Felicia's house?'

They looked into the yard. There were the three avocado trees standing watch over the small pool. There was the diving board that Felicia liked to lie on, reading a book that was held between her and the sun. A memory flapped up. A scorching summer day when they had ridden her scooter from the ice cream shop. He held a cone in each hand as she drove, stirring up a hot wind that attacked the vulnerable scoops. Twin trails of colorful splatter followed them as they raced for home, where their towels were spread by the pool. She accused him of eating them down to the cone during the short ride. It was just like *The Old Man and the Sea,* he explained. How the sharks got most of the big catch. She pushed him in the pool and he emerged with the mushy cones, which they molded to their noses and pecked at each other's mouths like angry toucans. Her brother, sitting in the shade with *The Wall Street Journal,* told them to get a room.

Get a room. Reliving the suggestion now pained him. He wanted to rewind and get back inside that assumption – that they would be doing what young couples do – before things got too tangled in his head and his body refused to follow. And it's not like nothing ever happened. After all, he had been her first, as she had been his. But it had taken a lot of trying, and it soon became clear that it wasn't just some kind of performance anxiety that he would get past after their bodies became more familiar with each other. Later, when she gently pressed him for an explanation, he could only say that he loved her too much. That her tenderness made him feel brotherly toward her. Yet he knew he possessed desire for her. It was there in his dreams. That's where they had explored each other, where he could answer her shape with his.

One time, she had been waiting at the edge of sleep, when

he dreamed they were entangled in the kind of embrace his waking mind wouldn't allow. She felt it animating him behind her, and she tried to cross into his dream by gently taking him inside her. His hands, heavy with sleep, came up to her waist and held her tightly as he rocked against her, pushing deeply into her so that she had to muffle her gasps by biting her arm. But as he surfaced from sleep and his mind began to reorganize his world, she felt him receding. Still half asleep, he fought against it, but his determination quickly took on a tone of anger, of violence. She tried to pull away but he rolled on top of her, pinning her. She fought him off, kicking at him. His head hit the wall. He backed away, then quickly gathered up his clothes and left. That was the last time they shared a bed. A few weeks later, after they had exhausted all possibility of talking their way through it, she pushed him out into the world, telling him to get help – a directive his shame prevented him from pursuing.

All this swam through his mind as he stood looking down at her parents' house, but it was displaced with the sudden, sobering observation that Felicia's dad was sitting on the porch. He could clearly see the man's dark form, backlit by interior light passing through the sliding glass door. Was he talking to someone? His mouth was moving, head bobbing slightly. Maybe he was on the phone? Strange, but nothing Chase wanted to explore at the moment. The thought of being spotted standing at the backyard fence of Felicia's house at two in the morning sent him running.

Three

Lila Ferrell knew from the Internet that it was happening.

Insomnia was a trending topic online. It had crept into everyone's status updates. People were posting videos of attacks on sleepers.

So she knew what was going on when she emerged from her room one summer morning to find her parents sitting at the kitchen table, positioned exactly as they had been when she had said her goodnight. They looked ancient in the golden light from the desert pouring in through the windows. Slumped over warm wine, eyes ringed and twitching. Someone had shredded the napkins.

She said, 'Oh my god, you have it.'

Mrs Ferrell said, 'Have what?'

'This insomnia thing.'

'What insomnia thing?' Dr Ferrell said. He was a therapist at the base – an expert on sleeplessness who worked with war-haunted Marines, trying to get them through the night. A bad liar too. Lila knew.

Dr Ferrell once wrote: 'In the dreams we have forgotten we have had many mothers. We have had many fathers, brothers, and sisters. Even as children we have parented many children of our own in our dreams – sons and daughters that gave us forgotten lifetimes of joy and torment, leaving only a shadow of a memory.

'Playing out of endless familial permutations is one of many tasks the mind tackles while we sleep, our bodies on hold.

'We know everyone we've ever seen with great intimacy.'

Most of the students at the new school were military kids. The girls were pretty slutty, in Lila's opinion. Seemed like everyone was a cheerleader. The boys were all what she liked to call soldier larvae, though her dad hated the term. Not soldiers anyway, he would say. Marines. Lila never saw the difference. They fight wars, don't they, wearing uniforms all the different colors of dirt?

Some of the girls on the soccer team were okay, but Lila came in halfway through the season and didn't really get to know them before summer vacation hit.

Lila decided she didn't need them. These days, you could just keep your old friends by staying connected online. She went home after school and logged in and there were Arielle and Matthew, waiting for her as avatars in their virtual hangout. Arielle looked a lot like she looked in real life, but Matthew had a tiger's head in that other world of theirs, where opting for an animal head was common.

This is not Earth, Mrs Ferrell thought when they first arrived in the desert. He has brought us to some desolate planet. She had abandoned the notion that she could continue her real estate career in this place. It's a landscape without selling points, she told her husband that first night. The only view it offers is that of the sun going down, the dying of the light slowing traffic like a fresh wreck on the side of the road.

'That's putting a pretty morbid spin on things,' Dr Ferrell had said.

It's not a place that you can carry off in your heart, she concluded. This is not what her daughter will picture, years from now, when she tries to remember home. At the very least, memories of an American home involve trees.

On the base, Dr Ferrell was working with a Marine who had rolled a grenade into a tent where eight men were sleeping. The Marine had been an insomniac, though the media overlooked this at the time and focused on his Arab ethnicity.

The doctor had his own struggles with getting to sleep. Lately, it had worsened as he considered possible causes of the epidemic. Many in the scientific community were focusing on a known disease – *fatal familial insomnia* – the idea being that this was some kind of mutated strain of the already mutated variation called *sporadic familial insomnia*. Whereas FFI was believed to be hereditary and limited to less than forty families in the world, and took up to two years to kill the afflicted, this new iteration seemed to be some kind of unstoppable upgrade. Accelerated, resistant, moving through the four stages of demise at three times the speed.

But this was just the leading theory. No real connections had been made, and the medical community remained confronted by its greatest fear: a mystery.

Could it be? Not with fire, not with ice, but because of a protein abnormality? *A change of amino acid at position 178?* His mind kept whirring into the morning hours, a pinwheel spun by the current of his speculations: Maybe more like mad cow. He had seen a report. A chronic wasting disease superbug triggered by a weaponized mammalian prion, ticking in the thalamus. Born in the meat of elk and deer. Bambi's revenge.

But what did he know? He wasn't a researcher or physician. He still practiced the talking cure, his mind tending toward more karmic causes: all those warriors he worked with, afraid to dream, heads crowded with scorpions. Maybe that's where it started and they brought it back from the desert, some kind of contagious psychic wound, guilt based – the empathy system hyperactivated by the policy of preemptive war, the outsourcing of torture. Maybe it was the ugliness that showed itself after the election, the town hall rage and rallies. Except it wasn't restricted to America. Her enemies were also pacing the floor.

Christ, maybe I did it, he proposed. Maybe it was taking this job. It was the last sellout the universe would tolerate. Trying to help Marines by asking them to write alternative endings to their nightmares.

The one interesting place was the aqueduct, Lila thought, which was basically a long concrete-sided canal that cut through the desert. It lay just beyond the cinderblock wall at the edge of their backyard. The banks were steep, also concrete, and when the water was low, it settled into a deep, mossy trough that ran down the middle. Dark, tinted water, silent and deceptively still. At breakfast one morning, her mother read her an article about a picnicking Latino family that was lured in, one after the other, all drowning in their attempts to save one another.

The current was strong, but invisible because there were no rocks to show resistance in the form of rapids or waves. Only a rusted post jutted out of the middle of the stream, and the water parted smoothly around it. A hawk was often perched there. In vast stretches, for miles and miles, there were few opportunities to climb out, since the walls were steep and smooth. She went there every now and then, daring to sit on the slanted cement bank, legs splayed out toward the water. She imagined the drowned family, passing by like figures frozen in the thick amber sap of the water, twisting and tumbling past the saguaro and chaparral toward the faraway sea. They would look like they were sleeping, she imagined. Like I was seeing into their dreams, the nightmare of their family drowning.

No one will understand this, Dr Ferrell was certain. The mainstream media was reporting on it now, making it real. The cities showing signs – commuter traffic dropping, two out of five employees missing work, hospitals filling up and first responders unable to respond. Numbers and trends, but no explanations. He turned off the TV and glanced at his wife, who appeared to sleep at his side.

The reasons, the source. No one understands the economy, or the climate either. If we've learned anything it's that we are in the dark. Come to think of it, maybe it's the dark matter. Makes up most of the universe and we can't even see it. Maybe that vast reservoir of dreams has been depleted.

In the posted video Lila found online, someone is rolling with a camcorder, filming a man with a chain saw. He revs it and the sound is too loud for the camera mike, causing it to distort. Then he starts sawing at a tree. The camera pans up and you can see a woman stirring high in the branches. Other people gather around. They look and sound like neighbors, but they are yelling angrily at the woman in the tree, shaking their fists. Even throwing things up at her. It sounds like Russian, or Polish. Lila can't tell. The woman is screaming down at the man, clearly begging him to stop. But he doesn't and the tree starts leaning, then falls with a loud cracking and moan, shuddering on impact with the ground. The woman comes down with it but the camera can't find her on the ground, in the branches of the fallen tree. Someone titled the video: *Insomniacs Kill Woman Sleeping in Tree.*

*   *   *

For the second night in a row, Mrs Ferrell was pretending to sleep as her husband paced the floor or watched TV in the bed next to her. Her thoughts flashed just on the other side of her eyes. A deluge of fears. What happens now? The body has to shut down at some point. It just can't keep going on and on, forever circling the drain.

She wasn't sure why she was keeping it from him. A cure would emerge before it got too bad. Or it would just stop, ending itself because the alternative was unthinkable. Sometimes she would act as though he had woken her. Then she would attempt to sound groggy as she asked him what the news was, what they were saying about it.

'Go back to sleep,' he would say with an odd urgency. And when he said it that way, it seemed to her that he meant 'sleep' as a place – a physical location, a state or country that she should take Lila and return to, as if it had once been their home. It was only exhaustion, she concluded, that made her hear it that particular way.

Lila pulled a blanket over herself in the backseat of the car. It wasn't cold in the dark garage, but she needed it as protection, as camouflage. Then, curled up, she did it without any problem – the thing everyone was trying to do. Sleep was the summer craze, the must-have of the moment.

She saw how it could be true, what her father had been saying about insomnia being real in some people and imagined in others. You worry so much about sleeping that you can't sleep. A self-fulfilling prophecy, he called it. It had this effect on her, but only to a point. Then exhaustion simply took over and she saw, in pre-REM flashes, the rusted post – the hawk's safe roost – in the aqueduct quickly approaching. She was sliding toward it on the raft. She knew she had to grab it and readied herself.

*   *   *

She can do it, her mother seemed to say.

Through the door, she heard her father say something low and calm, but Lila couldn't make out the exact words.

'She's doing it under her bed,' her mother insisted, after a long silence. 'And I bet that's what she's been doing in the car.'

Lila heard them talking in bed right before she opened the door, their voices sawing like stringed instruments through the wall. His low friction of worry, her high pluck of anger. Then there they were, still as statues. Pretenders. Eyes closed, flopped back on the pillows with the pale green sheets pulled up. She went to her mother's side and looked at her face, examining the stillness for signs that she was there, awake under the surface. She was beautiful like this, Lila thought, admiring the full lips, the smooth contours around the eyes, the swell of cheekbones. And her dad, his face almost unrecognizable without the worried creases. They both looked younger this way, even if they're faking it. Nice touch with the open mouth, Dad. Maybe I should drop a coin in there. What kind of song would I get?

Maybe it was the hurricane upsetting a sealed storehouse of voodoo, Dr Ferrell considered as his daughter hovered over them.

He distracted himself with his ongoing mantra of maybes.

Maybe it was the toxic dust from fallen towers, the ash creeping into our lungs. Maybe it was some ancient spore released by the melting ice. Maybe it was the earthquakes and the tsunamis they summoned. Maybe it was the hole in the ozone, the collapse of the upper atmosphere. Maybe it was the betrayal by the banks. Maybe it was the dead surpassing the living. Maybe it was the ground choking on garbage and waste. Maybe it was the oil blasting freely into the ocean, or the methane thawing at the bottom of the sea. Maybe it was the overload of information, the swarms of data generated by every human gesture. Maybe it was the networking craze, the resurrection of dead friendships and memories meant to be lost, now resurfacing like rusted shipwrecks to reclaim our attention and scramble our sense of time.

When they first arrived, Lila and her mother talked about all the pretending going on. Everyone was pretending they weren't living in a desert where no humans are supposed to live. It's one thing for Marines to train out here, so they can be ready for those faraway deserts where the fight is sputtering on, but regular humans? They had a little joke about it. They would go to the store and every time they encountered another person, they would turn to each other and say, conspiratorially, *Pretending*. Or when they drove past the new rows of identical houses, with their feeble parkway trees: *Pretending*. At the brand-new bank, Mrs Ferrell pointed to the little strip of lawn that lined the smoldering path. 'Look how it pretends there on the ground,' she said.

Lila got in on the action, pointing to a playground that jutted from the side of a fast-food restaurant. The brightly colored plastic playthings about to melt in the white heat. 'Pretending,' she said.

Her mother looked sad. 'Maybe more than anything,' she said.

Everyone was still sleeping then.

Maybe it was the death of an artist at the hands of a zealot. Maybe it was the preachers howling on the subways, or the political lies that hit us like the vibrating hand, killing us years later. Maybe it was the particles made to collide. Maybe it was the return of slavery. Maybe, like the nuts say, it was the chemtrails scarring the sky, the black helicopters, the UFOs hovering over sacred sites. Maybe it was the rewiring of our minds. Maybe the mapping of the genome. Maybe the blowing up of Buddhas. Maybe it was the death scream of dolphins ringing in our ears. Maybe it was the clash of gods, the tug-of-war over our souls, not one of them refusing to let go, instead opting to see us sliced in two by Solomon's sword.

Her father sat down heavily on her bed. She was online at the time, her avatar dancing on an iceberg with some penguins. 'Look, kiddo,' he said, 'we know you can sleep. You don't have to hide it from us. Well, you do, but unless we see you, nothing's going to happen. We'll make sure you do it in a safe place.'

She turned from the screen. 'So it's true that you can't. Both of you.'

He looked at her, then slowly nodded.

'Why can't you take something for it?'

'We have. It doesn't work anymore. Makes it worse, actually.'

Her eyes welled. She blinked against it. 'What's going to happen?'

The doctor slumped, rubbed slowly at his face as if trying to locate a strand of spider web he had walked into. 'I don't know,' he said. He kept his knowledge to himself: how they would start to lose their minds, how their bodies would begin to fall apart, their immune systems collapsing. How they would seek relief at any cost, as some of his Marines had done. She and the dwindling numbers of those like her were rapidly becoming the only reassurance, the only hope, they had. Maybe they were immune. Maybe just late to the party.

'Daddy,' she said, reaching out and squeezing his wrist.

He looked at her hand, configured with fear.

'We knew you were okay when you came in the room the other night,' he said.

'When you guys were faking it.'

'You didn't go ballistic, so we knew.'

She saw it happening like the stars going out, one by one. Her online friends dropping off and never showing up again. If it wasn't summer, she bet school would have been canceled by now. Everything was shutting down, going dark.

Her parents had taken to handcuffing themselves to the piano and giving Lila the key, telling her to sleep in the master bedroom because the door could be locked from the inside. She could hear them talking, sometimes arguing about whether he had betrayed his beliefs by working for the military, or whether they – Lila and her mother – should have moved out here to be with him. Maybe they should have given him more time and he would have walked away from the job.

They all sat down at the kitchen table. Lila's mother took her hand, squeezed it. The best thing was sometimes the hardest thing, they told her. They needed to protect her from the inevitable chaos, but also from themselves. More and more people were roaming the streets, trapped in visions. In other places, where they were further gone, they were tearing people apart. And yet Lila slept.

'I have been hearing about another base where people are gathering,' her father said. 'People like you, who seem immune to all this. You'll be safe there.'

Lila started shaking her head. 'I'm not leaving. I'm not.'

'I've talked to someone – a sleeper, too. He'll take you with him.'

'Listen,' Mrs Ferrell said, 'you'll be safe there. Things are only going to get worse here over the next few weeks. You won't even be able to trust us. Baby, you have to go as soon as we can arrange it. Just until things get—'

'*I'm not leaving!*' Lila shouted.

You could tell something was going on just by looking at the comments people were posting. Under one video, which showed a toddler sleeping on the floor, curled up next to the family dog, thousands had viciously called for the child's death, describing in shocking detail the outrageous acts of violence they felt the child deserved for sleeping. Another video featured a man passed out on a moving train, a subway, maybe. His friends had filmed him, taking turns scrawling obscenities on his forehead and arms with a felt pen. Again, the enraged comments numbered in the tens of thousands.

HIS SLEEPERS THROAT IS TO BE CUTTED!!!

They pulled the piano over one night. It crashed to the floor with an explosion of sound in the still night. Of course it woke her.

She unlocked the door and peered out. Had they been crushed?

There they were, still handcuffed but staring back at her, their eyes red, lifeless.

'Everything okay?' she asked.

'Oh, did we wake you?' Mrs Ferrell said bitterly.

'Oops,' Dr Ferrell mouthed, his eyes hooded under his angry brow.

They glared at her until she shut the door.

They say you start to hear things, voices. Mrs Ferrell considered this. She sat back, pressing against the leg of the piano. Shadowy people appear in the corner of your eye, at the edge of your field of vision. Eric tells me about his patients – Marines who haven't slept in weeks. He has a front row seat in how this all works, what it does to a person's mind. They start speaking strangely, he has seen. Mixing their words up, scrambling the order. But he claims it's somehow poetic, even endearing. I remember his mother, lost in a haze of Parkinson's, talking about a zero flying under the bridge, a war putting too much light in the sky. Going to the Grand Canyon, she told us, because they have a great coffee shop out there. It was chilling and, yes, she could see how the ramblings of insomniacs could have a certain incidental lyricism. But there's the violence too. The murderous rage they feel when seeing others sleep.

'We have to get Lila out of here while our sentences are still straight,' she said.

'I'm making the arrangements. I told you that.'

'For what, though? This place you've heard about? This rumor?'

'I'm trying to confirm it.'

'Where is it, this supposed sanctuary?'

He leaned close, and said in a whisper, though there was no one else around to hear them, 'Somewhere near San Diego. I think it's Miramar. The air station there. I think they are flying people out of there.'

'To where?'

'I'm not sure. Somewhere else.'

The water in the aqueduct didn't look very realistic. Lila had seen better water in virtual worlds online. Still, she dreamed about floating down it on a raft, through the desert, then through the city, and all the way to the beach.

* * *

She was sleeping under the car, not in it, when they found her. Her father rammed his head against the side of the vehicle trying to reach her. She woke to his garbled threats. 'You will never close them again no,' he told her, peering in at her. There was blood seeping down from his brow into his eye.

'I will break open your head,' he said. 'I will bite out your fucking eyes.'

She screamed and kicked at his hand, edging away. Trying to roll, but not enough space, so squirming up toward the engine.

Her mother shrieked from the other side, releasing a piercing, inhuman sound. Lila could see her feet as she kicked at the car, bashing her shins over and over. Then she saw her mother back away and the car started to rock. Her mother groaning, possessed, as she tried to push it over.

'*Stop it! I'm awake,*' Lila yelled. '*Stop!*'

What she ended up doing was taking a rubber raft her father stored in the garage with the camping gear. She pumped it up, then carried it to the aqueduct at dusk. She plopped it in the water and rode the silent current, paddling out into the middle, then grabbed the rusted post. She tied onto it and felt the water pulling at the raft as it swung around and aligned itself with the current. She lay down on her back, head resting against the inflated bow.

Recalling the apologies had made her cry. The raft shook with her sobs and slapped at the water moving under her. She had never seen her parents so devastated, both of them tortured, begging for forgiveness. It was almost as though they had actually killed her. It was not them, they were not them. She wasn't convinced either by new precautions they had taken. Her father bolting rings to the floor, chaining both of them to it. Leaving just enough slack to reach the bathroom, the kitchen. Dogs panting on a leash. The piano had collapsed. They had pulled the legs out from under it trying to get at her. The keys littered the floor like giant broken teeth.

The water moved under her, a black flow of melted glass. She heard the coyotes yipping their wounded lullabies. The thick electric wash of cricketsong, swarming particles of noise. Soon the desert stars seemed to blaze just beyond her reach. Her face was smudged, painted with dusty tears. She hugged herself, curling up, and was able to quickly drop off, exhausted by terror.

Just before dawn, she was woken again by an angry shriek. She looked up in time to see someone in the dim light flying out toward her from the bank, but falling short into the dark water with a heavy splash. Lila peered into the gray light, seeing only a flailing arm, a kick of leg, swallowed by the glossy water. Then, seconds later, the gargled coughs of someone drowning – a man.

She came crashing through the door and there they were, sitting shackled to the iron rings in the floor. Her mother looked at her with alarm, misreading Lila's anguish.

'Oh no,' she said.

Her father was afraid to ask, but put a sentence together: 'You sleep?'

Maybe it was food becoming a prop for food, the rise of corn and its many guises maybe it was the fluoride in the water maybe the author of us all decided to see what would happen maybe it was a distant comet dusting us with its tail of poisoned ice the moon was having its revenge someone uttering a combination of syllables that should never be uttered maybe it was the kids who weren't given a chance maybe it was the finger-fucking of the priests the rise of autotune the piracy the orgy of infringement all the bad books and movies the shift to decentralization the emergence of collective intelligence the flattening of the world. Maybe it was the turtle on whose back we all live slowly shifting its feet the Sasquatch sending out vibes sharks swimming far upstream the game we inhabit had a glitch.

Maybe the angel's horn had finally been blown.

Four

When Biggs first entered the main room of the loft and found her gone, he froze as his mind took in the evidence – the over-turned chair, the rope and bungee cords loosely nested on the floor, the socks he had used to pad the bindings, the open window. He rushed to it, shouting her name, sending it echoing through the alley. There was no sign of Carolyn below. As he checked the bathroom and the closets, he tried to see her fate as ambiguous, sidestepping the obvious: the only way out was down.

He searched the neighborhood for her, hoping to turn a corner and see her sitting on a stoop, confused, maybe scraped up a bit and babbling, but okay. Back in the loft, he sat in the darkness, suffering fits of guilt. Why hadn't he tied her more securely to the chair? Why had he left the window open? Of course, the biggest mistake was that he allowed himself to sleep for so long in the bedroom. How could he have been so weak when so much was at stake? The same way people fall asleep at the wheel of a vehicle traveling at high speed, he knew. Sleep, if held off for too long, had a way of overriding even the body's most basic directives to persist. And though it had lost its grip on everyone else he knew, sleep retained him as its servant. Why? He did not know. Nor did he know if there were others like him.

It occurred to him that Carolyn might have tried to return to her father's house in the suburbs. Maybe she had somehow found her way to the ground, maybe leaping to the fire escape – something she might have tried in her delirious state – and started out for her childhood home. They had discussed this retreat as the epidemic began, wondering if it would be a safer place to ride out the crisis, but he insisted on staying in the city.

His preference was always for the city, even though he was from an incorporated sprawl of housing developments thirty miles out. As early as high school, he had vowed to escape what he perceived to be suburban somnolence. Inheriting his father's insurance agency would be like agreeing to a lifelong coma. Throughout college, his experiences downtown – attending readings and workshops, mixing with artists, musicians, and filmmakers like Carolyn and her friends – confirmed his belief that cities were the flashpoint of consciousness; the suburbs were the geography of sleep. Even now, as the city howled and shuddered, he believed that it was the better place to be – that help, if it was coming, would surface here first.

She didn't buy it. She had wanted to retreat to her childhood bedroom in a city neighboring his own hometown. They had spent their first summer together in that room as she nursed her dying mother and distracted herself by animating The Dream, which had brought them together. Just over a year ago, she had hidden there for weeks, trying to work through what she called a creative block.

'We're safer here,' he tried to convince her. 'Six floors up, where no one can reach us. Plus, everything we need to survive is within a few blocks.'

'Everything that can kill us is within a few blocks too,' she told him. People were her greatest fear, and in the simple math of her reasoning, there were more here, around them, going slowly insane with sleeplessness. At least her father's sprawling property had walls, a gated entry, dogs.

He couldn't help replaying this conversation over and over in his mind, finding it hopeful. If she were to go anywhere, it would be there. Yet he was trapped by indecisiveness. What if he left and she came back?

He decided to wait another twenty-four hours. He put together his old hiker's backpack with items he surmised were necessities: a first aid kit, a flashlight, a tin plate and cup from a camping set. He excavated the closet to retrieve an old light-weight sleeping bag. Sleeping bag. The term already felt archaic and provocative. Sleeping bag, he had said to himself as he cinched it to the pack. Sleeping bag sleeping bag sleeping bag. That's a funny combination of words when you think about it. Sleeping bag. He let out a single bark of laughter and the sound startled him.

With the pack ready and positioned by the door, he returned to Carolyn's abandoned studio.

It struck him as he surveyed the props and tabletop set that she had made a career of being invisible. Carolyn was not present in her stop-motion films, but rather slipped in between frames – in the gap where time was vast and formless – and incrementally repositioned her actors, her landscapes and sets, before retreating behind the lens to snap the shot. 'The human eye can only see so much,' she once said in an attempt to explain frame rate to him. 'There are spaces between the events we see where things get past us. Magicians know this too, with their sleight of hand tricks. If you can find the rhythm of those spaces, the openings in time, you can hide whole worlds inside them.' Is that where she had gone? he wondered. Had she slipped into the gap?

The evidence of her presence was seen in the lifelike movement of her film worlds, the tiny furrowing of brows or gentle flicker of cellophane flames, or the ropy limbs of a warrior churning with momentum past the hand-cranked scroll of sky. It was impossibly time-consuming work, resulting in only seconds of screen time at the end of a week. She had enjoyed the magic of it, the power, but worried over every detail, continually burdened with that particular brand of inner torment reserved for artists. It eventually became too much, her patience or ideas depleted, he never fully knew. She hadn't attempted to make a film – neither stop-motion nor computer animation – in over a year. Not since returning from her stay at her father's house.

At midnight, he slipped out the entryway of the building, legs unsteady with emotion. Over the darkened city, the sky was vibrant, dusted with stars. He crossed the vast, empty post office parking lot as rats scurried from shadow to shadow and office paperwork sliced through in the wind. He called out for Carolyn one last time, then stood motionless listening for a response.

Behind him, his building howled like an asylum. Human voices in every mode of despair seeped through the walls after him. Biggs turned away, the pack bouncing on his back as he crossed the open pavement to the concrete channel where black water slid slowly by. Across the flood channel, the massive post office and train station complex stood silent and dark. He could see people stumbling across the unlit overpasses of the freeway. He knew he could move among them, passing as sleepless so long as he aped their jittery movements and circular speech patterns, their slurry delivery and convoluted logic. But his fear of accidentally falling asleep in their presence was enough to steer him away, knowing the rage it would trigger.

He took his bearings and aimed himself in the direction of Carolyn's childhood home in the suburbs.

*   *   *

At sunrise, Biggs realized he was only a block from the first place they had rented together – an apartment in an old deco building. Could she, in her confusion, have gone back there? He decided it was worth a shot and cut through a weedy lot, then ducked through a gap in a chain-link fence, placing himself on the street of their first address. The building stood under tall, creaking palms. There were doves cooing somewhere in the shelter of fronds and the narrow shadows cast by the shaved trunks stretched across the road. Theirs had been the third floor balcony on the pink stucco structure. He thought about calling up to it, but was reluctant to draw attention to himself.

The front doors were locked, so he set down his pack and hopped the low fence of the yard. Small bungalows lined the yellowy patch of lawn. He stood where Carolyn used to sunbathe, in her own modest way – shorts rolled up, a bikini top or sleeveless T-shirt, the sun bringing out the freckles on her shoulders. They both loved this place, which seemed to be stuck in the 1930s. The building had the qualities of a ship, with its nautical angles and prowlike façade. A church, which had been converted into a banquet hall, loomed behind it. On the cupola, a golden angel lifted a horn to its lips. Newer properties crowded in, including a bland cinderblock medical center next door, which drew anti-abortion protesters on weekends.

Once, standing on their balcony, Biggs had watched as a lone woman parked her car and removed a sign from the trunk. The sign featured the grotesque image of a mutilated fetus torn from the womb. The woman made exactly one pass in front of the building, heels clicking on the sidewalk, before throwing the sign back into the trunk and driving off. When he told Carolyn about it, she speculated that the woman was conflicted and realized she didn't feel right about her stance.

Biggs was less generous. He saw it more as a checklist gesture. Buy groceries. Check. Take car in for tune-up. Check. Protest abortion. Check. 'That's awful cynical, Mr Biggs,' Carolyn had said.

He went up the stairway along the side of the building and found himself on the second floor landing, peering into the windows of the apartment there. They both knew the floor plan well, since they had spent many hours inside with the elderly couple who once lived there. Carolyn had adopted the Whitneys, who were in their eighties when Mr Whitney had a stroke. Every day for nearly two months, she went downstairs in the morning to help Mrs Whitney wash and dress her husband. She prepared meals for four, and their casserole dishes and plates migrated downstairs. Biggs helped too, lifting Mr Whitney from his wheelchair and setting him gently into bed.

One night, he had found Carolyn on the balcony, crying silently.

'What's going on?' he asked.

'She wants me to contact their son,' Carolyn said. 'To find him.'

'He should know,' Biggs said gently, pulling her close. Moths ticked against the light. Beyond her, he saw the many planes – just a loose string of lights that extended toward the horizon – slowly advancing on the international airport, like lanterns on the tide.

She pulled back. 'You know what that would mean.' Yes, they had discussed it. The family would come and put their parents in a rest home, box up their belongings and conclude the couple's mastery over their own lives.

'They need the care, Carolyn.'

'I'll take care of them!' she said fiercely. She was acting very much like a child who had found a sack of abandoned kittens. He knew this was connected to her mother's sad demise. Yet that was different: the entire family had been there with her as she passed away at home. Carolyn, her sister, and their father. Maybe that's what Carolyn wanted for Mr Whitney – a death at home. Yet she knew that the children, whose failures and cruelty Mrs Whitney had detailed, wouldn't see their father through it.

As the situation arced toward the inevitable, Biggs began dreading what it would ultimately do to Carolyn, who was so slow to recover from grief. He was relieved when Carolyn honored Mrs Whitney's request and tracked down the son's contact information on the Internet.

Two weeks later, just as they had predicted, the Whitneys were gone. Their absence put Carolyn in a dark place for weeks, but she eventually pulled herself out of it by finding the loft on the other side of town and urging that they buy it. It was an escape, Biggs knew. But they had been talking about moving for over a year anyway, to get away from the protesters that picketed the clinic every weekend. And they knew they needed to stop renting and buy something. That's what grown-ups do. 'Bottom line is, I'm tired of waiting for that angel to blow that thing,' she said, staring up at the statue overhead from where she had spread a blanket on the little lawn.

The loft was mostly one large room, but it had two small walled-off spaces. 'One could be a studio and the other your office,' she insisted.

'Or a nursery.' He knew she wanted to hear this.

'Let's not get ahead of ourselves,' she said, but he saw the agreement in her eyes.

The move had the desired effect. She loved the new place – the studio and the fact that it had skylights. The walls were lined with shelves, and she insulated their nest with boxes of volumes collected over the years. Their décor was the many colorful spines. She threw herself into a new film and was soon able to wonder about the well-being of the Whitneys without descending into sadness.

Biggs had not returned to the building since the move. He took the outer stairs up to their old apartment, and it seemed as though nothing had changed. The kitchen door was unlocked. He hesitated, listening, then entered. The place was trashed. He waded through the clutter of their former kitchen, the living room where they had assembled their thrift shop furniture. The carpet was concealed under books and papers, cushions from the couch. Biggs picked his way through to the bedroom. There he was startled to find an obese man standing against the wall, blinking in his direction. Or, rather, the man, who was naked except for a sheet that he wore like a diaper, was pressing his back against a mattress that he had propped against the wall.

He looked directly at Biggs, drifting forward a bit so that the mattress sagged toward the floor. 'There is supposedly a guy there standing,' he said to no one. 'But magic of the mind is all it is.'

'No, I'm real,' Biggs said. He wondered what proof he could offer.

The man studied him from behind a wild red beard. His pink complexion flushed, his gut sagging over the sheet, which was held up by a belt. 'If so, then pillow me,' he nodded at a pillow at his feet and held out his hand. 'Pillow me, then we'll see.'

Biggs stepped closer, watching the man cautiously, and scooped up the pillow. The man snatched it from him and tried to put it behind his head. He seemed to be under the impression that he was lying down. The pillow stayed in place until the man leaned forward. It fell to his feet, and when he bent down to pick it up, the mattress folded over him. In a rage, he shouldered the mattress hard against the wall and kicked at the pillow. 'There it is where it was so you are useless,' the man said.

Biggs backed away.

'Yes! Get back to the other side of my eyes,' the man said.

Back in the living room, Biggs called out for Carolyn.

'Oh, Carolyn is who you are looking?' the man called from the bedroom.

Biggs returned to the bedroom and stood in the doorway. He had once stood here before, during an earthquake. Carolyn had refused to leave the bed. He studied the man, who stared back at him. Biggs said, 'Was someone named Carolyn here?'

The man scratched at his enormous belly. 'Here and lots of places. There even.'

Biggs frowned. This guy was out of his fucking head. Or maybe not. 'Listen, was someone here named Carolyn in the last few days?'

'She was here but very smallishly here,' the man said.

Did he mean that Carolyn is small? She is small. Petite. 'What did she look like? What did Carolyn look like?' he asked.

The man didn't respond. He pressed against the mattress and shut his eyes, as if to be sleeping.

'What color was her hair?'

'Ha! She has no hair but fur that's white and orange,' the man offered without opening his eyes. He added: 'Someone was calling her for her in the other room. She did not come that I know of but stayed under the bed.'

He's talking about a cat, Biggs concluded. The person calling for her was him, only minutes ago. The man attempted to toss and turn against the mattress, drunkenly acting out the postures of sleep. He will fall over soon, Biggs speculated. And he will not be able to get out from under the mattress.

Biggs retreated through the kitchen. Before leaving, he checked the cabinets and found a box of cake mix. He tore it open and ate a fistful of the powder while staring out the window, into the empty courtyard of the medical center next door. He could hear the fat man pretending to snore in the other room.

Even the quieter streets at the edge of the city offered evidence of crisis. The total collapse of infrastructure could be quickly read in the chaos – urban order rearranged into a collage of artifacts. The looted stores lined the junk-strewn streets, dark and empty. Occasionally, a telling stench would rise from under a pile of litter and debris tossed from windows, and Biggs would glimpse a bloodless hand, a foot or clump of hair, entangled in the clutter. Bodies were turning up everywhere.

There were living people too, aimlessly roaming the streets mumbling to themselves. They displayed varying degrees of sleeplessness, with those newer to it still somewhat alert to the world around them, walking fairly straight lines. Biggs staggered his stride, blinking as he moved past them. Others were further gone, shouting and growling in the shadows like Carolyn during that last week, when he failed to cure her with his placebo. The memory of her raging against her bindings until the chair fell over. He leaned against a wall, looking very much like the afflicted around him, hand covering his face, shoulders quaking.

She wouldn't want this. She had always said one of his great qualities was his reluctance to feel sorry for himself. It was the thing that had helped her endure her mother's long, terrible death as a victim of cancer, then grieve. She claimed she saw herself through his eyes, which had little tolerance for self-pity and were somehow able to find illumination from the sparest light. She would not be that creature he saw in The Dream, propelled by self-pity into the blackish sea. Just as he, now, should not allow himself to be drawn into the void of her absence. After all, he could still sleep, still dream. Who knew what those dreams had yet to reveal?

He started moving again and made the effort to target earlier times in his memories of her. Stumbling along the street and recalling how she would rest her head on his chest at night – the vanilla smell of her skin and the pleasing weight of her leg thrown over his thighs. Her exotic, short-lived food obsessions: green apple sandwiches, then crab Rangoons, then Vietnamese subs. The erotic and funny shadow plays she produced with her hands, projected against the far wall by the flood of evening sunlight.

He noticed more people on the streets. Maybe, lost in his thoughts, he had ventured into the busy center of this particular neighborhood. He headed toward the nearest intersection with the intention of ducking the crowd and taking the quieter side streets, when he noted that everyone seemed to be shuffling along in the same direction, a trend. This was an odd sight.

Biggs was drawn into the current. He did not fight it. Maybe word was out that there was help of some kind being handed out somewhere down the street. He followed the flow of people, which came to a stop as a small, loose crowd in front of a shop of some kind. Empty cars clogged the street and people climbed over them or pushed around them, filling in the spaces between like soft mortar. The crowd prevented Biggs from seeing the entry and whatever activity that was taking place there. He could see from the signage that the establishment was not a store. It was, or had been, a strip club called Delicious. The windows were painted over and a cagelike iron grille had been pulled across the entire storefront. Biggs climbed up onto a car for a better view. He could see a couple of massive men standing in the dark entryway, on the other side of the gate, looming like bouncers. Could this be about sex? Biggs wondered.

'What's going on?' he asked the man standing next to him on the hood of the car. The man turned, looking both dazed and puzzled. Biggs realized he had dropped his sleepless pose. He started to back away, then lost his footing and fell into the crowd. He hit the press of bodies backpack first, generating a chorus of complaints that was abruptly silenced by a loud clap of gunshot.

The sound hit Biggs like a slap. He righted himself, stunned. The crowd collectively ducked and, until they slowly rose back into place, Biggs could see through to the doorway where a small man with a pistol was now standing between the bouncers.

'Shut up and listen!' he heard the man shout. He had an Indian accent. The crowd quieted enough for Biggs to clearly hear his pitch. 'You want to sleep, you step up with gold. Just gold. Don't have gold? Go get some. Yank some hobo's teeth, rob your church. I don't give a fuck. Just get it. That's the only thing that will get you through these doors and into a bed, where Mother Mary will have you sleeping like a motherfucking baby.'

The crowd reaction was mixed. Some surged forward, either in anger or in desperation, Biggs couldn't tell. Others scattered. In the crush of bodies, he backed away, then turned and staggered down the street. He wasn't sure what to make of the offer, but to think there might be other sleepers compelled him. It seemed like a volatile scene, though. And why at a strip club? Best just to keep moving. Besides, he didn't have any gold, and he guessed that the gun-wielding bouncers at the door weren't open to negotiation.

Biggs walked on, but the strange neighborhood had turned him around. An hour later, he realized he was heading back into the city. Backtracking, he knew he had walked a loop when he found himself in front of Delicious, where a small crowd was still gathered. Night was descending. Biggs, exhausted and frustrated at having made no progress, sat on a car across from the strip club and studied it. The barred storefront, the blackened windows, the dim windows on the second and third floors. He was scanning the building, searching for a way to sneak in, when he thought he saw Carolyn at a third floor window. There she was flashing by – hair pulled back, arms bare – glancing quickly down at the street, at the crowd.

At him?

He stood, his eyes darting over the dark façade. Could it really have been her? He had to get inside. He covered his mouth with his hand, as if suppressing a scream, and felt a metallic coolness against his lips.

His wedding ring.

Five

Just past St George, in the basin of a valley walled with Irish-setter-colored stone, they were pulled over by a patrolman. The trooper sat in his dust-coated car for a prolonged moment before approaching, giving Chase ample time to turn pasty with fear. He grabbed at his own throat and squeezed. 'We're fucked,' Chase said. He began to hyperventilate.

Jordan kept his hands on the wheel and stiffly watched through the rearview mirror without turning his head.

'Just hold it together,' Jordan told him through clenched teeth, talking like a ventriloquist, as if to be seen conversing would somehow incriminate them. 'It's just about speeding. I think I was speeding.'

Chase turned in his seat to see the lawman approaching, edging along the driver's side, one hand sliding along the top of the car. He could hear the squawks of static coming from the officer's radio, a jangling. Keys, maybe. At the sight of the badge, the heavy gun belt and holstered pistol, Chase's chest locked up, his throat clenched.

'I can't breathe,' he said.

'Relax,' Jordan said calmly. 'Don't give him a reason.'

Now the trooper stood at the window, swaying slightly,

waiting. Jordan turned and rolled down the window. 'Hi,' he said cheerily. 'Was I going too fast?'

Chase could not see the trooper's face, only his khaki shirt straining against the swell of belly. The cop belt of weapons and restraints. The officer held out his hand. Chase heard him mumble, 'You know the thing.'

He fluttered his fingers, as if to say, hand it over.

'License?' Jordan said.

'Let's go,' the cop said. The fingers fluttered more impatiently.

Jordan retrieved his wallet from his back pocket and handed over the card. The officer shuffled back to his car without leaning in and inspecting the interior, without even seeing Chase imploding in the passenger seat. Jordan watched him in the rearview, then turned to Chase. 'See? He's just writing a ticket.'

Chase dared a glance over his shoulder. He could see the policeman's form behind the windshield. Sitting in shadow, head bowed, he did seem to be writing, or reading. Maybe staring into a laptop as it crunched Jordan's specifics.

'Don't stare,' Jordan said, studying Chase out of the corner of his eye. 'If he sees you, he's going to want to search the car. You look guilty as fuck.'

'We are,' Chase said. 'We are guilty as fuck.'

'I'm going to say you're sick, you're dying, and I'm trying to get you to the hospital. That's why I was driving so fast.'

'Don't say that. What if he decides to give us an escort?'

Jordan, still staring into the mirror, said, 'You watch too much TV.'

They waited. A truck blasted by, then the occasional car, moving past with a flash of color and glare, a whoosh of air. They heard the piping call of red-winged blackbirds from the roadside grass, the whistle of wind passing over the bristled expanse. A hawk circled overhead and its shadow slid over the road.

'If he goes for the trunk, we have to distract him,' Jordan said. 'You have to fall down and scream like you're dying. Grab your side like you're having an appendicitis or something.'

'Seriously?' Chase said.

'You have a better idea?'

Chase didn't. The cop would have to be very motivated to find the stash, which was under the floor of the trunk in the spare wheel well. A good portion of the pharmacy was stuffed there, in their signature trash bags, both black and white. Anyone searching would first have to remove the tent, clothes, a camping stove, and some boxes of canned goods and pouches of dehydrated trail food. They had tossed in some blankets and comforters, along with Chase's sleeping bag and some clothes, which formed yet another layer of hassle for anyone digging around.

None of this was of much comfort to Chase. There must be some kind of search going on for Jordan back home. This would come up on the cop's dashboard computer. Dots were being connected, he sensed. He closed his eyes and waited to be ordered out of the car at gunpoint.

But the order did not come. After fifteen minutes of nothing, Jordan said, 'What's he fucking doing back there?'

Chase took a quick look. 'He's still just sitting there.'

'What the hell?'

They waited another ten minutes. When the officer failed to reappear at the window, Jordan opened the door and stepped out of the car.

Chase shook his head. 'Dude. No.'

'Just wait here.' Jordan left the car door open, as if he might have to make a quick escape.

Oh, fuck. Fuck. Fuck.

Chase watched his friend raise his hands and slowly approach the cruiser. He heard him say, 'Officer? Is everything okay?'

Jordan approached the driver's-side window and peered in. Chase saw him wave his hand in front of the window, then give a one-knuckle knock. He bent over and practically pressed his face into the glass before stepping back and scanning up and down the stretch of highway. When he saw Chase looking, he shrugged and came back to the car. He slid into the driver's seat.

'What'd he say?' Chase asked.

'He didn't say anything. He just sat there.'

'What do you mean?'

'He's just sitting there, with my license in his hand.'

'Is he dead or what?'

'No, he's moving. A little. Like when I knocked, he kind of flinched. I can't see if his eyes are open because he has sunglasses on.'

'Well, fuck, what do we do?'

Jordan sat in silence for minute. Then he started the car. 'Let's go.'

'We can't just go.'

'What else are we supposed to do, just sit here all day?'

'What about your license?'

'I don't need it anymore. No one does.'

Jordan pulled away slowly. Both of them watched for a re-action from the patrol car, but there was none as it receded behind them. Jordan picked up speed and soon they were over the grade. The road shimmered with fumes behind them. There was no pursuit. They kept going.

'I bet he hasn't slept in days,' Jordan finally said.

Maybe there was something to this insomnia shit, Chase thought as they pushed on through Utah, the vast salt lake like a massive spill of light to their left. He couldn't explain the behavior of the patrolman. 'Maybe he got a call with some bad news,' Chase proposed, miles later. 'Like his whole family was killed in a crash or something.'

'Nope. He wouldn't just sit there,' Jordan countered. 'I'm telling you, he's gone sleepless and his brain is fried.'

It was the second inexplicable thing Chase had witnessed in twenty-four hours. During the drugstore heist, the cops had behaved in a more predictable manner, doing exactly what Jordan had hoped they would do. After Jordan had deliberately triggered the alarm by opening the loading dock door, the police showed up like good little monkeys to deactivate it and check the store for any signs of a break-in. Chase and Jordan watched them from across the lot, where they sat in the car, parked among the junked wrecks that formed a ring of automotive tragedy around the body shop. Through the dark storefront windows they could see the firefly bobbing of flashlights, the occasional sweep of beam, as the cops searched the premises.

Mel, the owner, played his part too. Failing to rise from his deathlike way of sleeping and drive to the store to reset the alarm. Chase couldn't blame him. It was three in the morning, after all. The cops pulled out abruptly, right on cue, and they were left with silence.

Chase had driven back down the access road to the loading dock door and dropped Jordan off, and it was while Jordan was in the pharmacy pillaging the bins that Chase saw the second strange thing. He had looped back to their hiding place among the wrecks to wait for Jordan's signal. From this vantage point, he saw that the lights in the music store were blazing, when only minutes before the place had been dark as a cave. He watched as his former boss, Sam, appeared in the lit show-room, wearing a T-shirt as he danced around the floor with a cello in his arms, his long beard swaying. Chase leaned forward, watching as Sam waltzed behind cymbal trees and stacks of amps, then reappeared in the window, close enough for Chase to see that he wasn't wearing any pants.

Before he could begin to make sense of the scene, a flash of light had caught his eye. Jordan signaling from inside the drugstore. He said nothing of Sam's behavior as they put their homes behind them, catching the 15 North, hot wind roaring in the windows when they dropped into the desert. They glided past suburban matrices of light as they cleared the planned communities of Victorville and Hesperia. Four hours later, after passing through a wide expanse of darkness, they saw the dreamlike city of Las Vegas blazing in the distance. It read like an illuminated monument of wakefulness – a hive of unsleeping souls all working under the assumption, however temporary, that there was no tomorrow.

They took a cheap room in Idaho Falls, at a motel across from the river park. They had been driving for eighteen hours straight, not counting the half-hour pause with the state trooper. They collapsed on the narrow mattresses and both slept until late in the evening, when a loud truck pulled from the lot, gears grinding.

'I've stayed here before,' Jordan said from his bed. 'With my dad.'

Chase looked over, checking Jordan for some sign of emotion. His father had been killed in a biking accident when Jordan was twelve. A year later, Jordan lost his eye. Jordan didn't like to talk about either incident, nor the fact that his mother had squandered the lawsuit money. Maybe the trip, being back where he had spent time with his dad, had shaken things up. But Jordan's face revealed nothing as he stared up at the ceiling. He asked, 'You ever fish?'

'No.'

'I got really into it,' he said distantly. 'There's something really weird about feeling an animal, under the water, biting at the bait. That little tug. It's like a mild shock, or a message coming from another world. I used to dream about it a lot, just that feeling in my hands.'

'I guess I did try it once, but I never caught anything.'

'Up where we're going, you can see the fish in the water. Trout. Can catch your limit in less than an hour and cook them on the spot. I used to live for those trips.'

Chase noted that a wistful tone had finally crept in. He tried to say something cheerful. 'Let's do that when we get up there.'

Jordan didn't respond. He continued to stare at the ceiling.

Chase stood and pulled on his pants. 'I'm going to get us some food,' he said.

'There's a pizza place next door.'

'I'll get us some sandwiches.'

'Get me a meatball sub,' Jordan called after him as he stepped outside. He crossed the parking lot, checking to see that the car was okay. The thought occurred to him to dig out the pills – his pills – from the stash. He was eager to try them, to see if they worked, though he wasn't even one hundred percent sure Jordan had bothered to get them. They had pulled over in the dark, as soon as they cleared the suburbs, and stuffed everything into the trunk. Jordan insisted he had grabbed the right stuff. 'Decades' worth of boners,' he said. Chase regretted not nabbing a few then. To do it now would put them at risk. Anyone could be watching.

He crossed the street and took the stone stairs down into the park. The river pooled there, where a small dam created a wide pond and water spilled like a layer of glass on the concrete banks into mild, stepped rapids. The sun had set, but there was still some seepage of light in the sky, beyond the black shapes of tall pines. Swifts darted over the water, through swarms of mayflies. The air smelled of forest and fish. Standing at the water's edge, Chase pulled his phone from his pocket and called Felicia.

As expected, he got her voice mail. She had stopped taking his calls. If they communicated in real time, it was limited to text. She held to her assessment that they had said everything they could possibly say.

Had she answered, he would have skipped over the hello and jumped right into conversation, saying, 'A year ago I was living under your bed.'

'Rent free,' she would probably respond, not missing a beat. It was true that, after his parents had rented out the house and left for Boston, he had had a gap of homelessness before he could move into the dorms. Their plan was to have him secretly stay in her room for a week, then relocate to a series of camp-sites on the beach. She would join him and they would live out the remainder of their summer in the same tent that was now in the trunk of Jordan's car. Her parents weren't fans of the idea, but they had little leverage since she was paying for college herself – with her saved-up waitress money, and now with her work-study salary as a lab assistant. She shamed him, really, with her drive and industry. His parents covered his tuition and he did not need to work, yet he sleepwalked through his courses and squandered his afternoons napping in his dorm room.

By the time they arrived on campus, all of their clothes and their hair smelled of campfire smoke and their shoes were filled with sand. They had spent their mornings waiting out the June Gloom, then tanning in view of the titlike nuclear reactors of San Onofre. In the evenings, they watched sparks fly from the fire ring. They had connected their sleeping bags and pressed together at night for warmth, but Chase would eventually pull away, defeated and frustrated when his body wouldn't respond to her urgings. Sometimes he would go back out and sit by the fire until she fell asleep, telling himself that he was guarding her from psychos and rapists that wouldn't hesitate to cut through the fabric walls and drag her into the night.

Now, hearing her voice instructing all callers – not just him – to leave a message, he felt the sting of losing her. At the beep, he said, 'Hey. It's me. I'm standing by a river in Idaho, believe it or not. I'm here with Jordan. It's been kind of crazy but I wanted to remind you that we're meeting up for your birthday, okay? It's going to be different, Fel. It's going to be so different. You'll see. Yeah.' He didn't know what to say, but didn't want to hang up. 'Hear that river? I'll hold up the phone. Oh, Jordan says hi. I'm a little worried about him. It's a long story, but basically he thinks the world is ending. Because of sleep, or people not being able to sleep. He's so sure that he almost has me convinced. But if something like that was really happening, Dr Dreamy would have told you already, right?' He immediately regretted saying that, so he deleted the message and said everything over, leaving out the dig at Felicia's boss before hanging up. There was no reason to bring up his jealousy of Dr Lee, whom she described as a genius, even if he had meant it playfully. It was time to at least act like he wasn't threatened.

He hung up and stared into the darkening water. A shadow darted through.

When Chase returned to the room, he found that Jordan wasn't alone. A girl was sitting on his bed, laughing at something Jordan had said. Maybe twenty or so in age, blond hair pulled back, and wearing a blue industrial apron over jeans and a sweatshirt. This explained the cleaning cart outside the door.

'She thought the room was empty,' Jordan said. 'She really wants to scrub our bathroom.'

'Oh, yeah, I'm just dying to do it,' the girl said, laughing.

Jordan introduced him. Her name was Michelle and her mother owned the motel. 'I like working at night,' she explained. 'Usually most of these rooms are empty, to tell you the truth, so I can even vacuum.'

'So you sleep all day?' Jordan asked.

'Most. Well, to about three thirty in the afternoon.'

Jordan gave Chase a knowing glance and he wasn't quite sure how to interpret it. Chase handed him a sandwich, which was wrapped in foil.

'So you're a vampire,' Jordan said, smiling slyly at the girl. He unpeeled the foil and took a huge bite of the sandwich. It was the old Jordan.

'Maybe I am,' the girl said, grinning, 'but I like ice cream, not blood.'

Chase said, 'Do you want some of this?'

He held out half of his own sandwich.

The girl shook her head. 'That's sweet, but I already ate.'

Jordan said, 'She's ready for dessert.'

'You guys finish those sandwiches, and I'll take you to the best place in town for banana splits.'

'Don't you have to work?' Chase asked.

The girl shrugged. 'That's what's cool about working for your family. I mean it's not like they can fire me,' she said with a laugh.

Jordan didn't put up much resistance when Chase said he was going to opt out of the banana split hunt. He was polite enough to ask twice if Chase was sure, but quickly let it drop. Again, he flashed a look that Chase now read as a signal that he was interested in this girl. It seemed he was able to put his apocalypse on hold to spend some time with a Mormon cutie in Idaho Falls. This relieved Chase, since it made Jordan more familiar. But it also confused him, after a conversation they had had a week earlier, following their late night drinking strolls along the horse trails, when Chase revealed why he was willing to help Jordan.

Chase wasn't exactly sure what he had said that night. He had drunk with the intention of bolstering his courage but had gone too far and eventually blacked out. He vaguely recalled uttering the names of the pills he wanted: 'Viagra, Cialis, you know, Spanish Fly, whatever.' By the time Chase had woken up in his room the next day, Jordan was already back from work and standing over him with a bottle of water.

'Better drink this,' he said.

Chase took it and sat up while Jordan pulled back the blanket Chase had hung as a makeshift curtain. He poured the cold water into his mouth, the water glugging musically as it spilled forth. It made his teeth ache.

Jordan had sat on the narrow windowsill. Chase glanced his way. It was hard to read his face. Had he agreed to do it?

They sat in heavy silence.

Jordan shifted his position and said, 'Didn't you used to have a mural on that wall?'

Chase stared at the butterfly pattern before him. 'It's still there,' he said. 'Underneath it.'

'What was it, some kind of animal, right?'

'A tiger.'

He recalled the rest of the painting – the abandoned city overwhelmed by jungle. The ruins of civilization. A sci-fi geek's apocalyptic vision before he fell in love with Felicia. Now it was more Jordan's thing, apparently, the collapse of civilization. He would see it as an omen, a prophecy of some kind, no doubt. But it was actually just proof that the mind moves on, that these dark preoccupations are really just retreats from coping with fears of growing up and that it's life itself that helps you get past it. His parents had told him it would happen. He had come to their bedside when he was sixteen, woken them in the middle of the night to say that he didn't think he could do it.

'Do what?' they asked in the darkness.

'All the things you're supposed to do.' He listed his fears involving relationships, having kids, a career.

His father was first to respond after a long silence. 'You're thinking too much,' he said. 'It works out.'

'Of course you can't imagine it now,' his mother said. 'You're a kid. That's why kids shouldn't do all those things. You're not meant to be ready.'

To help him get ready, they sent him to a psychiatrist once a week during his junior year. The doctor told him, on the topic of relationships, that what usually occurs is you start loving someone and a kind of alchemy happens, and all these fears, which are just fears of the unknown, turn into a desire to be brave or, even better, to move through your days, months, years, without giving all those dicey moments we all face too much weight. Sure enough, that's what had happened. Almost. He had almost reached that place with Felicia.

He stood up and stepped out of the sleeping bag that gathered at his ankles.

'Watch this,' he said.

Chase pressed himself against the cool wall, remembering the image underneath against the measuring stick of his body, the span of his arms. For one entire high school summer, he had worked on the mural every afternoon. It was another kind of therapy. He still knew the wall intimately, because of the spatial demands it had placed on him. So much so that he was able to measure out a distance from the center, crab-walking his hands, until he came to a spot of interest. He scraped at the wallpaper there, eventually pulling away a strip to reveal two green eyes, the size and color of limes, smoldering with predatory intensity.

It was a good trick. Jordan actually smiled.

He stood and came over to the wall. With his fingernail, he worked up a tiny flap just below one of the eyes and pulled at it. A strip came away, revealing the side of the tiger's nose. A stripe of tooth and tongue.

Within minutes they were tearing furiously at the wall, uncovering the tiger's face, the piercing gaze and tensed mouth. The rich orange of the animal's fur blazed out at them. They revealed the heavy paws and muscled shoulders of an animal regally posed in the heart of its reclaimed dominion: the crumbled buildings overtaken with vines, the entire scene lushly framed by the glossy, wide fronds and the curling tendrils of ferns. Over the beast's shoulder, partially hidden by vines, was the dark mouth of a cave – the tiger's lair.

Standing back, it looked as if someone had thrown a chair through a window, punching through to an alternate world. Chase saw his work with fresh eyes, thinking it would embarrass him. But it wasn't bad. He had always been a good painter. He had a way with images. But the subject seemed to him laughably childish. Hopefully Jordan saw it that way too, and recognized that he had now embraced the same common and trite fantasy in his world without sleep.

'Pretty lame, right?' Chase had finally said.

Jordan looked at the wall, then turned and put his back against it. 'Actually, I think it's pretty fucking cool. *Come, Armageddon, come,*' he sang.

And though he had leaned away, it seemed to Chase that he

had closed the distance between them, smiling the way he was, showing some hint of warmth.

'You know what else I think?' Jordan had asked.

'No idea,' Chase said. He had started raking up the shredded strips of wallpaper with his feet.

'I think I should kiss you. I think that would be the best thing for you.'

Chase looked up. 'What?'

'I said I think I should kiss you.'

'I don't get it,' Chase said. 'What? You think I'm gay?'

'No one isn't,' Jordan said.

'So you're into guys now? Is this what you're saying?'

'It's not even a thing,' Jordan said. 'It's one of the things we'll lose when we stop sleeping.'

Chase put it together. He must have given details about the problems he had with Felicia. Jordan had come to an obvious conclusion. It didn't exactly surprise Chase. After all, Felicia had suggested the same thing. But it wasn't true. If it was true, what about the dreams? To this Felicia had said maybe he was just suppressing it all. People are good at denial, she told him. It sounded implausible to Chase. Just something she had picked up from her psych classes. Or maybe something Dr Dreamy had told her. The thought that she had maybe discussed their situation with a stranger horrified him.

Chase didn't want to talk about it then or now, with anyone. But what was Jordan telling him about himself? He immediately thought back through Jordan's history, looking for clues. There were plenty of girls. Was this openness part of Jordan's new end-of-the-world outlook somehow?

Jordan stood.

'Get the fuck away,' Chase said, his fear spiking and urgent.

Jordan raised his hands and sat back down in the window. 'Whoa.'

'Why do you have to say such weird shit?'

A long silent pause passed.

Finally Jordan spoke. 'What I'm saying is you have to get down to the truth of things, and pretty soon that's all we're going to have, so you might as well get ready. Those pills you want are just lies. A lot of pills are just that – shiny little lies that we choose to swallow. They won't help you. Pretty dumb, or desperate, to think they will, don't you think?'

Chase looked at Jordan in the window frame. Behind him the air was unusually clear, blown west by a mild Santa Ana. He could actually see the jagged, moon-colored mountains that rose up like storm clouds over the valley. They looked muscular, dense, convoluted. Orange light from the descending sun colored the peaks. Jordan followed his gaze, turning to look out the window. The mountains were like a massive fist hanging over them. Somewhere along the way, living in the foothills of these often shrouded peaks, Chase had picked up the belief that truth was conditional and subject to change. Sometimes it was as real as a mountain range. Other times it was just a blank space in the sky. 'Look,' Chase finally said, glancing up from the floor. 'I don't believe in your stupid insomnia thing and I'm still helping you.'

Chase recalled how Jordan hadn't looked his way. He seemed to mull things over, then nodded slowly out the window. It was as if he was signaling someone on the mountain to let time keep rolling forward, if only to see how it went.

Now here they were, three states north, the heist behind them. Jordan had somehow managed to pick up a girl without leaving the room. The girl tried to entice him to join them by describing a local attraction: two graves side by side in the graveyard, one inscribed WERE, the other WOLF.

'It makes for an awesome profile picture,' she insisted.

'I'm really tired,' Chase said. This was true, but he had another motive for staying behind.

As soon as he was alone, he went to the car and began his excavation of the trunk.

Six

The sun would stop it from happening. There were no working streetlights anymore, no power in the lines. Drivers couldn't see in the dark – sleepless people who shouldn't be driving anyway. But it was coming, the sun, a dumb but faithful beast of fire, as though no one had told it everything had changed.

Lila could see the sky lightening behind the craggy mountains, a peach-colored hue slowly seeping into the pale canvas, bringing some definition to her surroundings. It was such a relief to see. The night had taken forever, and, though it was receding, the crashes continued. Over her shoulder, on a winding concrete overpass suspended high overhead, she heard the shriek of tires and the crunch of metal and glass as another speeding car joined the long chain of collisions. She winced, then lightly touched her swollen face. She was pretty sure the Marine driver was dead, if not from their crash, then from the eight or so crashes that had followed in the darkness. The car – which her father had given to the Marine for his willingness to drive her – had probably been gradually crushed in a vise of impact.

'The sun will stop it,' she said aloud.

Daylight revealed that she was standing in the basin of a wide, arid valley. They had lived in the area for a while, though many miles from here, when she was small. She only vaguely remembered it – a date tree in the yard, the elderly neighbors splashing in their pool behind the oleander hedge, coyotes close to the fence at night, a fire on the ridgeline and ashes snowing down.

The freeway cut through the valley and the loop of overpass, from which she had staggered down, swung close to a neighborhood. She could see that it was a development of identical tract homes, painted in gradients of beige and roofed with pink Spanish tiles. It was very similar to Lila's own neighborhood out in the desert, behind the treeless, moon-colored mountains that loomed in the background. The trees along the parkway were little more than frail saplings tethered to posts for support. She knew from watching neighborhoods sprout in the desert how it had evolved from skeletal two-by-four frames mounted on concrete slabs to stuccoed and shingled homes. How the lawns had been rolled on like carpet, how the crosswalks and yellow lines were spray-painted from a slow-moving truck. As she entered the closest cul-de-sac, she could see that the sidewalks were flat, unbroken by roots or earthquakes, and the gutters were dry and free of moss. Under the chaotic clutter of junk on the lawns and driveways, and a heap of ashes in the middle of the street, it was all brand-new.

As the sun inched upward, she felt wobbly in the legs and sat on a curb. What now, what next? How would she get home? Where was it, exactly? She was overwhelmed by a sudden sense of her smallness, her solitude. Crying into her hands, she was careful not to press too hard on her battered face. They had betrayed her by sending her away, her parents. For her own good, they kept saying, her own safety, to protect her. They hadn't been themselves for a couple of weeks now, alternating between fits of delirious rage and apologetic promises to have her taken somewhere safe. A base near the coast where her father had contacts. They have others over there, they told her. People like you who can still sleep. But where? The Marine driver would say nothing about it, though she had pressed relentlessly from the backseat.

God, this is so messed up.

She pulled off her left sock, which was soaked with blood from a gash in her thigh, and dropped it in the dry gutter. It looked gruesome, like an organ torn from a body. There must be a cut somewhere on her head too, because every time she pressed her hand to her temple, it came away daubed with red. Her entire scalp and swollen jaw pulsed with pain. Her lip was still bleeding; she could taste the blood. What frightened her was seeing part of her own face out of the corner of her eye.

A number of vultures were circling the overpass, like trash bags in a dust devil. Lila had counted more than two dozen when a woman came out of the house across the street and noticed her sitting there trying to decide what to do. She crossed the street, her oversized flip-flops clapping against her heels. Judging by the woman's frazzled appearance and darting eyes, Lila figured that she had been sleepless for some time. She was stout, wearing a simple denim skirt and a man's pinstriped dress shirt that was buttoned wrong. Her wide bulldog face looked sunburned and her lips were cracked.

The woman said, 'Why is it you that is sitting out here with these bloody socks in the middle of everything? Come home away from here!'

Lila allowed herself to be led into a nearby house, pulled along by the woman's grip on her arm. Not the one from which the woman had emerged, but the house immediately behind Lila. There, the woman sat her at the kitchen counter. The sink was filled with broken dishes. There were blackened pots and pans on the floor and what looked like shards of dried pasta everywhere, as well as dark soupy splotches. Lila wanted to plug her nose. Something was rotten somewhere close. On the windowsill, a dark avocado seed was suspended over a jar by toothpicks, like a dried and shrunken heart. There was no water in the jar, Lila noted, just a filmy residue. Maybe someone drank it. She wished she had water now, and food.

On the counter, there were several bowls of uneaten cereal. Someone, perhaps this woman, had placed one before each barstool. The woman glanced around. She opened the refrigerator to reveal its emptiness. Like the inside of a spaceship in the future, Lila thought, looking past the woman into the white plastic void. She picked out a cornflake from the bowl in front of her and put it on her tongue. It was soft and stale. She didn't care. It had been weeks since she had had cereal and almost two days since she had eaten anything at all.

The woman seemed surprised by the empty state of the fridge. She stood back and studied it, scratching at her heavy thigh. Her legs were webbed with purplish veins. She walked past Lila and opened a door, which Lila could see led into a dimly lit garage. Was there a car in there? Could she drive it home? Could she drive a car? It didn't look that hard, you just turn the wheel when the road curves.

The woman stepped into the garage and shut the door behind her.

Lila sat alone in the kitchen, painfully chewing fistfuls of the soft flakes and watching the door. Her hope was that a larger meal was coming her way, and the possibility of eating overrode all other concerns for the moment. Five, then ten, minutes passed and the woman did not return. Lila got up and tried the faucet. Water miraculously spilled from it with a steady hiss. She leaned into it and drank, though this made her head wound throb. She could feel water passing through her throat and sloshing heavily in her stomach. The water was cool and airy, almost fizzy, as it flowed from the tap. She finally broke away from the stream, gasping for air, and wiped her mouth with her hand. She looked out the window. The street was empty. She liked that – the absence of people. People without sleep were trouble, broken and dangerous even if they've loved you their whole life.

Before she sat down, she held the jar under the faucet and filled it so that the bottom of the avocado seed sat in water. Then she placed the jar back on the windowsill and returned to the counter, where she started in on another bowl of stale cereal.

Eventually, she heard movement from the hallway. The woman must have come back in through another door. The shuffling footsteps came closer. The woman who emerged was not the same woman who had led her into the house. This woman was tall with short blond hair – nearly as pale as her white top, which was streaked with orange and yellow stains. When this new woman saw Lila, she stopped, her deep-set eyes narrowing on Lila's forehead. 'Baby, what is it that has happened there onto your head?' she said.

Lila's hand went up to her wound, then to a gash on her left thigh. 'What is what what?' the woman said, now very concerned.

She went to the sink and wet her hand, then rubbed at Lila's head wound. The rubbing hurt. Lila pulled away. 'No it's not,' the woman said to herself.

She pulled off her top and wet it under the sink. The woman wasn't wearing a bra and her small, freckled breasts were even whiter than the rest of her skin. She held Lila's head against her chest as she scrubbed at the wound. It felt like her face was on fire.

When Lila squirmed, the woman said, 'Hold so that.'

Then more firmly: *'Hold so that I can.'*

After she had cleaned the wounds on Lila's head and thigh,

she put the shirt back on, though backward. Lila could see her bloodstains on the shirt.

'Go you with them and find wood that burns,' the woman ordered cryptically.

She shooed Lila off the barstool and into the hallway. It was a white-walled corridor with four doors and a low ceiling. Family photos hung on the wall and Lila studied them for a moment. The pale woman was there, and children with her deep-set eyes and light skin. One girl was maybe the same age as Lila. There were pictures of her dressed as a cheerleader. A man, bald and lean, also appeared in the pictures – the father. There were older black-and-white pictures too, the family before the family. The people like you who came before you, Lila found herself thinking, hinting at who you'll be. Clues to the answer that's you.

They had pictures just like this, she and her parents – her own family. Though they hadn't been taking pictures much the last couple of years, she realized. Probably, she considered, because her dad had moved out to the desert base to start his new job while she and her mother had stayed in San Jose. For a while, Lila wondered if her parents had separated. She was astonished when her mother casually told her that families weren't necessarily permanent. It was only after Lila tearfully demanded that she be allowed to live with her dad that they made the move. The desert turned out to be all her mother said it would be, only crappier. But at least we're together, they'd all say, to the point that it became a punch line in their wry attempt to transform any mishap or unsavory condition of the environment into a shared joke. When the air conditioner broke, when their neighbors shot automatic rifles into the air on the Fourth of July. Or once, while they were driving, when they spotted a dead fox on the shoulder of the road being torn at by coyotes.

'At least we're all together,' her mother had said with fake cheer.

Lila thought she heard a cough coming from the end of the hallway. One of the doors was cracked open. She went to it and listened, hearing the quiet sounds of someone in the room – the occasional sniffle, the squeak of mattress. When she slowly pushed the door open, she saw the man from the pictures sitting naked on the corner of the bed. He was staring at the TV, which wasn't on. Lila could see that he was wearing tennis shoes, no socks. He was remarkably thin, with his ribs exposed, his sinewy frame, the dark patch of hair and his penis like a bird in a nest. She had seen a lot of naked adults over the last few weeks, especially in the desert, and was surprised at how quickly she had gotten used to it.

The man caught sight of her out of the corner of his eye. He made no move to conceal himself. Without turning in her direction, he said, 'Go away, Dad. You can see that there is a nasty business here. Fuck, your beard is such a ruiner.'

Lila backed out of the room. Off to the left, another door was partly open. She pushed through and found herself standing in a dimly lit bathroom. To her relief, there was water in the toilet. The whole neighborhood must still have water. They had lost their water in the desert a few weeks ago. One well on an abandoned property became the source for the whole community, requiring her father to walk out to it every morning with a five-gallon gas can and fill it up, sometimes fighting with others who tried to hoard the source. When that became too dangerous, they started taking water right out of the aqueduct and boiling it.

Lila used the toilet, savoring the whoosh of the flush but watching with skepticism. Maybe that was the last flush ever. Yet the bowl slowly refilled.

Just like hope, Lila thought. That was what her mother would have said.

Then she held her breath and turned, daring a look into the mirror. She could hardly recognize herself. One side of her face was swollen. A cut ran from her scalp to just below her cheekbone. It was red and raised, but probably from that woman scrubbing at it, she thought. Both eyes were purple with bruises, though one was worse – puffy, the skin stretched tight, shiny. Her lower lip was swollen and split. There was the painful gash on her thigh too. She knew she was supposed to feel lucky to be alive, but she didn't feel much of anything. This must be what shock feels like, she thought.

She should never have allowed herself to fall asleep. The Marine driver wasn't a sleeper. She thought she had sensed it when he first arrived at the house, but he did a good job of hiding it. He probably saw faking it as the only way off the base, arranging with her father to serve as courier in exchange for medical authorization and the car. Who knows where he was really going, and when he planned to ditch her. It was the car and the clearance he wanted. Probably just made up the safe haven.

The Marine didn't say a word as her father threw her into the backseat. Her mother seemed to have forgotten their agreement, or her instincts took over. She started slapping and clawing at her father, screaming, 'You let her go!' But he already had Lila in the car, door slammed. He slapped the trunk and the Marine floored it, throwing her back as the car lurched forward and ignoring her screamed demands to stop and let her out. Instead, they rushed headlong and she watched her mother draw back into the distance, swallowed by the desert darkness.

She tried to reason with the back of her driver's head – a square block of meat, prickly with high-and-tight hair, rising from bulky shoulders. A faceless face with no connection to emotion. He sat stony and fixed, eyes squinting at the unlit road ahead. The engine whined as they shot up the on-ramp and onto the deserted freeway, the scarecrow forms of Joshua trees blurring by. She sobbed and screamed behind him, face glazed. His response was to stomp the pedal, throwing her back against the seat, her head banging against the door as he swerved to dodge something in the road. She sat upright and again he swerved hard, this time tossing her into the door to her left. Her head hit the window, rattling her brain.

'Better strap,' he said. These were the only words he spoke to her. It was his erratic driving that encouraged her to pull the seatbelt around herself.

The swerving continued, though she saw nothing in the road ahead of them. She should have known then that he was an insomniac, dodging imaginary obstacles. But instead she thought he was just trying to keep her off balance and out of sorts, or in such a state of worry about his driving that she would give up trying to get him to turn around. Still, she had no intention of falling asleep in the presence of this stranger.

But crying was like a sleep drug for her. About an hour into the drive, as they ascended the overpass, she nodded out. It was only for a few seconds, but it was enough for the Marine, who caught the dropping of her head in the rearview. He turned in his seat, reaching for her with both hands, completely abandoning the wheel and shouting incomprehensibly, and she jolted awake. She screamed, seeing the crashed car rushing toward them over his shoulder. The impact sucked him halfway out the windshield and spat him back into the driver's seat with a smashed face. The car crumpled toward her as she folded over, bashing her mouth on her own knees, then blasted back with the seat into the trunk, which held her like a coffin. She had had to kick it open to escape, then wandered a few wobbly steps before collapsing on the shoulder, out cold. Another crash – a car plowing into the trunk she had just fled – jolted her back onto her feet. She darted for the concrete barrier that lined the road and almost threw herself over before realizing she was several stories above the ground.

Now she was in the home of some strangers, staring into the mirror looking like a stranger herself. Maybe she was no stranger to them, she pondered. Maybe I just think I'm a stranger because I was in a crash. I'm just confused or something. Happens in movies all the time. Maybe I really do live here and have always lived here and that other life is just a dream I had. That's why they don't ask who I am. But she also knew that the sleepless are like that. They lose the ability to recognize people.

Plus, they get really stupid, Lila reminded herself as she stepped back into the hallway. You can talk them out of anything, except shipping you off to some imaginary safe zone, even though it's just a rumor passed around by a bunch of sleepless lunatics.

Oh, man, my face kills.

She found the next door closed, but not locked, so she ducked inside. The bed was unmade. There were posters of shirtless actors on the wall. Eww. That whole vampire scene that Lila hated. This must be the cheerleader's room. She went over to the desk where a laptop sat. She tried to turn it on. Nothing, of course. There were trophies on a shelf – cheer-leading victories.

Catching her reflection again in the dresser mirror, it occurred to her that she should change her clothes. She searched the drawers and selected a pair of jeans. Sitting on the bed, she stripped off her bloodstained shorts and slid into the pants. They were a little loose, but she cinched them tight around her narrow waist with a belt.

She decided she wanted a shirt with buttons so she wouldn't

have to pull anything over her battered and bruised head. When she pulled open the closet door, she was confronted by two large eyes in the darkness – unblinking eyes the size of saucers. She gasped and drew back before her brain could process what she was seeing.

It was a mask.

The mask of a team mascot. An owl's head with enormous eyes. Oh, yeah, she thought, recalling the local high school's team name from the trophies. The Night Owls.

Out on the street there was a commotion at the center of the cul-de-sac, where the ashes were piled. Several parents and kids had emerged from the houses and were gathering in the hot, shadeless street. Lila could see them from the cheerleader's window. She wondered if one of the kids was the cheerleader. Maybe they had food out there. The soggy cornflakes hadn't quite filled the void of hunger. She had been carrying it for weeks now – always hungry, always sleepy.

She made her way to the gathering, stepping over the clutter of objects the houses seemed to have coughed up on the yellow lawns – toaster ovens, printers, shattered televisions and torn-up books, soiled clothes, soccer cleats, documents blowing around. Broken shards of circuit boards and plates, barbecue grills. How had all this gotten outside? A couple of young boys came up behind Lila, running past her toward the ash pile, where two men were standing with rifles slung on their backs. Lila studied them. Could they drive her home? They wore only shorts and boots. One had a long, wild beard that hung down, dark and wet over his sunburned chest. 'The fire we want is higher than the houses,' the bearded man said.

The other began speaking before the first man had finished. 'The ones who don't are the ones who won't, better understand.'

Lila saw the woman who had first led her into the house. She came out the front door of yet another house, walking with an elderly woman in a bathrobe. Trying to lead her by the arm, but the two of them staggered drunkenly off the path into the lawn. The older woman slumped toward the ground, but the other woman held her up. Another woman was watching from her upstairs balcony as she threw papers into the air. There were about a dozen kids now. Most of them were younger than Lila – eight, ten, maybe. Boys and girls, thin and scraped up. Red-eyed and twitching with nervous energy, practically panting like dogs chained to a tree.

There were four teenage boys and three girls. A fat boy was shirtless, exposing his floppy breasts and loose folds of skin. Another boy with a scruffy goatee held a homemade spear. It looked to Lila like a curtain rod with a knife duct-taped to the end. He looked old enough to drive, not that messed up. Sleepless, she could see, but not that sleepless. Not too sleepless, yet.

One of the girls was wearing a tattered yellow prom dress. She could not be the cheerleader, Lila knew, because her hair was nearly black. The cheerleader, like Lila, had dirty blond hair. Another girl was wearing a one-piece bathing suit and running shoes. The third looked as if she could be going to school, with capri pants and a flowered blouse. She was holding a broken umbrella over her head, creating a circle of shade with a bite taken out of it on the ground. Everyone seemed to have a hammer or a hatchet, or even a monkey wrench, in their hand. They wavered where they stood, blinking at the light.

Without any apparent cue, the boy with the spear let out a whoop and started running down the street. Everyone ran after him, including Lila. She did not know what else to do, nor could she tell if they were running with or after the boy. But if it led to food, she would play along.

She ran with this pack of sleepless youths past the end of the block and into a nearby field of dust, charging down the shallow remnants of vague furrows and past the gnarled wicks of long-dead grapevines, the sky a pale blue parachute above them, the vultures churning over the ribbon of concrete suspended on columns like an ancient aqueduct. They yipped and howled. The older boys seemed to be racing toward some unspoken destination, with the teen girls trailing, the smaller kids already falling behind and fanning out.

Lila ran hard, trying to keep up. Each step caused her head to pulse with pain, her thigh wound to flash hurt like lightning. But she had been a junior varsity soccer player at school and some of that was still with her now, in her muscles and the targeting of her steps, as they crossed a dirt road and started down a slope of quartz boulders. Below was an undeveloped stretch of washland – a field of speckled rocks and mustard stalk. Lizards darted off sun-baked boulders as they approached.

Sleep inside them, she thought. Tiny doses. Lila could hear their dry skittering in the weave of dead grass.

The kids stomped like wild horses through the terrain, now heavy-footed, breathing hard. No one was whooping now. They fell a lot, crashing to their knees, skidding in the dust. Soon it was just the older kids. They ran down old winding motorbike trails, through the brittle scrub, scaring up grasshoppers. The land gradually tilted toward the bottom of the valley. In the distance, a lone tree billowed darkly among the thistles.

They turned toward it.

Is that the wood for the fire? Lila wondered. Are they going to chop it down?

The tree was a massive old oak and, Lila could see as they approached, it held in its branches a sloppily built tree house. Really it was a mishmash of old cable spools, plywood, and two-by-fours hammered and roped together. There appeared to be a main platform, suspended like a crude porch about twenty feet in the air, where the trunk split into three massive branches. Higher up were some actual semienclosed and roofed platforms, perched like crow's nests. Boards had been hammered into the trunk to serve as rungs of a ladder. Some of the tree house had already been dismantled and there were loose pieces of wood, prickly with rusty nails, among the layers of dead leaves all around the base of the tree. Not enough to build a fire, everyone seemed to know as they waited to catch their breath, standing stooped over in the shade of the tree.

Some of the smaller kids caught up and immediately started for the ladder. The boy with the spear pulled them down and started up himself, leaving his weapon propped against the elephantine trunk. The other kids followed while Lila lingered on the ground, hoping her head would stop hurting. The run had set her heart pounding, shooting pain through her scalp and down the side of her face. She delicately caressed her cheek, her face screwed up. Looking up into the dark branches above, she watched the boy in the lead reach the first deck, then start climbing toward one of the higher rooms. Others swarmed out over the deck itself and began hammering at it with rocks they had scooped up, or viciously attempting to pull up boards with their hands. She backed away as chunks of timber started flying down, bouncing off branches and landing in the dense compost of fallen leaves.

Crazy winged monkeys, she thought.

She had started for the ladder when a shout of raw anguish – of volcanic rage – came from above, followed by a scream. Lila flinched and backed away, knowing the sound. A sleeper had been discovered. Is it me? she couldn't help wonder, panic coursing through her. She scanned the branches and followed the movement of kids as they stormed up one of the ladders, climbing like rats up a rope. High above them, where the boy with the spear had gone, there was a struggle taking place in one of the crow's nests. Through the slats of the platform, Lila could see only hints of violent motion.

The boy continued to yell, a guttural, choking sound, as someone – it sounded like a woman – screamed, 'Get away from me!'

Then a body fell, scream trailing after it all the way down.

Lila could see that she was falling headfirst. A teenage girl. Lila turned away before the body hit and the screaming stopped. But the kids were still shouting from above. They threw their rocks and tools down at the body lying in the leaves. Lila backed away, then started running.

She ran back through the washland, using the overpass as a landmark. As she neared it, she heard claps of gunshot coming from above. They were killing something up there. She ran on, returning to the neighborhood, which again appeared empty. The house she had explored earlier was also vacant. She moved quickly down the hallway and into the cheerleader's room, where she sat on the bed and began to cry. She fell forward on the bed and sobbed into the cheerleader's pillow. It was just too much and it wasn't fair that she had to do it alone. How was she supposed to stay alive in this totally messed-up world? It was her, she thought. It had to be the cheerleader sleeping in the treehouse, then screaming and falling. The hammers and rocks raining down. She recalled the terrible soft thud the rocks made as they struck the helpless body, then shook her head violently, trying to work loose the memory, but was stopped by the pain it summoned.

She thought she heard someone in the hallway. Oh, crap. What if someone should come in? She wiped away the tears and looked for a place to hide. The closet made sense. She opened it and there was the mask, staring out at her. Eyes wide. Always open. Always awake.

*   *   *

When she emerged later that night wearing the mask, she was just as invisible as she had been before. No one questioned the unblinking eyes that covered her face. They were like badges, she thought. Sleepless people actually got out of her way, stumbling over one another. No one had the attention span or focus to investigate. A couple of kids leaned in, trying to see her face through the owl's open beak, but it was too dark to see much of anything. What would they see anyway? Just two black eyes, the pout of her mouth. Dirty, tear-stained cheeks.

A fire was eating at the stacks of wood piled in the center of the cul-de-sac, casting a Halloween glow. But it had already lived out the most luminous phase of its lifecycle, having flared up and roared, throwing a column of smoke into the breezeless air, then settled into submission. Now the neighborhood people piled on what looked like skinned dogs, strapped with belts to heavy grilles – repurposed iron window grates. They hooked and dragged the grilles into position over the flames with golf clubs.

The smell of burning meat made Lila's mouth water. She ventured closer to the fire and watched the neighborhood women turn the flayed bodies of birds on stakes. The birds looked like scrawny chickens. Then she caught sight of one of the heads when it flopped into view. They were vultures, she could see. They had shot vultures. The dogs, she realized, were probably the coyotes she had seen strolling up the freeway on-ramp at dawn. Of course they had eaten their own pets, just as they had in her own desert neighborhood. But this cul-de-sac had been blessed with a great lure for living creatures. The pileup of speeding cars on the overpass, the bodies as bait. The scavengers came in to feed and now they were feeding on them. She retched inside her mask, her appetite gone.

She sat on the curb, her back against a feeble parkway tree, and watched what had become of the human race through the mesh eyeholes of the mask. At first glance, or maybe from a distance, she thought the scene could be mistaken for an end-of-summer gathering. A block party barbecue. With people standing around, sharing food, talking about how summer was ending and school would soon start. But the reality was no one was talking about anything. They seemed oblivious to one another as they gnawed on half-cooked hunks of meat. They wore bizarre assemblages of clothing, or no clothes at all. They squatted like apes to shit on a neighbor's lawn or crouched to suck water out of a sprinkler.

She stood, head in a tiny globe of darkness, fronted by the same protective pattern found on the wings of butterflies and the flared hoods of cobras. She decided it was time to go. Drowsiness pooled behind her eyes, starting to press. It would be suicide to fall asleep here. What she should do was find a bike. She was only about two hours away from home by car, she figured. The desert lay beyond the wall of mountains. She could get there. Just follow the freeway back, up through the pass, right?

In her mask, Lila moved away from the fire, scanning the yard clutter for anything she could use. A map, maybe. She was prodding at a file cabinet someone had apparently pushed out a window when she heard a groan.

She squinted into the darkness, into the backyard of a large house. Suspended between two trees, she could see the faint form of a hammock. It sagged, its middle swollen with the weight of a body. Again, a groan.

She edged toward it.

His face was also concealed, behind a slick mask of blood, but she knew it was the Marine driver. One eye was mashed shut and the other looked out at her from a gummy slit. She could see that his legs were strangely bent, propped before him. Blood bubbled from his flattened nose and his lips were flecked with shards of teeth. She winced inside the mask. They must have brought him here. Found him during the hunt and now here he was, abandoned, forgotten.

She cautiously moved closer, afraid that he might somehow rise up and grab at her like the last time she saw him. But other than the movement of his eye, he did nothing to acknowledge her. The mask, she thought. She reached for it, then paused. But how could he be dangerous? He was so messed up. Her throat clenched and she fought the impulse to cry. She couldn't help feeling responsible. 'Oh, man,' she said.

She slowly lifted off her mask. He seemed to watch, but again there was no change to his anguished expression. She thought then that maybe he was paralyzed. She brought up her hand, covered her mouth. She had thought to ask him where he had been taking her, or how to get home, but what came out instead was an apology.

'I'm so, so, sorry I fell asleep,' she said.

He couldn't help trying to attack her, she silently acknowledged. That's just how they get. Nothing could stop it – not even the need to keep your eye on the road. Not even if the sleeper was your own daughter.

She was startled when his arm moved, dropping to his side. His hand began clawing at his thigh. It took a moment for her to realize that he was digging at the low pocket of his blood-soaked cargo pants. She waited for him to stop, but he persisted, groaning again. His eye darted from her face to the feeble business of his shattered hand. It pulled at the snapped flap, but failed to access the pocket itself. He wanted help.

She reached out and pulled at the flap until the snap released. She saw the white edge of an envelope. The Marine's hand fell away and he stared up at her expectantly. She drew out the envelope and saw her name written on it in her mother's handwriting.

The letter, which she read by the fire, told her never to return to the house. It said that they were already gone, that they went to sleep forever. Sleep! We will carry the memory of you, of every minute of your life, it said, into whatever place of dreams follows the terrible nightmare this world has become.

By the time she returned to the Marine's side, he was dead.

Seven

The transaction at the gated doorway took longer than Biggs thought it should. He had to twist the ring off his finger. They tested the gold by biting it. The ring had a serious ding to it – the result of once falling six stories from their loft window. But they didn't seem to mind its condition. Biggs did his best to maintain his sleepless pose, mumbling and swaying on his feet. They looked him over, saying, 'Mother Mary time, but you got to leave the backpack with us.'

Biggs stalled. He didn't know how to go about protesting this without revealing his lucid state, so he just violently shook his head. But they were already lifting it off him. 'You'll get it back,' they said.

He doubted this. But he could see how the pack itself could become a liability. The sleeping bag was practically an announcement. People would ask about it. No one else was walking around with luggage. He let it go. If Carolyn was in fact here, they would hike back to the loft and barricade themselves inside. After all, it was only a day's walk away – shorter without all the wrong turns.

He was led through the lounge, past the bar and padded oxblood booths. The lighting was dim and Biggs's eyes were slow to adjust. He could make out a few figures sitting in the booths, smoking in the darkness, as he scanned for Carolyn. There were no women in the room as far as he could tell. Biggs could smell the pornographic scent of peppermint cutting through the smoke. There was a low runway that ran down the middle of the room, fringed with tinsel, a pole at each end. The scene could easily be mistaken for a slow weeknight during more typical times. This wasn't a setting where he had imagined encountering sleepers, if it was really happening here. He wondered if Mother Mary was the street name of some kind of narcotic.

His guide, a massive man with a thick, dirty beard, pulled him by his elbow toward the stairway at the far end of the room. Biggs tripped over a chair, stumbling forward, but the man held him up. 'Easy there,' the man said quietly. His movements were solid and his speech clear. He was getting sleep somehow, this guy.

The stairs, hollow and narrow, creaked under them. Biggs and his guide went up two flights, their steps reverberating in the hard, small space. The landing opened into a hallway lined with doors. Biggs was led to a small room at the end of the corridor. The space contained nothing but a twin-sized bed. Biggs was startled to see movement in the dark window that hung on the wall, then realized it was a mirror and the form moving there was his own.

'Take off your shoes and lie down,' the man said.

Biggs hesitated. Should he tell this man that he was here looking for his wife? Should he ask him about Carolyn? It almost seemed safe.

The man backed out, shutting the door behind him, as Biggs lowered himself onto the bed. The mattress was hard and the room smelled faintly of incense. He sat still, waiting to hear the big man's steps shuffling away from the door, but heard nothing. His eyes adjusted as he glanced about. A simple room, filled by the bed. This is a brothel, Biggs acknowledged. He looked up at the ceiling, then scanned the blank walls. It felt like he was waiting for a doctor.

He found himself sleepily rubbing at the place on his finger where his ring had been for the last eight and a half years, with one brief exception. He recalled how the announcement that his sister-in-law was pregnant had triggered a complicated reaction in Carolyn. She had only recently returned from her self-imposed exile in her childhood bedroom when Biggs's brother, Adam, called with the news. The ensuing turmoil led up to a moment when, while lying awake in bed late one night, Carolyn picked up Biggs's wedding ring from the nightstand and casually dropped it out the window. They heard the small chime when it hit the brick alley six stories below.

'There,' she said. 'You're free at last.'

Biggs was already out of bed, pulling on his pants, working to stay calm. 'A band of metal isn't what keeps me here.'

'At this point, I have no idea what does.'

'Carolyn.'

'I'd feel cheated if I were you.'

'We've said all this enough, don't you think?'

He left her in bed and took the elevator down, flashlight in hand. In the alley, he scanned the ground under their window, which floated high above, a dim portal to their complicated world, the warmly lit space behind the glass dense with dissatisfaction. Yes, he had regrets, he wondered how it would be if, or if, or if. Imagining different outcomes, different lives. But he never considered leaving her. They were supposed to be together, weren't they?

The Dream, which had lit the fuse to their relationship, seemed to suggest a certain spiritual endorsement. He was *brought* to her. She was his calling. He had married her one bright day eight and a half years ago and meant it.

Then there was all that they had weathered together since. Were those experiences not the ingredients for a kind of emotional superglue, a fusion of sorts? The mystery of her held him as well. That she was still, in many ways, unknown to him. That after all these years, she still possessed uncharted regions, still kept him guessing. He liked how she refused to be predictable: slipping into his shower, drawing him as he slept, returning from a predawn walk, her head crowned with feathers. Climbing through the skylight to see the stars from the roof, her feet dangling high above their bed.

Throwing his ring out the window. Maybe not one of her more charming stunts.

He searched under the cars parked along the far wall of the alley. Maybe the ring had bounced there. The lane was narrow. During the day it was often blocked by trucks making deliveries to the corner store or nearby pub. He imagined one of these trucks flattening his ring. When he found it, in the gutter perilously close to a drainage grille, the impact had put a nick in the ring, but the integrity of the circle survived.

Biggs lay back, feeling that he was being watched. Maybe he should pace. Carolyn avoided being in bed after a week of complete sleeplessness, calling it a trap. In many ways they are, Biggs thought. Beds.

He attempted to sit up but his body seemed to collapse into itself in sudden recognition of his exhausted state. Biggs fought to stay clear-headed by listening for any evidence of Carolyn in the soundscape. He heard almost nothing through the walls, just the distant sound of music, a faint melody. He imagined an ancient Victrola spinning in a rosy room somewhere, a light swinging slowly.

He felt sleep reaching out for him and shook it off, forcing himself to stand. He went to the door and listened. It was time to find her.

The knob turned with a quiet graininess and he was relieved to find the hallway empty. He decided to move as quietly as possible but, if spotted, to slip right into his sleepless routine. He could hear the murmur of people downstairs. There were only two other doors to check on the second floor. He opened the first door to an empty office space. At the far end, a wide balcony looked over the floor area below. Biggs shut the door and moved on to the next one. Behind it, he was astonished to find a man sleeping soundly in the bed. The man was on his side, arm hugging the pillow, snoring lightly. His scuffed boots sat on the floor and his pants were hung over the rail at the foot of the bed. It had always been strangely odd, somehow invasive, for Biggs to watch a stranger sleep – on the subway, or waiting for a plane. Now he observed and admired it, as though the man was putting on a virtuoso performance.

Upstairs it was more of the same. One room contained an older couple, sleeping in each other's arms under a satin sheet that shimmered like abalone shell. There was another man, naked and obese, snoring up at the ceiling from behind the mound of his hog-colored stomach. Then, in the room at the end of the corridor, Biggs found a young family: father, mother, and two small children, crowded onto a narrow bed, limbs entangled and frozen in time. Their stillness unnerved Biggs a bit, somehow reminding him of the Pompeii death figures, eternal sleepers molded from impressions in the hardened ash of the volcano. A civilization snuffed out in the night. What happened to the dreams they were having when they died? Did those dreams continue? A vision came to him: a slow blur of light pulling away from the body, an unending narrative fleeing the broken cage.

Biggs quietly pulled the door closed and stood in the corridor.

There were no more doors to check and no sign of Carolyn. He decided to return to the second floor, and as he neared the steps, was grabbed by the elbow. It was his guide, the massive man with the beard, who had apparently discovered his absence. 'Come on,' he was told, 'let's get you back to your room.'

The man spoke to him as if he were a lost child. Biggs played along, saying, 'Sleeping is what I am wanting.'

'That's right,' the man said. 'You can't get to sleep walking around, right?'

He was led back to the narrow bed. This time the man waited, watching until Biggs was completely horizontal, head resting on the yellowed pillow. When he did leave, Biggs knew from the click of the door that he had been locked in. He brought up his hands and rubbed at his face. It had been an illusion, the vision of Carolyn in the window. It was absurd to think she would be here. Sad thinking. Just as the impressions of the sleepless were colored by exhaustion, his were by desperation.

He turned on his side, knowing that he should get out of this place, keep moving. But the sight of all those sleepers, like museum displays, had aroused his own need to sleep. He felt the weight of it in his body, in his mind, slowing his thoughts. It had been a long day of walking, after all. And, here he was, in a bed where he was actually expected to sleep. But I shouldn't before they put me to sleep, however they do it. Whatever Mother Mary is, the stuff seems to work.

He slapped at his face.

He clawed his arm, twisted his flesh.

Don't, he told himself, as sleep rose up like a warm tide around him.

Biggs woke to find a woman sitting at the foot of his bed. She was in her early thirties, Asian, with tired, somewhat bleary eyes. She had her black hair pulled back, and even in the poor lighting, Biggs could see that it had purple highlights. She wore a yellow tank top, exposing the relief of her collarbones and hard shoulders, thin arms. Carolyn had a top like that, a figure like that. The realization sank in, dragging down his hopes. This was the woman he had seen in the window, not his wife. He frowned, back in the murk, as the woman continued to stare.

Had she said something, or touched him? He wasn't sure. Something had woken him. Just her presence, maybe. She was assessing him, eyebrows raised, as if he had just said something potentially insulting and she wanted clarification before deciding she was offended.

'You were sleeping,' she said.

'No,' he said. 'Just waiting. I had my eyes closed.'

The woman looked him over. 'You can sleep.'

Biggs said nothing.

'How?'

A silence hung between them for a long moment.

'I don't know,' Biggs finally said. 'I just can.'

The woman turned suddenly, looking at the door, then resumed studying Biggs. 'Why did you come in here if you can already sleep?'

'I thought I saw my wife in the window. But I think it was you.'

'What does your wife look like?'

Biggs took out his wallet and showed the woman a picture of a smiling Carolyn. It was a few years old, taken during hopeful times. Her eyes shining. Carolyn's hair was much longer now. A lot like this woman's.

'No. I have never seen her.'

Biggs closed his wallet and put it back in his pocket, explaining how she went missing, how he was searching for her. The woman listened, blankly studying his face.

'What's your name?' she asked.

'Matthew Biggs. Are you Mother Mary?'

'That's what they call me, but I'm Maria.'

'You can make people sleep?'

'Yes.'

Biggs couldn't understand how that would work. She had entered the room with nothing. No pouch of drugs, no syringe or pills. No food or drinks of any kind, nothing to swallow. He wondered if the way to sleep had something to do with her body. Were they counting on orgasm, or rather the rush of drowsiness that followed it, to break the pattern? Is that why sleep was being promised in a whorehouse? He knew it didn't work. He and Carolyn had tried it in the first few days she found herself perpetually awake. Besides, what about those kids upstairs?

'How do you do it?'

She smiled.

'I sing them a lullaby,' she said.

He didn't believe her. It annoyed him that she would try to lie. Did she think he was one of them – the gullible sleepless? Did she not see that he was asleep only minutes ago? That his mind was sharp?

'Seriously,' he insisted.

'Man, I already told you.'

'A lullaby?' It was like he was saying the word for the first time. She must have heard how strangely it fit in his mouth. He frowned and she lifted her head in quiet defiance.

'It's the truth,' she said. 'Now you tell me your truth. How are you able to sleep?'

'I don't know how, I just can.'

'Why would the spell not affect you?'

'The spell?'

'Yes, a spell has been cast over the whole world.'

Biggs smiled cynically, thinking, Spells, magic songs. Pass the pixie dust.

'You have been blessed,' she told him.

'Some blessing.'

He thought of how often he had wished it was Carolyn who could sleep, his family, not him. He recalled the last time he had talked to his parents, only two weeks earlier. How they didn't seem to know who he was on the phone. His brother, Adam, had called, asking if he, Jorie, and their newborn could come stay with them, thinking it would be safer in the cities, since the military was being mobilized in urban centers. But he had said no to the idea. The baby would just make things worse for Carolyn. Everyone should just stay put and wait this thing out, he had felt. What had become of them?

Biggs felt a building rage suddenly wilt into sorrow as he thought about all that was already lost. He recognized now that a slow-moving catastrophe like this one was a series of surrenders. You lose something you assumed you couldn't live without, but then you do live. So you fall back to your next most cherished possession. Then you lose that too, triggering yet another retreat and adjustment of expectations. At some point it has to bottom out. You either lose it all or start slowly gaining it back. He looked at Maria with impossibly tired eyes.

'You need more rest,' she said.

He laughed, but this time there was nothing cynical about it.

They sat, staring at each other.

'So it really is a song that you sing?' Biggs asked.

Maria nodded.

'When did you discover what it could do, this song of yours?'

'Right when I learned it. I could make my father sleep, before he hurt my mother. That's why she taught me the song – to protect us.'

'Oh,' Biggs said. He looked at Maria and saw that a dark memory now moved through her. She looked through him at some ghostly scene.

'I want to hear it,' Biggs said. 'Please sing it.'

His voice brought her back. Her eyes focused on him. 'But you can already sleep.'

Biggs smiled. 'Hey, I paid for it.'

'You should get your money back.'

'If this really works, you could be the key to stopping this whole thing.'

She moved toward him, gently pushing him back until his head found the pillow. 'You could be too.'

Biggs thought about this, looking up at her. 'The difference is that I can't help others. It's contained inside me. It—'

He was cut off by a voice at the door calling for Maria. 'Hey, let's go. People are fucking waiting,' the voice rasped. It was the Indian with the pistol, Biggs could tell.

'Are you a prisoner here?' he asked.

'No.'

'So you can leave?'

'Where would I go?'

'Anywhere you want,' Biggs told her. 'If this thing works, you should be the one calling the shots.'

She shook her head and shushed him. He could see that she was fearful, that she hadn't allowed herself to go down that path.

Then her hand was warm on his forehead. She slowly brought it down over his eyes as she leaned in, so close that he could feel her breath on his cheek. Then she began to sing. Biggs braced himself, trying to open himself to suggestion. It had to work like hypnosis, he figured. Or some kind of frequency thing.

The words she sang were not English. He was not even sure they were words. They were soft sounds, smooth vowels, candle-melt. Eroded stone. The consonants were like footsteps in the snow, hands tunneling in wet sand. The melody was weirdly complicated and difficult. Not exactly appealing, because it didn't seem to follow any musical rules, like key or count. But she eased it gently into his ear, pushing it with a warm wind. He felt the warmth move into him and spread over his mind, bringing slow pulses of color – purple and blue washes, undulating streaks of cool neon dancing under his eyelids like an aurora.

Then he woke up and got to his feet.

Then he was untying Carolyn from the chair. She slumped into his arms. He lifted her and carried her to their bed. He could feel the weight of the sleep in her, like a soaked sponge. She was so heavy with it he feared the bed would break and she would crash through the floor and continue falling, onward into a glowing abyss. But he was able to lower her onto the mattress, which she sank comfortably into, nestled. He put a comforter over her and lifted her head for a pillow. The movement caused her to slowly open her eyes.

'Go back,' he told her.

She focused on him and smiled. 'You're tired,' she said.

He nodded and they studied each other. He worried she would notice the missing ring. It was better, he decided, to show her rather than try to hide it. He held up his hand, only to discover that the battered ring was there. He looked at it, confused.

She smiled knowingly.

'I'm glad you never had it repaired,' she said. 'It was made more perfect by damage.'

He struggled to make sense of the ring's return. 'Did you do this,' he asked, 'between the frames?'

'If you say so, my love. You're the dreamer.'

Eight

Then Jorie was standing in the doorway holding the baby, bouncing him lightly on her shoulder, trying to get him to sleep. She was wearing her fuzzy pink robe and athletic socks and her hair burst forth in every direction. The old floor creaked under her feet. Adam was watching from the musty nursing chair by the window. The baby was murmuring into his wife's terry cloth shoulder. He heard the baby say, 'Don't answer that. It's undoubtedly those telemarketers again.'

This struck Adam as a very odd thing to say since the phone wasn't ringing.

Then Jorie was in bed next to Adam causing a commotion. Adam had his back to her. He must have had microsleep. That's the term they had learned on the radio. Experts said it would happen. Jorie was pushing and kneeing at his back. Was she trying to change the sheets without asking him to leave the bed? He felt he would never leave the bed. It was difficult to even imagine standing, walking about. The bed was now their white place of perpetual torment, a starchy pressure at their backs.

'Baby,' he said calmly, 'you'll never get to sleep going at it that way.' She hadn't slept for five days. When she didn't respond, only whimpered, he sat up to find her frantically searching the blankets. He assumed that she had lost her wedding ring. He said, 'Do you remember when it was our thinking that we had lost it up at that rest stop in the redwoods and we drove back down the map half a day's distance to dig through the trash with our hands and no gloves on them? We gave up and went on in our car up and up into the north and then it dropped in your lap from the map when you unfolded it to see what was that lake.'

'The baby,' she said, turning on him savagely. 'I can't find the baby that is ours!'

Then Adam was on the couch with the baby like a dense beanbag on his chest. There was pale light coming in through the window. His hand rested lightly on the baby's warm back, patting lightly on the little drum of tiny human torso. He was ashamed to find himself praying now, after all those years of silence. It's not like I'm asking to have anything done for me, he insisted to no one.

Then she was pregnant with the baby again. She knew that he was sitting right in the booster seat of her belly. How odd to know his face and fingers and toes, his tiny little fleshy hinges of wrists and ankles, and the feel of his hot little mouth pulling at her breast. All this before he is born again. She could not see over the mountain of her belly where Adam was holding the baby in the nursing chair. She could not move with the baby like a boulder in her middle. She felt confused and grounded at the same time. That was why, she recognized. Because everything is happening now *at the same time*. The mechanism that puts one minute after another has broken so that now it's just forever in all directions at once.

*　　*　　*

Then Jorie found the baby on the floor, between the sofa and the armchair, alive with battery-operated movement and a clear plastic mask on its face.

Then she went into the nursery to check on the baby. The nightlight projected an aquatic glow over the walls. She peered into the crib, careful not to wake her sleeping son. She did not know if other newborns could sleep at this point, nor would she let it be known that their baby was still doing it several times a day. The insomnia epidemic had made people hungry for sleep and, in their starved state, capable of anything. They were always standing in the corner of her eye, until she looked at them directly and they vanished. She believed they would consume any vessel in which sleep was found, hoping to absorb the ability. Yes, she believed they would eat her baby.

The baby heard her think this and started to cry.

Then Adam came out of the bathroom empty-handed, with the toilet gurgling behind him. She asked him, 'Is the baby something you have?' He went back in and came out with the baby wriggling and squawking in his hands. 'Oh my god, Adam,' she shouted. 'That you cannot be doing!'

He wept and said, 'Forgive this from me because my deficit is red.'

Then sometimes she had the baby or knew where the baby was and sometimes he had the baby or knew where the baby was. Then the baby was sometimes perched on them, driving them like oxen, using a hard yoke of emotion. Then, sometimes, more and more often, neither of them had the baby or knew where the baby was.

*   *   *

Then the baby turned up in Adam's sock drawer. It had learned how to meow. Adam closed the drawer, but not all the way. It occurred to him that it was better to hide the baby from the two of them, since he now realized he would trade the baby for sleep without much hesitation.

Would he trade the baby for a year of sleep? Yes. Would he trade it for a week? Yes. Would he trade it for a day? Maybe, after all, he did not know the baby all that well. They had only met a few weeks ago. It's not like they went way back. And babies didn't have the value they did before. Just a month ago, they were so treasured. People would go to great lengths to get one. Look at Matt and Carolyn. They were desperate. Poor Carolyn. A complicated person, Jorie once said about her.

Something must be complicated about her because the way to get a baby was not at all complicated since all he and Jorie did was fuck a few times and they got one. Carolyn's insides must be a labyrinth. Put two bodies next to each other and it practically happens on its own. Cock rises and plunges. Stuff comes out. They could make another one anytime they wanted, even in the shower or the car or the kitchen. 'We could give the baby to Matt and Carolyn and live off the ground six floors up for a trade,' he said to Jorie when she may or may not have been in the room. Some shadow was there.

The city is where help will come, they believed. And it was less dangerous because the law dries up away from cities first like a puddle evaporating along its edges. The law was almost vapor just a few miles out at this point.

But Matt had said no, it's too dangerous.

'It's because the baby will upset Carolyn,' Jorie had said sadly, when Adam got off the phone with his brother. 'And when this ends and our lives come loping back like a lost dog we tried to ditch in the woods she won't talk to us.'

*   *   *

Then Jorie wanted to know what the officers had brought that would turn off their heads for a while, knock them out and let the aching in their bones move one way or another off an unreachable place.

The police couple was sorry but they had brought nothing. 'That's because there is nothing,' they said.

Adam stood up, the chair falling back behind him, and snapped into a rage. He fell to the ground and bit at the table legs. 'You have sleeping in you, the way you talk and your eyes are telling me so fucking obviously so!'

Then the baby told Adam a bedtime story into his chest. The words went through the sieve of skin and bone, leaving behind a pool of drool. The baby said, 'Even though you had heard reports of the giant sparrow, you brought me to a certain park in the carriage. You and mother had a picnic when the bird came down from the black trees and landed on the handlebar of the stroller. Its weight – because it was the size of a dodo – caused the stroller to spill forward and I flew into the bird's beak. I was wailing into the sparrow's dry tongue, which smelled like fresh mud. The beak was locked down on me, solid as furniture, and in a tumble and roll, with flapping like an umbrella opening again and again, we were aloft. Your shouts and Mother's screams were muffled and growing distant but not gone. It took me up into the trees where it perched and tipped back its head, working me into the tight suitcase of its gullet. It was like being born into darkness. You and Mother hunted for us in the trees with your eyes, but the bird had roosted in the girding under a bridge, tucking its head under a wing. I was inside, refusing to be digested. I knew what to do since the bird, on the inside, was not unlike Mother. I introduced a maddening nursery rhyme into the bird's tiny brain, preventing it from sleeping. Deprived of food and sleep, the bird became very susceptible and it was then that I began a campaign of unreasonable suggestions. When the bird was weakened and the belts and tethers of its dark interior had gone slack, I assumed the role of pilot and puppeteer. I pulled sinews from the weave of the fleshy fabric and, using nubs of bone from digested animals as spools, built an array of pulleys that controlled the bird's every move, even after it had died. At the time, you knew nothing of this. The police couple that came to investigate were outraged by your claims. You were alternately persons of interest, then suspects. They separated you and lied about what the other had said. But you and Mother held firm, when not quaking with grief. You were with the police in the park with their cadaver dogs when the bird appeared above you, flying with the jerky movement of a marionette. I landed it in the grass with a tumble. The skin, which was now as dry as paper, tore upon impact and I tumbled out, little fists curled around the bone handles and levers I had devised. Mother scooped me up and attacked the remains of the bird with her boots, until I made it clear to her that the animal had died a long time ago.'

Then the police came to the door. It had been four days since Jorie and Adam had reported the baby missing. The police that came were a couple. They knocked at the backdoor with a flash-light and Jorie thought they were shadow people. She looked at them directly, through the window in the door, and they did not disappear. She went right up to the glass and stared at them for a long time. They stared back, a man and woman in uniform, holding light in their hands. 'Open the door,' the man was saying. 'We're here about a missing baby.'

Then Jorie cleared dishes out of the sink with the intention of giving the baby a bath and was startled to see the drain at the bottom of the basin. Of course it made sense that it would be there, but she found its existence oddly surprising and novel. She recalled a time when she and her brother, only four and five years of age, would wander around their home and point out things that were always there – light switches, door stoppers, vents in the floor – saying, Remember this? Remember this? It was as though they had already lived a thousand years and had forgotten the basic, utilitarian details of their surroundings after initially learning their purpose, marveling at them, then moving on to other discoveries.

Now, sick with exhaustion, Jorie felt the same sense of rediscovery, looking into the drain. And, like her child mind, she marveled again at the practical details. Who could ever have thought of it all and how did human living get so cluttered with detail? For a lucid moment, she believed she understood that the epidemic was somehow connected to this accumulation of practical – not ornamental – details. A threshold had been reached.

Then Adam wondered out loud why he could never make a kite that actually flew. 'Maybe it's time to try to make love to each other,' he said to Jorie. He didn't care if there were people sometimes standing in the corners of the room. In the corners of the world, Adam thought. Shadow people was what they were calling them on the radio. Just figments of the sleep-deprived mind.

Then he was so tired that he vomited. There were things in it that he didn't remember eating.

Then they had to start taking averages of their perceptions. If they saw the baby on the left side of the couch three times and on the right side three times, they would conclude the baby was in the middle of the couch. If it was two times on the left and three times on the right, then their conclusion put the baby slightly to the right of the middle of the couch. If the baby said, This can't go on, but the baby also said nothing, then what they heard was more like Go on or Can't go or This can't.

Then the baby was gone. They tore the house apart looking for him. Adam searched the garage, took apart the car, while Jorie checked every can, carton, and box in the pantry and squeezed out every tube of medicinal pastes. In the yard, there was a pile of leaves that they gently combed through. They did not blame the other. The search, in some ways, brought them together. They made love for the first time since the baby was born. It was safe to do so.

Then Adam insisted that the officers tell them what the news was regarding the epidemic. 'What would be good to be knowing,' he said, 'is how we're finding the things we need to make it stop us from ever sleeping at all.'

The policeman and policewoman said that things were tough, explaining that it took them four days to respond because the entire city was being served by less than a dozen police officers. There were rumors about help from the government, but also rumors that the government had collapsed. The only thing they could do was their jobs, which is what they had come here to do. 'Let's just tackle one problem at a time and find your baby,' the policewoman said.

Then the baby told Jorie a story while flopped over her shoulder for a burping. 'I became fixated on the notion that I was going to hurt you,' the baby told her. 'I knew that as I grew I would encroach on that which was you. If things continued and I was never to emerge from you, I would take from you beyond what your body was prepared to give. Life would slowly transfer from me to you and I would eventually shed you like a snake sheds its skin. All this resulted in a great deal of worry, made all the more excruciating by the fact that I could not willfully refuse nourishment in the attempt to end the escalation of presence. I loved you even before I was led to you. It broke my tiny heart to know I could not stay within you, since that would mean your demise, nor could I leave you without causing damage and pain. If you recall, being birthed is much like being drawn slowly toward a gaping drain. You feel the pull very subtly at first. Before long, it has taken you like a riptide and it's in everyone's best interest not to resist its demands. I had to recognize that the moment of surrender had arrived and all I could do is keep my head down, my shoulders hunched, and hope I didn't cause a tear in making my exit. And it worked, or so it seems. I was so relieved to learn that a cut at the opening was not necessary. I can only hope that this was in some way a result of my efforts since I love your flesh as though it were my own. More so, actually, since it continues to provide nourishment and mine already strains toward decay and dust.'

Then the police couple walked into the living room, looking at the mess Adam and Jorie had made in their searches for the baby. The couch was overturned and the shelves emptied of books. The TV was in pieces on the floor. CDs and DVDs were scattered about like fallen leaves. The policewoman looked at the policeman and then both looked at Adam and Jorie. 'When and where did you last see the baby?' the policeman asked.

Adam pointed to a place on the floor, which was approximately the middle point between the two places where he believed he last saw the baby, but Jorie patted her shoulder. The police officers exchanged looks again and ordered them to stay in the kitchen while they searched the rest of the ransacked house. They came back into the kitchen and Adam shouted at the officers and fell on the floor, thrashing and biting like a sick animal. 'We smell that you have sleeping in you!' When they tried to handcuff him to the table leg, Jorie screamed and threw herself on the back of the policeman. The policewoman grabbed her by the throat and slammed her to the floor. They were both left facedown on the floor, hands cuffed behind them.

The police couple went outside and began searching the yard, the shed, the garage. Adam could see their flashlight beams cutting at the air. The officers must have split up, searching different areas of the house, because they could hear the policewoman call to her partner, saying she found something.

'Oh, Jesus,' they heard her say.

Then they were staring at each other with the same idea burning behind their eyes.

Nine

They crawled up the switchbacks until they could park and stand on the edge of the mountaintop plateau. Below they saw the jagged range extending toward the horizon, the Beartooth biting at the sky, and the curve of the earth. Glaciers hung like blue-white banners in the sunless crags. Lakes, down in the pockets of hanging valleys, shining back at them. A storm seemed to crab-walk over the plateau, rushing toward them on crooked stilts of light, and wind filled their mouths with thin, cold air.

Then the descent.

Jordan rode the brakes all the way down the treeless heights, careening past the towering banks of talus. Chase told him three times that he was drifting over the line. What if a truck was coming around the curve? Soon they passed through shadow and forest, then found themselves between foothills, where the land flattened out enough for cattle ranches and, only miles away, the town imposed a feeble grid on the landscape. The campground was where Jordan remembered it being – the numbered campsites cut into the brush and pines along a loop of a narrow rushing creek. Each site came with a carved-up picnic table and a blackened fire ring. There were no rangers, only a drop box and some envelopes for the fees. It was the honor system and Chase insisted they pay.

Biting deerflies attacked them as they set up the tent. They worked quickly. Jordan knew the drill and directed Chase with terse commands. The clang of tent poles and the hammer ringing against the spikes announced their presence to the scrub jays, who responded by screeching in the trees, and to one other group of campers: a pale family with faded Jesus stickers plastered on the back of their trailer. They did not come over and offer a neighborly welcome as Jordan predicted they would.

The tent was from another era – canvas, not nylon. It smelled musty and was stained with rain. It was shaped like a pyramid. They threw clothes and the sleeping bags inside it and, after stepping out of their shoes at the entry flap, flopped down on the bed of clutter. The nearby creek sounded like wind in the trees or the wind in the trees sounded like the creek. Chase couldn't decide. He was already thinking about how he would get back home in time for Felicia's birthday, now that he had what he wanted.

Jordan was lying on his back, forearm over his face to block out the light. 'Let's go into town around dinnertime,' he said.

'How far is it?'

'Like ten minutes, tops.'

'Cool.'

Chase wondered when Jordan would tell him how things had gone with the cleaning girl in Idaho Falls. He had not volunteered a report, so Chase assumed it went badly. However it went, it took all night to get there. Jordan had returned from their ice cream run in the morning, ready to resume the drive north.

Chase tried to nap, since it seemed that's what they were doing, but the sitting in the car for nine hours had made him restless. He rose and announced that he was going to check out the creek. 'Don't fall in,' Jordan said from under his arm.

*   *   *

The water rushed past his feet, causing reeds to bow and tremble. The rumbling hiss and the churn of bubbles suggested surprising force. It was a narrow creek and the opposite bank, ornamented with smooth stones and high grass, looked landscaped to Chase. He crouched and reached out to the water, sinking his fingers into the effervescent wash. It was icy cold. Actually, it seemed colder than ice. Was that possible? The notion to drink the water passed through his fingers and up his arm into his head.

Yeah, but not just a drink.

He reached into his pocket and drew out one of the pills. Shaped like a dull diamond, colored a dull blue. He placed it on his tongue and reached down to scoop up a gulp of creek. He had taken a pill the night before and nothing had happened. Maybe he just needed more. Maybe the stuff just needed to work its way into his system. He drank from his hand and tipped his head back. The chill ran through him as the pill tumbled down. He chased it with another icy swallow.

'I wouldn't drink this water.'

It was Jordan, behind him. He looked up from his crouch, squinting. Jordan stood between him and the sun. How long had he been there?

'I thought you said you drank right out of the streams? You and your dad.'

'Yeah, from those lakes in the mountains, where no one goes. But down here you have cows shitting and pissing in this water. Or worse, lying dead in it.'

'Oh,' Chase said. He looked into the water, as if trying to spot foul microbes rushing by. He didn't know much about how this place worked. Was he already feeling ill? He focused on his stomach, his hand resting on it, trying to sense if any trouble was already brewing.

Jordan came forward, stood next to him in silence. He was quiet for too long.

'Once,' he finally said, 'when we were up there, I jumped over a stream like this and my foot hit something hard in the grass. I looked and it was a huge bone, half sunk in the mud. I pulled it out. It was like holding a dumbbell. I thought it was something prehistoric. It was mossy and stained brown and yellow. My dad was still on the other side of the creek, talking to our guide, so I held it up. I thought he would be interested in it because that's exactly the kind of shit he loves, but he just kind of squinted and went back to talking. I was like, Okay, fucking whatever, and I tossed it in the water. Then, he finally finishes his conversation and jumps across and he's all, Where is it? Where's what? The bone? He goes, Was that a bone? When I said I threw it in the water, I could tell he was disappointed. I mean, he's looking for it down in the water. So, I just jump right in thinking I would find it. Right into the freezing water! As soon as I hit it, I can't breathe. It literally takes my breath away. Next thing I know the guide has pulled me out and he's telling me to get out of the wet clothes. He starts building a fire on the spot while my dad is just yelling, Where's your goddamn head?'

Chase didn't know what to say. He sensed that this was a meaningful disclosure, but he didn't know what it meant, other than the fact that Jordan's dad sounded like a real asshole. It was hard to imagine Jordan being so interested in pleasing his father, or anyone. He hated his mother especially. 'How old were you?' Chase asked.

'I must have been about eleven.'

Chase did the math. That would be two years before he lost his eye, maybe a year before his dad was killed. Hit by a car while biking to work. 'Fuck' was all he could think to say. He tried to put some feeling into it, but the word offered a short runway for empathy.

'Yeah,' Jordan said.

'I wonder if it's still there.'

'The bone?'

'Yeah.'

They both looked down at the water rushing by, as if this was the very stream from Jordan's story. Or maybe as if the bone could have traveled through the network of snowmelt rivulets, urged along by the insistent current and gravity, to this very spot.

'I doubt it,' Jordan said. 'I'm not even sure if all that happened. I mean, I remember it, but what am I remembering?'

The town's main drag looked like the set for a classic Western, with its raised boardwalk and hitching posts, windows framed by shutters that would surely be swung shut during gunfights in the narrow street. Chase even speculated that maybe the overfamiliar structures were just flat movie set façades, supported from behind with long diagonal posts of local lumber. They ventured into many saloons to test their authenticity. Sure enough, there was floor space, tables ringed with diners, bars lined with locals.

Chase was shy about pushing through and ordering. They were both underage in California and they had no idea what the drinking age was here. Apparently they exceeded it, at least in appearance, because they were never carded. The beer was unbelievably cheap, too. And people were friendly, asking them what brought them to town and looking very impressed when they said they were from California. There were many offers to point out the best places to fish, or buy bait, or hike and camp. Chase's initial feelings of unease quickly dissipated. He had expected they would be eyed with suspicion and shunned as outsiders. He had expected cowboy hostility. But these people were just people, like the people at home.

Still, Jordan was watching them closely, for reasons different from Chase's wariness. 'Some of these people aren't sleeping,' he said, eyes scanning the room as he drained a mug.

'Just about all of them look like they're awake to me,' Chase said.

'You know what I mean.'

Chase studied the scene with insomnia in mind. There were indeed tired locals nursing drinks at the bar. The workday had exacted a visible toll. They slumped over their beers, glancing at the small TV in the corner. Brighter-eyed tourists were clustered around tables, flaunting their vacation energy with bursts of laughter and fevered backslapping. Chase's eyes settled on a stuffed bobcat that was mounted over the bar. The fur looked weathered, bordering on mangy, and there was something unnatural about the pose. Shoulders too stiff. Legs too woodenly arranged. Only the eyes, which gleamed with a convincing wetness, seemed to hint at a life once lived. They stared out over the scene, unblinking. What sights had they witnessed?

Jordan gave Chase a nudge. He nodded toward an elderly man who had appeared behind the bar, relieving the burly biker who had served them. His eyes were not unlike those glued in the head of the stuffed wildcat – glassy, staring into nowhere. He was remarkably filthy. His hands and thin arms were mapped with grime, and a black crescent sat under each yellow fingernail. There was dirt on his face and in his woolly, graying beard, actual grains of dark soil dropping from it when he turned. His hollow cheeks and brow appeared to be stained by dirt-colored sweat, giving his flesh the finish of a church pew. Little streams of dirt trickled from the creases in his clothing. There was a tiny mound on his right shoulder, as if it had been gently troweled there. He smelled like freshly exposed earth and moved stiffly, as though maybe he too was stuffed, only with soil instead of sawdust.

Jordan mouthed, What the fuck?

They watched him attempt to open a bottle of Irish whiskey. His fingers smeared the neck of the bottle. Before he could manage the task, a woman rushed behind the bar and took the bottle from his hands. Chase had noted her earlier – a waitress, probably in her early thirties. Kind eyes, long black hair, maybe Indian. Beautiful, yes. Like Felicia ten years from now, maybe even prettier.

'Come on, Wells,' she said softly, pulling at the man's arm. 'Come have some food. Before it gets cold.'

She turned and yelled with surprising force across the room, 'Rollins!'

Rollins was the biker bartender apparently, because the man emerged from the side door, blowing smoke out the side of his mouth. He skulked back to his post behind the bar as she led Wells past him. 'Just stepped out for a smoke,' he said.

'He can't be behind the bar,' she told him.

'I know. I know.' He looked at the older man sorrowfully. 'Go eat something, buddy. Got to keep wood in the stove.'

Chase and Jordan watched Wells being led away through the swinging door to the kitchen area. When Rollins approached to take their order, Jordan said, 'What's wrong with that guy?'

Rollins looked the two of them over. 'Well,' he said, 'I don't see how it's any of your goddamn business what's wrong with him.'

'Hey, just asking,' Jordan said.

'Ask for a drink or move along.'

The bartender gave Jordan a long hard stare. Chase felt the danger of it, even though he was once removed from its focal point. Rollins was a large man with a shaved head and a red goatee. He wore a denim shirt with the sleeves cut off, weathered jeans, and dusty biker boots. His arms looked like what most people would call legs. They were blotchy with bad jail-house tattoos.

'Maybe we should—' Chase began, but Jordan cut him off.

'Didn't mean to be nosy,' Jordan said. 'How about two more?'

Rollins scooped up two cold steins from under the bar and put them under the tap, eyeing them as the mugs filled. 'Those are on me,' he said, setting them on the bar. 'Drink them and go.'

They did as Rollins suggested, moving to another saloon only two doors down after chugging the beers. 'Not the friendliest of dudes,' Jordan said of Rollins.

'No, it was a perfectly normal question,' Chase said. 'I mean, that guy was fucking caked.'

'Looked like he'd been buried alive but fought his way out.'

'Maybe he has a garden and he's way into it,' Chase suggested.

'Maybe he can't sleep.'

'Here we go,' Chase said. He wanted to know what that had to do with a guy being covered with dirt.

Jordan thought about this.

'Fuck if I know,' he finally conceded with a shrug.

When the bars all closed and the town was shuttered for the night, they stumbled back to the car. They had some work to do. Their plan was to bury all the stolen pharmaceuticals in the old Coleman cooler under cover of night. But on the drive back to the campground, they missed the dark turnoff from the highway twice. They finally found the exit at the end of their headlights and started the bumpy journey down the rutted access road. They were passing through pastureland under a half moon when Jordan slammed on the brakes. Dust clouded the headlights and obscured the shapes of beasts in the road. Horses, eyes glowing in the headlights and looming in an illuminated aura of dust, stood with indifference in their path. They stared back at them in wonder. After a few minutes it became clear the horses had no intention of moving on and letting them pass.

'Maybe honk,' Chase suggested.

'I don't want to start a stampede. Let's just give them a minute.'

They sat looking at the horses. This was not something either of them had encountered before, but the scene, at least for Chase, read like a memory. The horses, sentinels along the road into the wild dark, their animal wisdom and ancient life force, humbling the two suburban boys. The bestial presence seemed to accelerate their return to sobriety as they waited. To Chase, they appeared larger than normal horses, but he wasn't sure of horse sizes. Maybe they are a type of extra large horse? he wondered.

'They're giant,' he said. 'Aren't they?'

Jordan said nothing. He settled back into the car seat as if he was prepared to wait out the vast span of night behind the wheel.

Maybe, Chase thought, they should go another way.

After a stretch of silence, Jordan said, 'I'm thinking I should go back and get her. Just take her for her own good.'

Chase knew he was talking about the girl in Idaho Falls. Not his mother.

'Did you ask her to come with us?'

'She shouldn't have to suffer.'

'You mean from insomnia.'

Jordan was silent. After a few minutes he got out of the car and staggered toward the horses. He stood among the animals, patting their flanks and urging them off the road. To Chase's astonishment, the horses obliged. They shambled off, away from the headlight beams and joined the roadside shadows.

Later that night, Chase woke up to find Jordan standing in the tent. 'I should never have touched them,' he said.

* * *

In the morning, Chase found that the pills had finally worked. He had taken more throughout the night, in various restrooms of the many saloons they had visited. The tightness of the effect was actually somewhat painful. He squeezed himself and marveled at the hardness. Wow. He could rape a boulder with this thing. Maybe the thing would burst. It was like putting too much air in a tire. Would there be an explosion of blood?

Jordan was fully clothed, sprawled on top of the blankets that served as his bedroll. He was out cold after what was apparently a long night. Chase stood and carefully pulled on his pants, pinning the swelling under his waistband and pulling down his shirt. It was not very noticeable, but not at all comfortable. He left the tent and decided to check on their handiwork from last night. They had loaded the meds into a cooler and buried it in brush. They had covered it with dirt and loose branches. They had done this in the dark while drunk and, seeing it now, Chase had to shake his head at how conspicuous it looked. Couple of retards did this. He worked for a while at making it look more natural.

It occurred to him that he should take advantage of Jordan's unconscious state, given his body's reaction to the pills. He did not feel at all aroused, despite what his groin was telling him. Still, now that he knew it worked, no reason to lug this thing around all day. There was no way he was going to jack off with Jordan in the same tent, so he sat in the front seat of the car. There he unbuckled his pants and conjured up some memories of Felicia, using them as fodder for a fantasy that involved his triumphant return and her surprise at what he had brought for her. He imagined himself fucking her mercilessly. Yet he had trouble seeing Felicia's face. This was not new. When he first fell in love with her, she became increasingly elusive in his waking fantasies, but more vivid in his dreams. His desperation to see her features somehow muddled the access and garbled the pictures. Even now, he was seeing the waitress – Macy, claimed her nametag – just as clearly as glimpses of Felicia. He focused on the older woman and quickly climaxed.

This did nothing to undo his engorgement.

Chase decided to go into town. There was nothing to do at the campground. Besides, it might be nice to run into that Macy. He couldn't find the car keys and figured they were in Jordan's pockets. In the tent, he gave Jordan a nudge with his foot, but this failed to rouse him. Instead, he snorted and turned his face away. 'Dude,' Chase called. 'Where are the car keys?'

Jordan didn't stir. Chase reached out with his foot and gave him a light kick. Still nothing. It was clear that he had taken some of the sleep meds. The guy can't get to sleep one night and he thinks he's an insomniac, Chase thought. Fuck it. I'll walk to town.

He figured it would take him no more than an hour to reach the town if they were able to drive it in ten minutes. There was no sign of the horses from the night before. He tried to identify the exact spot where they had their 'equine encounter,' as Jordan had later called it, but it could have been just about anywhere along the road. There were hoofprints in the dirt, some mounds of droppings as well, alive with beetles. Were they left by cattle or horses? Chase couldn't tell.

Soon he came upon a barbed wire fence that marked the edge of the property. It ran along the highway forever in both directions. He watched a shrike impale a grasshopper on one of the barbs, then crossed over the cattle grid where the paved road began. It was hot and he was tempted to take off his shirt, but remembered that a private part of him was jutting out from under his waistband. Don't want to frighten the locals, he thought. Besides, there were swarms of small insects hovering over the roadside, and Chase assumed they were mosquitoes.

Chase wandered the town and found himself staring up at the stuffed bobcat. Yes, this was the place where they had seen the dirt-covered man, where the bartender had essentially kicked them out. Where that waitress, Macy, worked. He scanned around for the bartender, realizing he could have drifted back into the biker's sights. He was tempted to turn around and walk out, but the thought of seeing Macy again drew him forward. He sat in a booth. There was another waitress serving sandwiches and beers to the diners. The bartender Rollins appeared and, though he took in the room with a sweeping glance, he didn't seem to recognize Chase, or to have an issue with his being there. After all, it was Jordan who had offended him. That's who he probably imprinted in his mind – Jordan, the kid with the fucked-up eye. The kid with the boner was okay.

Chase nursed along a plate of onion rings and some Diet Coke. The server, a heavy-set girl with tattoo sleeves, was diligent with the refills. She asked him where he was from. When he said California, she smiled. She had a sister out there, in Fresno. Chase said he had never been to Fresno and the woman found this hard to believe. 'I suppose it's a big state,' she said. 'Not as big as Texas,' she added.

'No,' Chase had to agree. He shifted uncomfortably and adjusted himself under the table, where his erection was lancing at his belly.

He waited another hour, putting off ordering dinner. Then he saw Macy appear, tying on her waist apron. She was stony and serious as she pulled her hair back into a ponytail. She could definitely be Felicia's older sister, he observed. It wasn't just a beer-goggle impression. Thankfully, it seemed Macy was relieving the other waitress. They were conferring about the transition, looking over at each table as the tattooed girl explained the status of service. Chase looked away as their gaze arrived at his table. Then he watched the chunky woman go behind the bar, draw herself a beer, and press against Rollins. Rollins gave her a firm spank on the ass.

Macy eventually made her way to him. 'How we doing here?' she asked, distractedly, he couldn't help but note.

'I think I'm ready to order dinner,' he said. 'What's good?'

'I'll bring a menu,' she said, then walked away. He watched her go.

Damn. How was he going to get past this strictly business bullshit? He thought about telling her how much she looked like his girlfriend – his former girlfriend. He could even show her a picture on his phone. But wasn't that probably the lamest way ever to start a conversation? Maybe the California thing would work. Maybe she has a relative there. Or maybe she's been there and loves it. Probably not where he's from – what was there to love? – but the beach maybe, like San Diego or Malibu.

She came by and handed off the menu without a word.

He looked through it and settled on a cheeseburger, then closed it as a way of summoning her back. He was repositioning himself under the table when she suddenly appeared, pad at the ready for his order.

'I think I'll have that cheeseburger,' he said.

'Fries?'

'I just had a bunch.'

'So no fries?'

'Hey, what was with the guy last night?' he suddenly blurted.

'Guy?'

'There was a dirty old guy behind the bar. I mean, he was covered with dirt.'

Her wince turned into a vague, wistful smile that quickly

faded. He thought this was an unbelievably pretty thing to do. There was feeling behind his extruded physiology all of a sudden. 'Yeah,' she said, 'that was Wells. He owns this place and he hasn't been feeling too good.'

'It was cool how you were taking care of him,' Chase said.

'Someone has to,' she said flatly. 'So, no fries?'

Back to business. Fuck.

'Sure, bring fries,' Chase said, feeling defeated.

When she came back with his food, he was ready. 'Any chance Wells is an insomniac?'

She looked at him and frowned before turning and walking off.

Two minutes later she was sitting across from him. 'How did you know that?' she asked.

When he told her it was an epidemic, that the story was about to break, she put a hand over her mouth, but he still caught the wobble of her chin. And above this mask, her eyes, stricken with an emerging awareness as pieces fell into place. It wasn't that she was scared, or even that she fully believed him. But the possibility of it all was enough to send her inward. She said, 'I thought I caused this. By pulling my hand away that time . . . it started happening around then.'

She wasn't really talking to him, and when she realized the volume was on, she hit the mute button in her head. Her shift had ended and she had led him to a table in the kitchen area. Wells would be up soon, she explained, for food.

'Up? I thought you said he wasn't sleeping.'

'Up from under,' she said.

When she offered no further explanation, Chase went on, parroting Jordan's warnings, citing his obscure Internet evidence. He claimed he didn't believe any of it at first. Sure, lots of people couldn't sleep, but that was always the case. His own mother had trouble, sometimes waking at four in the morning and not being able to get back to sleep. That's how she got so much reading done. Insomnia was a common topic all along. But stuff he had seen added up to something strange: his boss prancing around with a cello in the music store, his ass and balls exposed to the world. The weird behavior of the cop in Utah. His ex-girlfriend, she worked with sleep researchers at the university, and all communication had been cut off. What was that about?

'It's like they discovered something, and someone, the government probably, quarantined them,' he said, sounding more convincing than he expected. Really, this thought hadn't occurred to him until now, but maybe there was something to it. Would Felicia really just shut him out like that? Not on her own.

'Okay, you think that's weird, come on,' she said. She led him to the venue's small banquet room and showed him the excavation Wells had dug into the floor. The hole was like a grave, cut right into the middle of the plank wood floor. Macy explained that Wells used an old outhouse door on a pulley to winch up the mounds of dirt. He carted it outside and spread it under the pines at the far edge of the parking lot. 'He claims he sees a light down there,' Macy said. 'He won't stop tunneling toward it.'

Chase could hear him in there now, beyond their view in the tunnel, grunting as his shovel, or maybe a pickax, hacked at the wall of dirt in the darkness.

'What's that?' he said, pointing to a dark stack of something, maybe firewood, against the wall. Macy had not turned on the lights, so the room was dim. Wells had ordered her to keep it off at all times, she told him, since it made the light in the earth harder to see.

'Bones,' she said. 'He keeps bringing them up. Rollins says

they are buffalo bones, that he must have hit an old Indian dump site.'

Chase went in for a closer look. Yes, they were like dumbbells.

'Wells thinks it's an extinct animal, a deformed beast that no one has ever seen,' Macy said. 'He probably hasn't slept in almost three weeks.'

Wells could not confirm this when he finally appeared and Macy led him to the table. He was too far gone, holding his spoon in his fist like a caveman. His knuckles were scraped and the soup Macy gave him was soaking his beard. He stared just beyond Chase's shoulder as Chase talked, telling them both how he and Jordan had come up from California, how they had enough serious meds to get them through this, and they were willing to share, for a price. Wells didn't seem to grasp any of this.

Macy tried to explain. 'He's saying it's an epidemic, Wells. That other people have it and it's going to get worse for all of us.'

Wells said, 'A long time before I stopped then too. I came up on the ridge with rainbows slapping on a string at my leg and lightning had killed a bear like a grave mound with smoke in its fur and the eyes like hard-boiled eggs. There was another eye in the hole staring up at me and I couldn't sleep for weeks and weeks after I saw it down there big as a softball I thought oh a puddle until it blinked.'

Macy grabbed Wells's hand. She said, 'I thought you couldn't sleep because you were thinking about me. But it turns out it's something else. So much for romance.'

Wells looked at her as if she had just spoken in some alien tongue.

It was difficult for Chase to get up from the table without putting his anatomy on display. He was sure Macy caught sight of it, but he almost didn't care. He told her where she could find him. 'We're willing to share,' he said again. 'But not for money. It has to be something that has value after all of this is gone.'

He hoped that wasn't too direct, yet just direct enough.

Ten

Felicia was seeing things – Chase, for example. First, out on the deck, staring at the indifferent ocean, shirtless and skinny. Then a glimpse of him sitting at the edge of her bed, head bowed as if reading something in his lap. Or she could just hear him peeing in the bathroom, his little allergy cough revealing his identity and disrupting the noisy stream.

She saw her mother and her orthodontist down on the beach, peering into the tide pools and strolling at the edge of the water, their footprints fading behind them in the silvery gloss. A pelican too, with a laugh identical to the horsy guffaw of her childhood piano teacher. It sat on the railing no more than three feet away, winking at her as if they shared a scandalous secret.

It was worse for some, since they all had succumbed to the symptoms and progressed through the phenomenon, as the researchers insisted on calling it, at different rates. There were people in the Sleep Research Center talking to shadows and others who were only now starting to slur their words. The doctors – Kitov, Lee, Porter – were showing signs but not publicly admitting to it. Porter appeared to be the furthest gone, but maybe that was just because Kitov and Lee were generally harder to read. Even before the sleeplessness hit, the old goat-faced genius Kitov had rambled nearly incoherently, peppering his speech with Russian and shuffling down the laminated corridors not unlike the insomniacs on the streets.

Meanwhile Lee had largely persisted with his robotic demeanor, at least in public, though Felicia thought she had heard him scrambling his grammar at the last morning meeting. Then again, she was also hearing strains of music emanating from the ocean, as though a sea monster were playing a giant cello just beyond the continental shelf.

Whatever they were going to do, these researchers, they had better do it quick. This implant scheme of theirs. They had briefed everyone. A wire in the head. It sounded like a workable plan, until the Q&A, when Warren – one of several grad students who had gravitated to the lab to work with the famous Soviet-era exile – pointed out that none of them were surgeons, let alone neurosurgeons.

'Is not exactly brain surgery,' Dr Kitov tried – the joke being that it was. 'But serious,' he insisted, 'is not so complicated. Two holes drilled in skull, electrode leads threaded into brain, then wired up to stimulator that is put under skin, here in chest.'

Dr Porter, now like an angry drunk from lack of sleep, took a swipe at the principal investigator. 'Maybe when we're in there, we should go ahead and stimulate the place where fucking articles are stored.'

Felicia, and the handful of others still operating within a framework of cultural norms, felt obligated to laugh in an attempt to undermine Porter's weird venom. But it was a losing battle, this effort to uphold manners – let alone common decency – in the face of the ravaging epidemic. Emotions were raw, nerves exposed by exhaustion, and the morning meetings, lunches, gatherings of any kind were becoming increasingly hostile and unpredictable.

The irony of their situation inflamed matters. After all, here they were, the staff of one of the world's most famous sleep research facilities, and they were just as clueless as anyone else. Much of the anger and disappointment was directed at Kitov, since he was the world-renowned expert in the field of sleep and insomnia who had drawn millions in grants to the university over the years yet claimed to be completely blindsided by the phenomenon.

'It is,' he proclaimed, 'attack on cathedral of human mind, perhaps of alien origin.'

His eccentricities were no longer endearing quirks in the eyes of the sleep center inhabitants – a group of two dozen researchers, lab techs, undergrad assistants, and a small security team. Instead, his slightly askew worldview, along with his attempts at humor, was seen as a diversion, drawing the eye away from his incompetence. People had begun to look to Dr Lee, but he deferred to his master, publicly supporting Kitov's implant scheme. Indeed, he had indicated to Felicia that he thought this mechanical fix was their only hope at this point.

For a while, before the meds stopped working, they had had to separate the sleepers from the sleepless and security was an issue. Now no one was sleeping so there was no need for lockdown. People strolled the hallways at all hours, some verbalizing their delusions in mangled sentences or crashing into the walls on wobbly legs. Felicia felt compelled to guide her fellow residents safely through the labyrinth of corridors, to be useful while she still possessed the presence of mind to navigate the center. They, in return, projected their visions upon her.

Some were subtle, but telling, mix-ups, such as when Porter addressed her as Felina. In his confusion, a tech named Miles called her Terry – the name of his sister, she knew. She gently corrected him as she nursed a cut on his nose, after he had walked into one of the glass doors. He peered into her face as if trying to make sense of the details.

When her friend Francine emerged naked from her room, Felicia took her by the arm and reversed her course. Francine called her Mommy as she helped her step into a skirt. They both laughed about it, before Francine collapsed into sobs.

She had taken to cooking the food after Claudio, their cook, nearly burned down the center after attempting to cook a pot of rags, which he believed to be salted cod fillets. By helming each meal, providing the small crowd of delusional diners with plates of pasta and hunks of bread, or salads made from whatever vegetables were foraged from the grad student apartment gardens, she secured her place as the small community's mothering presence. An odd position given that she was, in fact, the youngest resident.

They were drawn to her not only because she was still mentally sound, at least comparatively, but also because many assumed she had the inside scoop on the doctors, particularly Lee. Even before the phenomenon, many believed that she and Dr Lee were having an affair, regardless of her vigorous denials. Yes, there was some small measure of smoke, but no fire. She was a student, after all, and Lee carried himself with a relentlessly uptight professionalism. If he had been harboring any interest, let alone something resembling desire, she had seen little evidence. Maybe a lingering gaze, a hint of uncharacteristic warmth, but nothing more. Her friends claimed he treated her differently.

Whether or not they were intimate, they insisted, surely she must know what the doctors were up to, since she was around them so much. Assisting with their procedures and lab work, privy to their schemes. They can sleep, some insisted. 'They cooked up a cure that they're keeping to themselves,' Davis, a security officer, proclaimed. 'They're just letting the rest of us fall apart so they can study what happens to us. Pretty soon they'll start giving us God-knows-what and say it's a cure and we'll grow fucking asparagus out of our foreheads.'

With increasing frequency, she felt compelled to defend the doctors. 'Look at them. They're suffering just like us,' she told them. 'They want a cure just as badly as everyone else.' It wasn't hard to quell their suspicions, since sleeplessness had made her fellow residents unusually open to suggestion. The fact that she was already held in high regard, mostly due to her ongoing attempts to care for them as they unraveled, gave more weight to her appeal for reason.

'They're trying to fix this,' she would tell them.

And, at least for now, they would believe her.

Though she no longer slept, she retreated to bed out of habit. She was fortunate to have her own room, assigned when Kitov urged everyone – those who hadn't already fled to their families – to stay. It was his promise of a cure that held her. She could very well be in the right place at the right time, she told her parents during their last phone call. She would come for them when it was clear they could be helped. But that moment had yet to arrive, and she could feel the margin of possibility rapidly narrowing. The tide of sleeplessness was advancing, consuming all the sand castles of coherency and logic as it crept forward. Even now, sitting on her bed, she sensed dark figures standing in the periphery of her vision. They seemed to be watchers from another dimension, now somehow visible due to a tear in the veil. Always present unless looked at directly, pressing in on her.

She quickly turned her head, hoping to catch a glimpse of her observers before they slipped behind the blind of dark matter, and was startled to find Dr Lee standing in her room instead. He looked terrible, with heavy bags under his eyes, a washed-out complexion. His cheeks and chin were peppered with stubble and his black hair was uncharacteristically tousled. He persisted in wearing his white smock, though it was unbuttoned to reveal a T-shirt and olive cargo pants. He was falling apart just like everyone else, yet he continued to make his self-imposed rounds.

'Hanging in there?' he asked.

She stared at him, her heavy eyelids slowly dropping, then snapping wide open. She nodded, afraid to speak, not wanting to reveal the distance she had descended by providing a sample of eroded language.

'Do this,' he said. He performed a minor feat with his fingers, a roadside sobriety test that he had asked her to do before. Counting one through four and back again as he touched each finger to his thumb. He had no trouble with it. Maybe the others are right, she considered. Maybe the doctors had come up with an effective cocktail of serotonin and glycerin and they were keeping it for themselves. A part of her hoped this was true. Maybe they were just testing it before going public.

She did as he asked, running through the drill, fingertips to thumb. She was relieved to see – as if watching from outside herself – that she did it well despite her burden of exhaustion. Lee was pleased too, faintly nodding encouragement. He took her by the wrist and she felt the spark of his touch. She couldn't tell if he was taking her pulse or finally making some kind of pass at her.

Now he was looking intently into her eyes, leaning forward.

Here it comes – the kiss that she had been told was inevitable. Or had she? She suspected she was having a false memory. Remembering a dream, maybe, as though it were real.

'Settle down. He's just checking your eyes,' Chase said. 'The dilation.'

She turned her head to the right, where her former

boyfriend's voice hung in the air. But Dr Lee reached up and gently nudged her chin so that she was looking at him again. He pushed in close, his breath on her lips. She waited. Nothing. It appeared that he was indeed checking her eyes, the dilation.

'You're not so bad,' Lee said. 'Probably still of all them the best.'

There it was. The messed-up syntax.

He quickly corrected himself: 'The best of all of them, I meant.'

As if he had heard her thoughts.

'We're going to need your help,' he said.

'What with?' she dared to say, when he stood back and stared for a long silent moment, blinking and swaying slightly on his feet.

'The procedure. With Kitov. He is insisting on it for the implant. That it's him.'

She understood. The old man was going to go under the knife – or actually the drill – first. There had been talk of this. Some thought it was a brave and noble thing to do, given that it was untested. Others thought it was like the captain of a sinking liner being first into the lifeboat. It was hard to tell how Kitov saw it. He seemed capable of both motivations, possibly at the same time.

'When?'

'Tomorrow at eleven. Get some rest.'

She could not tell if this was meant to be a joke.

She had gotten in the habit of watching the sunrise from the deck. Though, looking west, what she saw was the flat plain of the leaden ocean slowly separate from the sky as it took on color. The sun rose behind her, behind the compound on the bluff and the university towers above. In the evening, it lowered itself slowly into the Pacific without a sound, igniting both sea and sky with pink and orange.

When they first arrived at the university, she and Chase had become participants in a daily ritual, sometimes driving down from the school and joining others who parked along the coastal roads at dusk. It delighted these two inland kids – refugees from the smoggy suburbs – that the locals would do this: gather at the edge of the earth, go still and quiet to watch the sun die its daily death. They would witness it together, everyone sitting in the padded pews of their cars. Then, as if a service had ended, turn their ignitions, check their rearviews, and drive off into their lives.

'It *is* religious,' she had once said.

'It's better,' Chase responded, though minutes later, after driving in silence back up the bluff and into the dorm parking lot. She recalled sensing his growing disdain for the place. It had killed her that she was partly responsible for his increasing detachment at school. But there were forces, like the shifting plates of the earth, pulling them apart, however typical and predictable: his need for insulation and control, her desire to have new experiences, to live beyond their plastic past. There were other problems. His – she didn't know what to call it – sexual hang-ups? She could so easily recall the dark weight of him in the bed next to her, sinking deeper into shame as his body failed him yet again. 'You don't understand,' he said in the darkness, 'how much I want you in here.' She heard the thud of his fist against his bare chest.

Where is he now? she wondered, as the sparrows in the coral trees began their dawn chorus. Last she heard from him was a voice message from Idaho. He was on his way up to Montana with Jordan, their friend from high school, insisting that she see him on her birthday, back at her parents' house. She had agreed, but wondered if she should have. Maybe it was best to make a clean break. Or maybe he was changing, as he said. These are the kinds of things she used to worry about. That was only a week or so before the insomnia story became the only story, before she learned that her dad hadn't been sleeping. Before survival became everyone's occupation.

She stood at the railing and looked down the bluff at the rocky beach below. Her eyes scanned the water's edge and she realized she was looking for the body of an administrator – a Swede named Annika – who had thrown herself over the edge a week earlier. A refugee from the main campus, she had become increasingly distressed at being away from her homeland as the crisis escalated. As sleeplessness overwhelmed her, she began insisting that she was being held in America against her will. Her leap, Felicia assumed, was her idea of an escape.

The body had been spotted on the rocks far below. Kitov had sent out members of the security team to retrieve it. But somehow, between sealing the corpse in a body bag and returning to the center, they had lost it. Their rambling and conflicting explanations could not be sorted out, and Franklin, the security chief, refused to risk sending anyone down to search for it, fearing they wouldn't be capable of finding their way back.

Felicia kept the black body bag in mind as she studied the shoreline. Would she, in her state of mind, be able to distinguish the bagged administrator from the seals sunning on the rocks? She became absorbed in scrutinizing the dark formations below.

By the time she made it to the meeting, Kitov had already announced that he would be first to have the electrodes implanted. The procedure would take place within hours. Only a dozen people had been clearheaded enough to remember the meeting time and place. They were alternately slumped over with apathy or aggressively challenging the plan.

'Why Kitov?'

'Because the research that he is researching must be going on,' Lee explained.

Felicia winced at his delivery.

'But why take the risk of being first? Isn't it dangerous?'

'Is not dangerous. We have planned very much,' Kitov answered.

'Why not just try it out on someone else's brain first?' Phil, a lab tech, wanted to know. The bags under his eyes like wasp stings. 'Someone more expendable why not?'

At this Kitov's face reddened. 'Who is this, this expendable someone? You would like that we just grab one of you and tie you to table and open your head?'

'Not us,' Phil said. 'Someone we find. Out there.'

Kitov cast an angry glare at the tech. Only weeks ago, such a withering look would have cut like a laser through flesh and bone and triggered the tendering of resignations. Now it was met with the blank stares of people too exhausted to fear.

Porter filled the silence, saying, 'There's no time for that. Every day we wait we lose the faculty to do this kind of procedure because, in case you haven't noticed, we're losing our goddamn minds.'

'I am not a Mengele,' Kitov finally said, reminding everyone present that he had seen the end of the world before – that everything he knew as home had been burned to the ground when he was a boy, or stood against a wall and shot. Yet here he was, attempting to stare down yet another Armageddon.

To gear up for the procedure, they had been looting equipment from the university's abandoned hospital, cobbling together an operating room in the main lab of the research facility. They were concerned about electricity, even though all the research facilities were powered by an experimental system that tapped wave movement and riptides. The turbines, which sat just under the surface among the kelp beds, were revealed every day by the receding tide. The elegant electromagnetic system had earned its inventor a Nobel Prize, even though it had never been adopted as a viable alternative energy solution anywhere beyond the research wing of the campus. Kitov had very publicly despised the late Frenchman who created the wave-powered plant and had abused his famous colleague at every opportunity. Now, as they shaved the back of his head, he joked that the plant would fail during the procedure. 'This bastard Cloutier will have last laugh,' he grumbled, his words slurred.

They enclosed Kitov's large head inside a metal frame, locking it into position with pins that bored into his skull. Felicia, who had mastered the use of a syringe when injecting countless rats and dogs for Lee's research, was recruited to administer the local anesthetic at the four points where the pins penetrated the scientist's papery skin. He winced when the needle went in, telling her that she was queen bee, who, unlike the drones, can sting repeatedly with no fear of death. The moment had summoned enough adrenaline to override her exhaustion and steady her hand. She numbed the top of his head too, at the drill points, then stood back. There would be no more anesthesia, local or general, since the brain itself does not feel pain.

Lee and Porter moved in, locking the electrode driver onto the frame. The driver would ease in the electrodes with the precision and steadiness of a machine. Normally, its movements would be largely automated – informed by calculations made from computer analysis of MRI and tomography scans. But no one remaining at the center knew how to get the driver and the computer to talk to each other, not in real time, so the task fell upon Lee, whose machinelike comportment seemed a good fit. For guidance, he would listen to the firing of nerve cells, which were picked up by the electrode and amplified. He would also ask Kitov to count, or list animals, or raise his arms, in order to determine the location of the implant as it traveled to its destination.

There was some blood when they drilled, even though they had flapped the scalp. Felicia was ready with gauze, quickly sponging off the area. The drill's high-pitched whine filled the room. A wisp rose from the contact point and Felicia couldn't tell whether it was mist from the liquid coolant the drill expelled or bone dust. Before long, there were two nickel-sized pieces of skull in the tray and two openings, like a peephole for each eye, in Kitov's skull. They could all see his brain under the lights – a slick, pale coil of fat worms, thinly stained red.

'And so,' Kitov asked sportingly, 'what do you see? My childhood is there? My Vera there on bench by river? See how we found so many mushrooms? I hurt my shoulder falling on the ice in front of the institute.'

'It's your head,' Porter said, 'not a View-Master.'

Lee, from behind his surgical mask, glanced at Porter, then Felicia. Was Kitov delirious from lack of sleep or just giddily rhapsodic over clearing the first hurdle? he seemed to ask with his raised eyebrows, with his questioning pause.

They did not answer. Instead, Porter asked Kitov if he was comfortable. The older man laughed. 'My face has before been trapped in tighter places! But, yes, soft places.'

Lee sat and studied the driver monitor. With a small joystick, he lowered the recorder electrode lead so that it sat only millimeters above the brain tissue. Then, with a nod to Porter, he edged the joystick forward and the thin, stiff tendril of wire slid slowly between the wet convolutions with a faint electric hum. He paused.

'All good?' he asked his patient.

'Yes, of course,' Kitov growled. 'Start it already!'

'We have,' Porter said with annoyance.

Now the hard, slow work began. Lee advanced the lead in micrometer increments, listening for the firing of nerve cells, which crackled like static until Felicia helped move Kitov's legs and arms. Then the waveform on the monitor spread across the screen like a dark stain, and the resulting firing of nerve cells was voiced with a loud, sustained creaking – a cathedral door slowly swinging open. Because they did not have the live scans of Kitov's brain, Porter cross-checked the coordinates against a generic model of a 3-D brain – a preset from the application's library. When they decided on an exact location, they swapped out the recording electrode for an actual pulse lead and again slowly advanced as Felicia monitored the EKG and observed Kitov's response to Lee's tests: extend the index finger of your right hand, tap your feet together five times, look to the left, to the right.

This went on for three hours, until by all available calculations they believed they had arrived at proper placement of the electrode.

'You ready for some downtime?' Lee asked Kitov.

'When I see Hypnos,' Kitov responded, 'I will persuade him not to abandon us.'

Then, when Lee gave the nod and Porter manually triggered the sleep pulse, they watched as Kitov's eyes dropped shut.

They checked the EKG. The heart marched on.

All three looked at one another, eyebrows raised. It seemed as though it had worked. They were removing their surgical masks when Felicia noticed the tremor in Kitov's legs. They watched it move up his body, into his hands, into his chest, where it caused a flutter in his breathing. Then spasms hit, the body convulsing. Lee threw himself over his mentor, trying to prevent him from tearing out the pins on the stereotactic frame that caged his head. But Kitov's body kicked and bucked, knocking over bedside machinery, the rolling tray of tools. Felicia screamed as Porter pushed her out of the way and tried to wrangle their patient's scissoring legs. The pins tore into Kitov's head as he twisted. Minutes later, the celebrated scientist died behind a veil of blood.

At first they hid, staying in the lab long after the projected duration of the procedure. There were knocks at the outer door, then banging. The others. They wanted to know what was happening. When Morales, one of the security officers, used his keys to open the door, Porter yelled, *'Get the fuck out!'*

The officer retreated.

They sat. Felicia would not look in the direction of Kitov's body, even though they had covered it with a blanket. She had cried, but quickly found herself too tired for emotion.

Lee could only stare into space, or down at his hands.

'If we tell them,' Felicia said, 'they will lose hope.'

After no one responded, she said, 'Annika I mean.'

Time passed, marked by the whirring of hard drives, the beep of monitors. The sporadic flurries of pounding on the door.

In the dead space between them, a question floated. Should they lie? If so, what would the lie be? No one said this, but Porter responded as if it had been spoken. 'We say Kitov was an epileptic. He told us never and this made it unsafe.'

Felicia looked up from where she sat on the floor. 'Was he?'

'Maybe,' Porter said. 'It's possible he was. How else can it be explained to anyone? All the math was right. It was fucking elephant math. Elegant.'

'It wasn't the math,' Lee said sullenly. 'An epileptic no not he.'

'Well then, what?'

'The generic model was wrong. Too young for Kitov, un-developed, unaged. Possibly I don't know.'

'The model was wrong,' Porter repeated sarcastically. His sleep-deprived venom surged. 'Or maybe you had your girl dose him so the alpha is you now?'

Lee would not be baited. 'Listen to us,' he said, slurring. 'We're too far deep to do this, just too tired. But we have to try now again. Stories won't help.'

Porter disagreed. 'You spill the truth and no one's going to sit in that chair.'

There was more pounding at the door.

Lee went to it, with Porter charging after him. He grabbed at Lee's shoulder, but Lee shook him off. Felicia came up behind Porter, rested her hand on his arm. It was her power, this touch. He looked at her, shaking his head, yet standing down.

Outside, everyone was waiting, a red-eyed, blinking mob, stooped and warped by exhaustion. Francine, now in her Smurf scrubs. Warren and the other grad students, bearded, ragged, sitting on the floor of the corridor. There were a few security men, some of the others that had come to them and were not turned away: students, university employees, Miguel from plant operations, Maritza from the neighboring institute. Some of them now three weeks without sleep. They looked past them, scanning for Kitov – for proof that there was a door in the black wall before them.

'It was not successful,' Lee said flatly. 'The procedure. A mishap happened.'

This was a first. Relief that sleep was impossible. She feared reliving Kitov's death in her dreams. The white, thick spittle gathering in the corners of his mouth, quickly churned into foam by the gnashing of his teeth. His eyes had rolled back when the spasm hit, so that he looked blind. So that it looked as if the inside of his head was lined with white plastic and pressure was causing the membrane to bulge out the sockets. His body jerked electrically, a marionette manipulated by an angry child. It was one thing to recall this. The horror was somewhat subdued. To dream it would be devastating all over again. To dream it is to feel it.

She had never seen someone die before, and this was a gruesome introduction to life's departure from the body. She knew, from stories the security team had brought back from the outside, that human death littered the cities, suburbs, open fields and forests, the side of the road. Corpses scattered throughout the landscape like scarecrows blown from their stakes. Annika's body, rising and falling on the waves. Had she actually seen this? The vision of it, real or imagined, was a quieter horror. So distant and in some ways resonating with a suggestion of release and the possibility of return. A metaphor – there in the arms of the wide blue expanse – that, yes, was like the promise of religion, not the threat. Kitov's death bespoke a torment that persisted beyond an extinguished pulse. His posture in death, the agony of his lines, suggested that it would continue forever. That he was born into a new realm of unceasing suffering.

'That's kind of a weird thought,' she heard Chase say from the bathroom.

'You didn't see it,' she said.

'Is that why you won't do it? Because you're afraid of dying a horrible death again and again?'

'Do what?'

'You know. The thing he wants you to do, your boss – Dr Dreamy.'

Felicia looked through the bathroom door. She could see the edge of the sink, the rim of the mirror. If she turned her head away, looking forward at the wall but concentrating – not focusing – on the margins of her field of vision, she saw his shadow on the wall. She knew Chase was talking about Lee. She knew the thing he meant was volunteering for the procedure. She felt the gravity of it, pulling at marrow in her bones, even before Lee went into the corridor and asked for someone to step forward. She dared not move, frozen with fear. Having seen what she had seen, no. She couldn't.

'You need to do it,' Chase said. 'For one thing, you promised you would see me on your birthday. If you don't do this, you aren't going to make it.'

She decided to ignore him.

'And if you do it, everyone will like you. And isn't that what matters the most?'

'Shut up, Chase.'

She lay back in bed and closed her eyes. He came in closer. She felt him standing at the foot of her bed. He told her a story.

'Your parents,' he said, 'are sleepers. Both of them. The sleeplessness your father mentioned during that last call was nothing more than his usual nighttime restlessness. He thought he was really in the grip of this thing, but he fell asleep in front of the TV one night, as the stories of the epidemic droned on in the dark. Your mother has never had the slightest problem sleeping, though she hid this from him at first – knowing what was happening when sleepers were discovered by insomniacs. But when she found him sleeping on the couch, she curled up next to him and the two of them slept through the night. In the morning, they tried to understand why the two of them could sleep while their neighbors and friends were succumbing to insomnia one after another. They spent three days going through everything in their environment, and everything they did throughout the day, to try to figure out the thing that had made them immune. They weren't on any special medications. They didn't have health conditions that would be unusual or rare. They thought about their diet, but it was the same stuff everyone else eats – lots of meat from the grill, bread and tortillas, diet soda and beer, produce and dairy from the super-market. They started considering the less obvious – maybe it was the new carpet they had installed when you started school. Some chemical in the shag, maybe. Your mother's religious nature kicked in, deciding it was God's way of rewarding them for living a good life. "Maybe," your father said. Or maybe it was because they had uttered some rare combination of syllables at some point in their lives, or eaten some weird combination of foods. They have no way of knowing, no way of tracing all the unexpected combinations they might have created. So they go on sleeping, not knowing how or why, keeping it a secret from everyone else.'

'If it's a secret,' she asked, 'how do you know about it?'

'Because I have moved to a place where I can see it happening. I'm there, just like I'm here, standing in the corner of their eyes, a shadow just at the edge of the frame. Watching and listening like an observing animal. Sleeplessness is a portal. But only for a little while. It's just a phase of the phenomenon – one that occurs right before things, well, get worse.'

She thought about his story. 'If you can see everything,' she said, 'what is it that makes them able to sleep?'

'If you look closely at your house,' he explained, 'you will see tiny, dark particles drawn from the air into a hole in the rafters. Stand closer and you will see that these particles are bees. Press your ear to the wall and you'll hear a deep, constant drone, like the sound of a giant drill. Push into the hole and you will see that the entire house is functioning as a giant hive. The walls are filled with bees and honey, all living in the waxy, brainy folds of honeycomb. It's the drone, reverberating through the frame of the structure, that creates a deep sound that is felt, not heard. Those cheap suburban houses, the way they're made. They are very similar to musical instruments, with a thin shell or skin stretched over a wooden frame. The vibration – a one-note lullaby – carries sleep in it just like the pulse Lee wants to wire into your brain.'

'So they are fine,' she said. 'My parents are fine.'

'For now,' he said. 'But it isn't going to last. I'm sure you've seen the reports. The bees are dying and no one knows why. Soon the walls will be filled with husks, just dry shells of the dead. And the drone will go silent.'

'No!'

'Yes.'

He paused and she thought maybe he was gone.

'Besides,' Chase said suddenly, startling her, 'you promised to meet me on your birthday.'

She sat in silence for the remainder of the night. Earlier, when they had emerged from the operating room, Lee was visibly disgusted that no one stepped forward. He ordered them to select someone by the morning meeting, which was now only hours away. Otherwise they would do a random drawing. By sunrise, standing at the railing, she had decided Chase was right, even if it wasn't the real Chase. Her mind was the sharpest, though her fear probably the greatest. She was the one.

She found Lee in the lunchroom and began trembling as she offered herself up. She somewhat expected him to refuse, to insist that someone else would volunteer. Or point to the random drawing as the only fair way. She had maybe even hoped he would insist it was out of the question, that she was needed to help with the procedure. Only she could do what was needed, only she had the experience, having witnessed their failure.

He looked at her blankly, as all her anticipated responses

seemed to scroll past his eyes. As each point was possibly considered, then trumped by the unequivocal fact that they were simply out of time. Instead of saying these things, he leaned forward and kissed her softly on the mouth.

Eleven

The insomniac woke Biggs, shrieking like the braking of a train and rattling the cage. His would-be attacker was a middle-aged man with bruised arms, ruddy hairless head, and ragged beard, a wiry frame under a filthy yellow T-shirt. He had his fingers through the tight mesh and he was pulling hard, as though he were the one trapped inside. Biggs scanned for others in the massive space. Sunlight poured down from the skylights above, gleaming off the steel conveyor rollers. He figured he must have slept only a few hours – the exhaustion still sat heavy in his body, slowing him.

The cage was solid, the mesh refusing to bend or bow despite the efforts of the attacker. It was a security cage designed to be a safe partition in an electronics warehouse. It should hold, but there was no reason to just sit there waiting.

Biggs got to his feet and grabbed the heavy flashlight he had picked up in an abandoned hardware store. The weight of it was reassuring. He took two steps forward, looking grave. His proximity sent the insomniac into an even more animated fit of rage, bashing at the wire with his head. Biggs recoiled, tense. The animal screams echoed in the vast interior space and Biggs wished he would shut the fuck up.

'I'm going to break your fingers if you don't let go,' Biggs told him flatly. 'You understand?'

The man's response was to press his face against the cage and bellow, his mouth open wide, exposing his silver fillings, his white tongue. Biggs wanted to shove the flashlight down the insomniac's throat to silence him.

He stepped forward and beat at the man's fingers until he let go of the cage, wailing and staring at Biggs in disbelief.

'I warned you,' Biggs said.

The insomniac charged again, pounding on the mesh. When he made the mistake of grabbing the wire, Biggs was there with the flashlight.

'Don't!' Biggs yelled, swinging hard at the fingers and hearing the sickening crack of bone.

Again the man backed away, whimpering at his damaged hands, before making another charge, urged on by his own war cry.

For a while, Biggs batted at anything that came through the mesh, then sat down, actually winded from the effort, as the man raged on. From his makeshift bed, Biggs watched the insomniac kicking at the cage, ramming it with the canvas carts and boxes that littered the warehouse floor, flinging fistfuls of loose circuits that hit like a spray of insects. Biggs flinched with every blow. Yet the cage showed no sign of yielding. It would hold.

At least no one else was around, Biggs observed. Who would be? The warehouse was one of dozens in the middle of other-wise undeveloped washland. The only thing to do was wait it out. If he sat here long enough, wide-eyed and alert, maybe the insomniac would forget that he had ever seen Biggs sleeping. At this stage, he knew, they were a mental mess – the sleepless. Their thoughts seem to cycle madly through a headspace bustling with contradictory signals. Unfortunately, he had seen that they only came into focus when in this highly agitated state, a sustained rage triggered by the sight of a sleeper. This could be a long and dangerous wait.

The man circled the cage. He tripped over boxes and slid on the motherboards that cluttered the ground, but he never took his eyes off Biggs.

Who are you? Biggs wondered, studying the man for clues about his pre-epidemic past. Veined, worn hands. Maybe a contractor or maybe a plumber, an electrician. Or most likely someone who worked here, in this warehouse. Forklift driver or what? Foreman. Maybe a father.

The man continued to shriek and, when he threw himself at the cage, to groan as his legs churned, plowing him forward against the immovable structure. Biggs regretted not having a real weapon. A gun would be best. But even if he did, he doubted he could shoot this wreck of a human, now grating his own head against the tight gauge of mesh. He had never even fired a gun. Now, he promised himself, it seemed necessary to find one. If I ever get out of this cage.

'You going to let me leave?' he asked the insomniac.

This set off a deafening volley of shrieking that, much to Biggs's relief, tapered off at the end. The man was screaming himself hoarse. That would be a good thing.

'Yeah? Then what happened?' Biggs said, now goading.

The man let out a ragged cry that bounced off the high ceiling. He bashed at the gate with his shoulder.

This response presented Biggs with a strategy. He got to his feet and provoked a series of fits, baiting the man by standing just on the other side of the wire wall, until he succeeded in reducing the outbursts to nothing more than gravelly expulsions. The man's body was starting to give out as well. He was drenched in sweat and it took him longer to get back on his feet after tripping over boxes or bouncing off the mesh to the floor. Yet he persisted in circling and launching himself against the cage.

Biggs returned to his bed. He too was exhausted, and groggy from his own, more conventional sleep deficit. It had been the first time in days that Biggs felt safe enough to make an attempt. After finding the cage in the warehouse, and testing it much in the way it was being tested now, he had doubled back a few miles to a ransacked Home Depot he had spotted earlier. There he found four heavy locks, still packaged, and stuffed them into the pockets of his cargo pants – also a prize of looting. Back at the warehouse, he found some foam packing cushions and boxes and layered them on the floor. It wasn't a bad bed. His plan was to get a couple of days' sleep, then continue on to Carolyn's father's house, where he was hoping she had fled as she had done before.

Now he drank some water that he had stashed, watching the man over the top of the plastic bottle. He lay back on his elbows and considered his predicament. Weird how a cage seemed like a good place to make a home, however temporary.

When you think about it, the whole setup – life as we know it – is one cage inside another inside another, he remembered telling her. This was at a time when his slowly accumulated disillusionment with ad work had begun to ferment. What he found he could no longer tolerate was the seriousness of it all: the desperation of clients to please their corporate overlords, the desperation of the agency to please the client. How a currency of such shallow ideas was treated as gold. It was all an illusion. 'Well, it's either a cage or a cave,' Carolyn once told him.

He recalled how she showed him the difference between the two. It happened at the most unlikely time: when they were trying to get pregnant. Biggs would sometimes come home from the office at lunchtime – if Carolyn's calendar indicated it was that optimal phase of her cycle. She would be waiting, often washing up in the bathroom if she had been painting props or puppets in her studio. He would come in and sit on the Murphy bed in the main room of the loft, kicking off his shoes and peeling off his pants. They joked about how clinical things had gotten, and somehow the joking made it less so.

'Your sperm donkey has arrived,' he called glumly through the door after an especially dreary morning at the agency. 'Let's make a zygote.'

'Be right out,' she responded over the hiss of the sink and the gentle splashing of her scrubbing.

'Your sex Eeyore,' he mumbled.

'Oh boy,' she said, stepping out in her bra and panties – a sight he never tired of, even during those days of constant trying. She sat next to him, sensing, he knew, that he wasn't in the right frame of mind. No doubt taking in his pants bunched up at his ankles, the slump of shoulders, not to mention the lackluster delivery of his jokes. It wasn't like him to brood, but today it felt like a default setting. She leaned into him and kissed his cheek, sniffing his stubble at the same time.

'Yep, it's you,' she said.

She claimed he had a unique aroma – a pleasing one that was part soap, part coffee, with a dash of some faintly musky perfume generated in his pores while he slept. Only she could smell it. It was strongest in the mornings, she insisted, often telling him that her sniff test was a surefire way to screen for dastardly clones and doppelgangers.

She threw her long thigh over his lap. Her shin was smooth, even shiny. She still had hope, an engine of possibility still purred inside her. This was her upbeat era. Their efforts at conception had yet to foreshadow the desperation to come. She leaned back and looked at his face, reached up and scratched lightly at the back of his head – unhurried, calibrating his mood. Invisible colors passed between them. She knew this was about his job. There was no reason for him to say anything. They had covered his career frustrations many times over – the meaninglessness of it all, the enslavement of storytelling, he had once melodramatically labeled it. The artless art, he once proclaimed.

'You know what we should do?' she asked.

'What's that?'

'We should drag the mattress into my studio where we can block out all the light. We'll make it pitch dark and silent. I have those thick black curtains, you know, and sound blankets. Then we should get under the covers and just sleep.'

'Just sleep.'

'That's it. No baby making, no talking, no thinking. Just sleeping. And we should try to sleep for as long as we possibly can. Days, maybe weeks.'

'What about my job?' he asked, though he was already buying in. 'I have a call with Chicago at two.'

'You won't need a job where we're going, baby.'

'You mean in our dreams.'

'You'll dream up a whole new life. What's your dream job?'

He thought for a moment. 'I always wanted to be the guy who delivers mail to some tropical islands by rowboat.'

'Really? Huh.'

'It would be a good daily workout, and imagine the tan.'

They followed through on the plan, converting her studio into a sleeping den. A cave deep inside a snow-covered mountain, she suggested.

After fifteen minutes, they found themselves making love in the lightless chamber. He fell asleep soon after. When he woke, he felt for her in the darkness, expecting her to be gone. She rarely slept during the day and barely slept at night. But she was there, warm and silent next to him. He drifted off again and woke up when she was sniffing his neck, the room still thick with an impenetrable darkness. 'Is it me?' he whispered.

'Aren't you wondering if it's me?'

'How long did we sleep?'

'I don't know.'

'What time do you think it is?'

'What day, you mean.'

'Day? Really?'

He started to sit up but she pulled him down. 'No, let's stay here,' she said. 'Don't you see that we're completely lost in time and space?'

'Hey,' he said, finally getting it. 'Yeah.'

'I never want to leave,' she said. 'I always want to be here with you.'

He went back to work the following Monday, after sleeping through most of Friday. But it was as though a seed had indeed been planted. It took only two weeks to bloom. He resigned and packed up, all in one afternoon. She met him downstairs, and brought along her equipment dolly to help him bring up the boxes of his personal belongings. It was the beginning of a new era, maybe an era called the end.

The assault was losing steam when Biggs reset the man's rage by yawning. At first he froze in astonishment, then was overwhelmed by violent convulsions. His rage took the form of a seizure and he fell to the ground, kicking and punching at the cage. He pulled himself up against it and climbed his legs up the wall, so that he was upside down, seething with an epic tantrum. Yet his cries were now mere hisses.

Biggs looked on sadly. It was a terrible thing that had set upon them all. His own father and mother must have passed through this stage as well, if not everyone else he knew. He did not know the fate of his brother. If he couldn't find Carolyn, he would make his way to Adam's house and see what had become of him.

Maybe he's like me. A sleeper. Why not? We have the same blood, same wiring – if that has anything to do with it.

When Biggs yawned again, he simply rolled onto his side, turning his back on the human explosion it again triggered only a few feet away. He allowed his head to sink into the balled-up clothes that served as his pillow.

Maybe it was only for a few minutes, maybe an hour.

He thought he heard someone say his name.

There was a clinking, the crunch of footsteps on the circuits scattered all over the floor. He sat up on his elbows and turned toward the movement. Maybe, Biggs wondered, I am an insomniac too. The shadowy figures, the voices. That's what you eventually experience. He watched, surprised, as the figure emerged into view.

It was Carolyn, dressed in black – her studio clothes that hid her in the darkness at the outskirts of the frame, or allowed her to puppeteer some quick on-camera movement while obscured against a black felt backdrop. She would then use a pen tool and tablet to manually erase every pixel of herself from each digital frame of the footage, replacing the hint of her shape in the darkness with a truer emptiness. It was grueling work that she called *cleanup*, this removal of herself from her worlds.

Now time seemed to be held up. Not frozen solid, but quivering in a tight loop. The scene flickered, pulsed, as though the cosmic playhead was jumping between two nearly similar frames. The insomniac's back seemed to shudder violently, flickering along the edges. Biggs wanted to warn Carolyn that the man was dangerous, but his mouth would not open at his mental urging, nor would his throat issue a sound. She glided toward his attacker without pause and stood over him, studying him. It was an expression of concentration he had seen before, when standing at the door of her studio, well past midnight, to ask her if she was coming to bed. She leaned in, tilting her head, squinting, then reached out. He heard her hands at work – the moist molding of clay, a sudden cracking as she grit her teeth and bore down. There was a burst of light. The man's form jolted, then settled back into the looping shudder.

Carolyn stood back and studied the figure sitting before her, again squinting, considering. She leaned forward and made some adjustments. Satisfied, she turned and said to Biggs, 'What next, dreamer?'

'Next?'

'Everything happens in your head first.'

'How did you get here?' he asked.

'I dropped in,' she said. 'From the skylight. No one ever looks up.'

She moved toward the margins of his periphery and seemed to settle there, just out of view, a soft dark edge to his field of vision.

He tried to follow her, turning his head, but the dark area moved with him. Rising to his knees, he shifted focus and scanned the room. There was no sign of Carolyn anywhere, other than a strange dark feathering to the extreme right corner of his eye. He rubbed at it, thinking there was something there – a hair, a mote of dust – but it remained. Had it always been there? Why hadn't he noticed before? Then the thought that was always there too: Was he finally succumbing?

The insomniac was now still and silent, slumped on the floor, his back pressed against the cage. Biggs stood and nudged the man's back by kneeing the wire wall. Nothing. He bent over and stuck a knuckle through the mesh, poking the man in the spine. Still no reaction. He yelled and kicked hard against the cage.

When the insomniac remained still, Biggs grabbed the flashlight. He dug in his pocket for the key to the lock. The gate opened with a creak and he stepped out onto the silent warehouse floor. When he came around the cage, he was startled to see the insomniac staring up at him. He raised the flashlight, ready to swing. But the man's eyes were locked in an empty stare. His mouth was frozen open to an unnatural degree. His jaw was clearly broken, and his chin was still wet with drool. Biggs could see that he was dead, yet he crouched over the body and slowly sent out his hand to touch the man's cool, lifeless flesh.

He stood and searched the warehouse for signs of Carolyn. She was watching him, he was sure of it. But from where? Like his wedding band, which had reappeared on his finger when he awoke at Delicious, there was physical evidence of her presence. He studied it now, half expecting the ring to be gone. But there it was, as real as the corpse sitting before him.

Twelve

Upon stealing the truck, Chase found himself in possession of sheep. He could not tell how many, daring only to glimpse up at the rearview mirror as he negotiated the many curves in the mountain road at an unsafe speed. Maybe four or six or nine, sliding around back there. He could hear the flinty sound of their hooves scuffing against the metal floor of the open bed, their woolly bodies thumping against the sides. The animals complained as they were herded by centripetal force into corners of the careening vehicle. Chase caught flashes of their pale gums and yellow teeth, their wild eyes. His sheep: maybe plural or maybe just one, carouseling past the window. No, at least two. Wow, they were stressed out, braying or barking or baying – whatever kind of sound that was.

He was freaking out too, not knowing if the insomniacs were right on his tail. Here he was driving a truck, naked, fingers and toes shriveled by the icy creek water. Creased soles matted with pine needles, bejeweled with jagged pebbles. Still, he stomped on the worn pedals. The hot seat seared his palest flesh and the steering wheel felt like a red stove burner in his hands.

Yet his erection persisted. It had bobbed out in front of him when he had leapt from the creek and run through the meadow.

It was like a tranquilizer dart someone had shot into him, purple as of a few days ago and craning up at the wheel as if trying to see over the dash. Tight and aching, the engorged appendage was a constant reminder that he had overindulged. A physical, artificially induced formality that had no linkage to desire. As if insomnia wasn't bad enough, he had this additional, armless cross to bear, a cruel miracle of persistence. Death-defying in its own way, since it had not become gangrenous, as Jordan said it would. What does Jordan know, anyway? He's a pharmacy cashier, not a doctor.

The creek had helped, sitting in the bitingly cold water as long as his body could endure. But now he had no creek. Nor did he have the other stolen pharmaceuticals – the sleep drugs that they had been using to ward off the inevitable.

No drugs and no pants. What he had was some desperate sheep rancher's truck, and his sheep. The guy must have joined in the caravan of insomniacs that raided the campsite, hoping for at least one good night. Maybe he'll get it. Maybe they'll find some loose pills in the creases of the sleeping bag, or in the dust by the water jug, where surely some fell from Jordan's trembling hands. If they looked hard enough, they might even find the cooler buried in the brush. They're going to be pretty pissed when they find out those pills don't work very well. They'll work a few times, then the sleeplessness comes back stronger than ever, settling like a ball of sparks in your brain.

Macy! Macy must have sent them!

The road straightened for a stretch and he looked back at his sheep, huddled against the wind, struggling for footing. Some of his sheep were panting. Yes, *his* sheep. He had claimed them, eager to secure possessions, being so suddenly a person with nothing. And there was something else at work – a strange allure of animals, as if the notion of other living creatures was somewhat novel. It was, in a way. After all, he was a kid from the L.A. suburbs who had little experience with livestock. But in his sleep-deprived mind he sensed something marvelous and cosmically awesome about their animal presence. It was possibly a subtle form of emotional hallucination, or maybe he had pulled on a thread of some great, hitherto invisible truth. He didn't know. He felt ownership, and with it a vague and complicated sense of transcendent wealth.

He owned beasts.

But that didn't mean he had no need for pants.

He knew as soon as he got behind the wheel – even before he had discovered the sheep – that he was going back to California. Felicia's birthday was only days away and he intended to be at her parents' house, where he knew she was sure to return. The epidemic had most certainly altered the timing of things, but if anything, it made her trip home even more likely, he figured. He aimed the stolen truck down the road he and Jordan had taken weeks earlier, which meant riding the highway back up and over the towering range before dropping into Yellowstone and angling toward Utah.

The truck had some muscle, powering up the switchbacks to the summit, which was a plateau covered with thick tundra-like scruff and a low haze of purple flowers. Small rivulets cut meandering courses through it like long, dark cracks. The road was lined with tall painted sticks, which measured the height of the snow during winter. He could see the craggy blue peaks of the range all the way to the horizon and, tucked in canyons and craters, white bibs of glaciers and lakes shining like chrome. Thunderheads piled up in the distance, threatening to topple and spread like a canopy of loose wool over the pale sky. The wind passing through the cab was suddenly cool, the air thin. It was a relief to the sheep, it seemed. They were no longer panting.

The only sign of civilization at that altitude was a trading post called Top of the World – a log-and-sod structure with a broad plank porch and a tin roof. Behind it sat a small prairie house, which seemed to serve as merely the foundation for a radio antenna that telegraphed upward several stories like a giant hypodermic needle. Beside the house sat a green swing set, and the ground was littered with brightly colored toys – a surreal sight, given the desolate location.

Pulling to a stop in the parking lot, he shut off the engine and looked around the cab for something – anything – that could pass as clothing. He found a pair of massive mud-caked boots behind the passenger seat and struggled to put them on. Behind the driver's seat was an open-top toolbox containing a hatchet and a car jack. There was nothing else. Not even a map in the glove box, which he had intended to wear like a towel wrapped around his waist. Given his anxious nature, this was a worst-case scenario. His youthful years were plagued with recurring nightmares of finding himself naked in public. It wasn't the most persistent articulation of his many fears, but certainly one that came to the forefront of his mind as he exited the truck, hands cupped to conceal his aroused state, thinking, Oh, jesusgod, this is insane.

He stomped toward the storefront in the cool wind, then glanced back at the animals in the truck bed. They peered at him through the racks. There were definitely more than six of them, it seemed. Gaunt, elderly faces – movie villager faces, Chase thought – and black eyes rimmed with gold. So hard to tell how many because they all looked exactly the same and they kept shifting around, changing position, their hooves scuffing at the grit on the floor of the bed. He envied their woolly coats. And what did they think of him? How many times, he wondered, had they seen a totally naked human?

He clomped up the creaky stairs and peered inside the

window, past the Yes-We're-Open sign and those promoting bait, maps, and supplies. He scanned the store for people but his eyes found no one. To open the door, he quickly allowed one of his hands to abandon its post and turn the knob, then pushed his way in, feeling the cold glass of the door's window against his shoulder. The interior was dense with clutter. An archaic cash register sat below a massive moose head. The walls bristled with antler wreaths. There were a few short aisles of groceries and camping supplies, plus a wall of souvenirs. A jackalope had been mounted atop some glass cases that held fishing flies and pocketknives. There was no one else in the store.

Rather than call out, Chase moved quickly to the back of the store, where, among the fishing gear, he caught sight of a mannequin dressed in waders, essentially rubber overalls with built-in boots. He kicked off the massive boots he had worn into the store and started stripping the headless figure, peeling the waders off and discarding the flesh-tone plaster corpse. It hit the hard floor with a clatter, chips of its enamel skin scattering on the tile. Fortunately, the waders were large in size, perhaps even extra large. When he pulled them up around him, cinching the straps down like suspenders at his shoulders, the fit was roomy enough to accommodate his stubborn erection.

He looked around for a shirt. In the souvenir portion of the store there were Top of the World T-shirts. He chose one that said I'VE BEEN TO THE EDGE on the front, pulling it over his head.

Now he was suddenly conscious of the fact that, should the storeowner materialize, he might not be able to walk away with the goods. It's not like he could buy anything. He had no money. The best thing to do was get the hell out of there before anyone showed up. He started for the door but decided to scoop up several boxes of cornflakes. For my sheep, he figured. Probably thirsty too. Near the register, he spotted a bowl of matchbooks. He might need fire. He grabbed a book and tucked it into the front pocket of the waders. There was a metal tub by the door, filled with what appeared to be hand-carved Christmas tree ornaments. Chase bent and flipped it, emptying the tub. He tossed in the boxes of cereal and carried it out. He could stop anywhere for water now.

Walking in the waders was odd. He moved stiffly through the wind in an impenetrable sheath. It was like wearing a diaper made out of an X-ray bib. In the places where his skin made contact with the material, there was a potentially chafing friction. He was already in a highly sensitive state. In the short walk to the truck, he knew this was going to be a real problem. Some underwear would sure be a lifesaver. He looked back at the store, then at the house.

He was startled to see a man sitting on the porch.

Chase's first instinct was to run. He resisted the urge and instead walked as quickly as possible around the truck to the passenger side, where he put the tub on the seat. Then, closing the door, he started back around the front of the truck, where he noticed a colorful display of insects stuck to the front grille. He waddled around to the driver's side.

All of his attempts at stealth were in vain, however, because the man appeared to be looking directly at him. He was watching Chase steal from the store but, judging by his slumped posture, didn't seem to care. His head swung slowly from Chase to the highway and back. It seemed to Chase that the man's lips were moving, that he was talking to himself. He recalled how he and Jordan had seen Felicia's dad sitting on his backyard patio at three in the morning talking to himself. That was before Chase believed in the insomnia epidemic, dismissing Jordan's warnings as slightly psycho ramblings.

He stepped out of the truck, but paused, trying to think up a semiplausible excuse for his actions. Anything that could get him some real clothes. He could tell the guy that he had tried to pay but there was no one working the register. If the man demanded payment, he could leave a sheep as collateral, saying he had to drive back to town for his wallet. He hated the thought of losing a sheep, though. He wasn't sure how many he had, but whatever the number, he did not want to see it diminished. Fortunately, the subject of his thievery never came up. As he approached, the man had other things he wanted to talk about, confirming Chase's suspicions about his state of mind.

The man, his eyes heavily bagged and bleary, squinted up at Chase and said, 'You can see from up here what they're doing from being this high up when the clouds aren't in the way. You can see all their business being conducted clear as day like it was. I watched them change the cards and I'm telling you they swapped those cards like nothing hard. They literally swapped the cards no ifs about it if you can believe that or buts.'

'I can believe it,' Chase said.

'Yessir! They switched the cards to God-knows-what and you might as well burn the black curtain!' He made the whooshing sound of something going up in flames. 'No one ever's going to pull that curtain closed with those cards switched.'

Chase had no idea what the man could mean. He studied him, trying to determine whether he was dangerous. Maybe he'd just push past him and go in the house, pick out something to wear. The man was probably in his late forties. He wore a dirty baseball cap, and his hair, or what could be seen of it hanging out the back, was going gray. He had a big cop mustache that hung over his upper lip, and small icy blue eyes. Those eyes were almost smiling when he said, 'So I shut everything down on my own with my own hands one by one because

I'm not letting them do it! I'm going to do it myself goddammit and I think it went okay I think it went okay.' .

He stood. 'Look for yourself and you tell me.'

The man beckoned Chase up the steps to the threshold of the house, where he held open the door. Chase obliged. The rubber soles of the built-in boots softened his footsteps on the hollow porch. Inside the dim space, Chase could see three children and a woman lying on the floor, faceup with their hands at their sides. Their eyes were closed and they had been arranged in order of size: a toddler, then a boy, an older girl, and a woman. Sleeping? He felt a rush of envy. But as his eyes adjusted, he saw that the only movement in the room was that of some flies, flitting about the blank faces, landing on alabaster eyelids. Chase went cold.

'It went okay don't you think seeing them there that it wasn't too bad?' the man was asking.

'Wait here,' was all Chase could think to say. He backed away, then trotted down the stairs. He said, 'Be right back.' But it was more of a whisper drowned out by the creaking of the rubber waders as he made for the truck.

He drove with the fear swelling up inside him. It was in his stomach like a mass of cold dough, expanding into a tight void. It generated a disorienting feeling like standing on a ledge, going woozy at being so close to the drop. The guy's face, his eyes – those small squinting eyes. Something animal was there, and a human thing missing, seeped out, so dumb to the horror. Did he strangle them one by one? A sleepless killer with animal eyes. Chase's hands shook, so he gripped the wheel and pumped the gas, then the brakes, then the gas again, taking the tight curves through the mountains. The sheep groaned as they slid around, knees locked, like end tables. The shifting weight felt like gusts of wind hitting the truck and Chase wished they didn't insist on standing.

'Get down!' he yelled out at them though the rear window.

Or was he yelling at himself, that part of himself that still stood? How could he still be aroused after what he had just seen? His state was some kind of punishment, he was now sure. Payback for some ill way of looking at the world. Because that's the stem, the fuse to a lifelong implosion, the hook for dreams and the on-switch of death. And now there it was, the thing normally most hidden, out in front of him and insisting with its posture, its wicklike attitude, on being lit.

He began sobbing but he wasn't sure what, exactly, was bringing forth the tears. It wasn't the children he had seen, so still and waxy like dolls. Nor was it pity for the man who had, because of some sleepless delusions, somehow executed each of them. Fuck, he just needed to see Felicia.

He encountered few vehicles on the road, even after completing the descent and moving through more populated areas. As they passed, Chase tried to read the faces of the drivers for insomnia. They blurred by too quickly to tell. There were several cars abandoned at the side of the road. He overtook an RV that was weaving and saw an elderly woman at the wheel, an old six-shooter on the dash. The road took him through a few towns, which were alive with people, some of them staggering on the streets. Chase couldn't tell if they were drunk or sleepless, but after the incident at the Top of the World, he was too afraid to stop and investigate. The occasionally shattered window of a storefront or streets clogged with haphazardly parked cars seemed to indicate that the epidemic was in play. There was no sign of authorities, not even a ranger.

As evening approached, he could no longer ignore the fact that he had to piss – a basic function complicated by his condition. He looked for a place to leave the highway, eventually deciding on a dirt road that ran alongside a creek through wooded terrain. The sheep, which had quieted as the highway straightened but were now jostled by the rutted road, resumed voicing their annoyance with congested bleating. 'Yeah, yeah,' Chase said. 'We all need a break.'

The place he chose to park was a grassy opening along the bank, a gap in the trees that lined the creek. He pulled to a stop and walked into the water as the sun set, tossing his shirt to the bank and peeling down the waders. They served their true purpose, protecting his feet and legs from the cold water as well as from his own fluid, which he released in uncomfortable, arcing spurts. When he finished, he continued to stand in the water, his face slack in a stupor of exhaustion. He felt the current pulling at his legs as he watched the mayflies swarm. Frogs started up their chorus and bats dipped and flittered overhead. He recalled how he and Jordan had used a fishing pole and peach beetles to hook bats when they were kids. Standing on the roof of the restrooms at the neighborhood park, casting up at the sky. Chase wondered where Jordan was now. Had he gotten away? Not likely, since he was so dopey with drugs these days. Turns out Jordan had grabbed morphine along with the sleep stuff. And it was the only thing that was giving him any kind of relief. Chase insisted that he wasn't really sleeping on the stuff, but only hallucinating that he was sleeping. 'What's the difference?' Jordan had asked.

He turned and looked at the truck. In the dusky light, the sheep were huddled in the bed, some with their faces turned his way. He wondered if he could let them out so they could eat the grass and drink from the creek. But how would he ever get them back in the truck? They would probably scatter in all directions. They would roam the woods and one by one fall victim to predators – wolves, bears, pumas. He couldn't let that happen. Not to his sheep.

He waddled out of the creek and around to the passenger side of the truck, where he pulled out the metal tub and corn-flakes he had stolen. Everything he owned, he had stolen, he realized. And to think that he had been so uptight about stealing the drugs from the pharmacy. He would have to steal gas too, he knew. The thought of it made him anxious. He told himself to stay focused on feeding and watering his sheep.

When he came around to the tailgate with a box of corn-flakes, the sheep moved away from him, pressing into a tight scrum at the opposite end of the bed. They were afraid of him. He tore open the box and scattered fistful of cornflakes on the floor of the bed, which was smeared with droppings. The sheep showed no interest in the cereal. Who would? he conceded. No one wants their food mixed with shit.

He tore open all the boxes and poured the cereal into the tub. Then he lowered the gate and slid it along the grooved floor. Still the sheep kept to the other side of the bed. The closest had their backs to him. He reached in for their stub tails, but they nudged and squirmed away, fighting to be farthest from the gate, from him. The truck shook under their desperate maneuverings. Had they learned to be this fearful? he wondered. Or were they born with the fear built in?

He stared at them, glazing over – their pungent odor and presence somehow soothing and hypnotic. To his exhausted eyes, they were identical. All clones of the same self-replicating animal. There seemed to be more of them than there had been earlier, and they appeared to be smaller. He tried again to count them, but their roiling movements and their uniformity made it impossible. In the failing light, they seemed to merge, then pull apart, entire creatures engaged in bodily mitosis.

Maybe he could no longer count. He seemed to find it difficult. He studied his hand, counting his fingers, but lost interest before completing both hands. What he should do, he realized, is move away from the truck. Maybe they would eat the cereal if he wasn't standing right there.

From the peak of the grassy bank, where he sat in the waders, he watched the slow churning of the sheep in the truck bed. They had no interest in the cornflakes. They didn't seem to recognize them as food. After a long while, Chase stood and shuffled back to the truck. He pulled out the tub and grabbed a handful of flakes and stuffed it in his mouth, crunched vacantly, and swallowed hard. He ate more, then tipped the tub, spilling the flakes into a pile on the ground before walking the tub into the darkening waters of the creek. It filled quickly but he found that it was too heavy to carry when full. He poured out all but about three inches of water, which sloshed against the tin sides as he carried it slung against his thigh.

This time, after he had slid in the tub and backed away, the sheep came forward. They mobbed the tub, lowering their heads into it and lapping at the water. Or, it seemed to Chase, they sucked up the water. The fact that they were drinking what he had provided moved him, causing his chin to quiver with a strange current of emotion. The event seemed to prove that all of this was sustainable, that it could go on forever so long as they were all allowed to play their roles.

Again, the animals jockeyed, shouldering and nudging others aside as they struggled to drink, pushing in and complaining.

'Hey, easy,' Chase called to them. 'There's a whole river of water right there.'

Oddly, they all froze and looked his way. He was startled to see all the gleaming eyes swing in his direction, and lock in on him. They looked him in the eye, which he found unnerving. How do they know that these are my eyes? Or that eyes are where you should look on a person? What teaches animals that eyes are where to look?

'What are you fucking staring at?' he shouted. He heard his own voice echoing in the distance.

What are echoes? he wondered. Another me shouting in a different dimension.

One by one, the sheep slowly disengaged, returning to the business of drinking.

He knew they needed food too. His hard-on stabbed at his stomach as he bent over and tore a fistful of grass from the sloping bank. He pulled up a few more handfuls, then tossed the tiny bundle into the bed. They went for it, sniffing with caution, and then lipping it up and into their mouths.

They bleated for more, so he started ripping at the hillside and lobbing loose fistfuls of grass over the side racks. He could hear the rhythm of their chewing, the crunching followed by a chorus of hard swallows. Then they would look out at him, eyes full of longing. They must be starving, he figured. He tried to keep the grass coming. But harvesting was difficult in that it involved stooping over and his inflated anatomy and rubber wardrobe got in the way. He took to bending at the knees and tearing at the grass at his sides. Handful after handful until he had a bundle in his hands, which he would toss in from afar. The sheep would devour it before it had settled on the floor.

He kept at it late into the night, moving robotically in the darkness as though in a dazed state. At one point, he tried to use the hatchet from behind the driver's seat, swinging it at the taller grass along the water's edge. This quickly exhausted him, so he went back to pulling at the grass on the bank. His efficiency dwindled to the point that at times he was throwing nothing more than a few blades, fistfuls of air. The animals ate whatever he managed to land in their tiny mobile corral. Finally he realized how hungry he was himself. He searched the ground for the cornflakes he had poured out earlier. They had been trampled, pressed into the moist earth by his own rubber-soled feet. He picked out what he could, then lay back looking up at the stars, his erection painfully tenting the rubber pants. The sheep, he knew, were watching him.

He felt sleep trying to arrive in his body. It was like watching a wave rolling forward, advancing on the shore, but never actually crashing. Just rolling in place, endlessly. Frustration welled inside him. This is how it had been ever since the drugs stopped working. This is how it was for the entire world – sleep hovering over, feeling as if it would drop down over you any minute but never falling. It seemed to tease, playing little presleep movies, flashes of visions, yet the full show failed to unfurl. It was like realizing that some vital part of you had been lost. Like waking up in a hospital bed without your legs, or knowing your face has been forever altered by fire or violence. You were grotesquely diminished without it. You would die without it.

He sat up, sobbing mechanically. The night intimidated him. His fearful mind conjured up the usual scenarios – people coming along, bad things happening. He had always been like that, his thoughts running dark at night. Worst-case scenarios playing out in his mind, an endless reel. His anxieties blooming. Now that no one was sleeping, he thought, there's no need for night.

He remembered how Felicia worked the late shift, waitressing at a coffee shop. He couldn't bear the thought of her driving home alone and insisted on picking her up at three A.M. every night. He couldn't sleep knowing she was out there. He started carrying a knife in those days, when he first fell in love. For the first time in his life, he knew he could drive a blade into someone's chest. He fingered it in his pocket as he watched strangers attempt to flirt with her at the counter. She found it in his glove compartment while searching for a map and threw it away – literally tossed it out the window as they drove through the desert, traveling to her family reunion.

He sat on the hood of the truck, missing her. Maybe not even the real her, but the dream version of her. In waking life, it was too complicated. He was hit with flashes of scenes – their bodies moving together, that fitted connection, the heat of her. That's the only place – inside a booth of sleep – where he could fully act upon his desire for her. He obeyed an urge to address the always-aroused part of himself, there on the hood of the trunk. The wader squeaked against the metal as he rolled it down to his knees and spat into his hand.

He finished quickly, though no resolution phase followed. His readiness persisted. It was as though he had told his cock an incredible story and it had laughed and cried, then turned to him and said, 'Then what?'

Later he checked on the sheep and found them sleeping. The sight of them crushed together, a huddle of gray mounds in the darkness, angered him. He pounded on the side of the truck and shouted, 'Wake up!'

Again, the echo.

'Fuck you!' he yelled to the other him.

It yelled back, *You will sleep if you kill those sheep!*

He thought, 'Maybe it's Jordan messing with me.'

The animals bounded to their feet and scrambled, some trying to escape by leaping up at the racks. Kill them? No way. What they needed was a shake-up. He jumped behind the wheel and tore down the road, bouncing the sheep around the bed. They screamed like teenagers on a roller coaster, slamming against the racks, sliding face-first into the rear window when he abruptly braked. The tub flew into their thin legs, bowling them over.

He had cooled off by the time he reached the main highway, the tires quieting to a soft thrum, the ride smooth. The cries of injured and rattled animals chased him down the road. After a mile or two, he was sobbing an apology into the rearview mirror. 'It's because I can't sleep,' he told them. 'It's because no one can sleep.'

He caught a glimpse of himself in the rearview. His jittery face, the heavy rings around his bloodshot eyes. He felt himself becoming one of the many sleepless he had encountered over the last few weeks. His outburst at the sleeping sheep was the most blatant symptom so far. He would be babbling incoherently soon, stumbling around the landscape. It was hard to say how long it would be, since he and Jordan had slept more than most, leveraging their drug stash. But rather than extend the timeline of demise, it seemed to now rush at him with a vengeance.

There was something in the road. A dark form darting from the shoulder.

He slammed on the brakes and the truck skidded and started to spin. The sheep hit the cab, a lumpy wave of heavy flesh. They moaned hoarsely. He peered into the darkness around the truck, but saw nothing.

As the sun rose, he found himself driving through a vast prairie. He passed two abandoned checkpoints, where hulking military vehicles crowded the gravel median. He sped through, fearing they would confiscate his animals, but there were no personnel in sight. Far to his right, he could see the tawny pattern of a pronghorn herd, speckling the broad canvas of yellowing grass. It occurred to him that this would be a good place to let the sheep graze. He could see them for miles, should they wander off. But he would try to keep them close. They'd probably just stand around in a frightened cluster, chewing on the grass. That's what sheep do, right?

The bed needed to be cleaned out, he knew. They were probably up to their ankles in shit by now. They are shit machines.

He drove on, hoping to see a pond or creek, looking for the ideal setting. Like a homesteader, he thought. Looking for a place to put down my roots.

But the land offered no ideal spot for settlement. He decided to pull off and drive the truck onto the prairie itself, away from the highway. It was a bumpy ride but he did it very slowly. Still, the sheep complained. He winced every time the truck was rocked by the terrain and shouted an apology through the back window. 'Sorry, guys! Hang in there. Just a little bit more and we'll park.'

He kept his word, pulling to a stop at the peak of a gentle rise. It was early morning and the truck cast a long shadow. He could see the low blue wall of craggy mountains in the side mirror, far to the north. Ahead, the prairie extended to the horizon. Fat clouds floated overhead and their shadows were like dark shifting continents on the flat parchment map of land. He stepped out onto the withering grass and stood blinking in his built-in rubber boots. The air was still and cool, carrying a hint of fall – the end of the summer without sleep. Maybe winter will freeze it out, he thought distractedly. He thought it again. Maybe winter will freeze it out.

Time to let them out.

He went to the tailgate and peered in. The animals were in bad shape. Roughed up and battered, more tightly huddled than before. In fact, he could now see, they were transformed. The many traumas of the road had caused them to collide and fuse together – a broad-backed woolly spider, conjoined torsos with many legs and heads, rib cages interlaced, spines inter- twined. Some noses were bloodied, some eyes swollen shut. A few legs protruded unnaturally from the cluster. He was horrified at the sight of them as he lifted out the rear racks, then dropped the gate and backed away. My sheep, he thought tearfully. My ruined sheep!

The hatchet, he thought. I can separate them.

The sheep came forward, a globbed-together mass rushing out of the truck in a stampeding clatter, their stiltlike hooves hammering through the layer of dung. They dropped to the ground, grunting on impact, then ran off – a small, low-flying cloud. He started after them, calling, 'You'll die out here! Surviving won't be allowed out here!'

His echo shouted back, *'See, dickhead? Now you have nothing to offer! Catch them!'*

It was impossible to run in the waders. They were too heavy and stiff to allow his legs to really churn. It was like running through tar. His movements were further slowed by the dry weave of grass that clung to his ankles. A hundred yards or so into the landscape, he fell to his knees, chest heaving. The sheep ran on, down into the basin of the plain, toward the faraway antelope. He watched them go, grasping at his hair. His face warped. His sheep gone.

They were swallowed by distance. He watched the place where they disappeared, waiting for them to reemerge.

The sun moved over him. The day passed.

At one point he yelled up at the sky, 'God damn it!'

'I'm watching you,' his echo said. *'I never sleep. My eye is always wide open.'*

'So?'

'So I know.'

Eventually he stood. It was nearly dark again. His legs were sore from kneeling. He studied the distance for the sheep, but they had disappeared long ago. So he stood as the sun dropped toward the edge of the world, warming one side of his face with an orange light.

When he went to close the gate of the truck, he found that they hadn't all abandoned him. There was one left, lying on its side on the floor. Its body was heaving, and when he leaned in, causing the bed to dip, the animal looked up at him. Two trickles of blood ran from its nose. 'My sheep,' he said. 'You are my sheep. My last sheep you are just one. The only sheep of the sheep of mine.'

Forty miles down the road, he passed a sign for a rest stop. This was funny to him. He laughed hysterically, his spittle flecking the windshield. Rest! So ha-ha-ha! He called the sign to the attention of his sheep, though it lay curled below his limited sight line in the back of the truck. 'It doesn't happen anymore for us humans,' he tried to explain over his shoulder, his laughter dissolving into a dry coughing fit. The sight of so many vehicles gleaming in the parking lot surprised him. Maybe they really were, he thought. Maybe it was where rest was really happening of all places on the planet.

He took the rest stop exit and rolled into the heart of an insomniac carnival. The scene was charged with manic energy: cars, trucks, and buses crowded tightly together, people roaming among the picnic areas and restroom structures, shouting, gesticulating insanely. Intoxicated by exhaustion or maybe something else: there were many semi trucks in the crammed lot that had clearly been looted, and at least one bore the logo of a beer manufacturer. Wide-open trailer doors revealed empty cargo holds, the ground littered with loose pallets and flattened cardboard. Colorful shreds of product packaging tumbled by, carried along by a steady wind. All of it the larval stages of a landfill.

The rest stop was ringed by a wide lawn, where the prairie had been routinely mowed close. People had already dug in, setting up a shantytown of makeshift lean-tos and campsites. Some had tents and canopies, while others had fashioned structures out of boxes and other items apparently from the looted trucks, including office furniture and inflatable rafts. Beyond this improvised residential zone, the prairie extended across the broad plain. Chase could see faraway figures wandering the expanse.

The lot was congested, cars closing off all but a narrow artery of pavement that unevenly parted the jumble of parked vehicles. As he struggled in his sleepless state to navigate through, the truck lurching and stopping, a couple of men who had been standing off to one side began to follow him. Slack-jawed, with heavy-lidded eyes, they kept pace, staring into the bed. He sped up and found himself facing another barricade. This time, his way was blocked by the many cars that had been driven down this narrow passage before him into a dead end and abandoned. All a trap! He threw the truck into reverse, badly grinding the gears.

Driving backward, however, proved to be beyond his present capabilities. His foot was too heavy on the pedal, his hand-eye coordination out of sync. He smacked into a parked car, the back end of the truck biting into the hood. The impact whipped his head back and left the truck sitting on an angle in the tight lane, wedged in on both sides and stalled. The sheep was silent, but he felt its distress and went to it, leaping out the door and climbing into the befouled bed. His foot hung up on the rack and he fell forward, face grinding into the piss and droppings that gathered in the grooved floor of the truck bed. The animal, crammed on its side in the corner of the bed, did not raise its head. It watched with heavy-lidded eyes as Chase sat up on his knees in the waders, spitting frantically, wiping at his face. He edged toward the creature, which appeared to be paralyzed, and pressed his hand into its warm back. Still, it did not lift its head or scramble to its feet. He patted the sheep and dust rose out of the fleece.

'Looks like you got something to give for all this wrecking you did,' someone said. There were several people now, gathered around the truck. They looked through the bars of the side racks: Chase caged, along with his sheep.

'Get away,' Chase said.

'That's pretty good those kinds of animals once you take the fur off,' someone said, 'if you can find the zipper.' It was one of the men, Chase could see, who had followed the truck as he drove in. He glared at the onlookers. All of them sleepless.

'And cook it with some fire, you have to do that to it,' someone said.

A large woman, who reached in with her heavy arm, said, 'You give us that animal because it's the way it works around here especially after you crashed up this person's car so now it's all crunked up.'

'Not going to happen,' Chase said, throwing himself over the sheep. He kicked at the woman's arm and held the sheep tightly under him, but rose when he heard them fumbling with the gate. He scooped up the filth from the bed with both hands and flung it in their direction. He did it again, splattering those pushing in for a look. They backed away in disgust, cursing at him. 'You don't want this sheep,' he yelled. 'This sheep is toxic! You can see that this sheep is toxic!'

'*He's lying,*' his echo said.

But the sleepless heard only the word 'toxic.' It burrowed in and their fear pulled them back. They wiped desperately at their faces, their necks, wherever he had struck them with the manure, spitting and gagging.

'You are so fucking inappropriate!' someone said.

A woman pointed at his groin. 'Look how it arouses him to be so vile like a dog!'

'Oh my crap it's true look at that gearshift there so jutting!'

Chase continued to scoop up the shit pellets and sidearm them at his tormentors. But they had moved back, out of range, even though he charged at them and leaned far out over the racks. 'We are toxic!' he yelled. 'Don't come touching us!'

'*He sleeps!*' the echo shouted.

'Now who's lying?' Chase said. But he didn't yell this. He didn't want a response. He sat back, his legs splayed out. The sheep was next to him. It wasn't breathing right. Its side was rising and falling too quickly, Chase thought. Every now and then a little bubble of blood would form from one of its nostrils. It was panting. Chase pushed the animal's pale tongue back into its mouth, clamped the mouth shut. He patted the sheep on the face, his fingers jabbing it in the eye. 'I won't let them don't worry,' he whispered, gripping the animal's ear and twisting it toward his mouth, so only the animal heard. So it was just between the two of them. 'They aren't going to get to do anything.'

He lay back hard against it, knocking the wind out of the dying animal.

They came several times in the night for the sheep. Each time he was able to fend off the insomniacs by screaming and throwing sheep shit scooped off the floor. Sometimes he remembered to say his line about the animal, both of them, being afflicted with some kind of toxic disease. Other times he just savagely lashed out at the vague figures that emerged from the darkness, edging in from the boundaries of his vision. He kicked up at them as they closed in, but his feet never made contact and they vanished when he squinted and focused.

In the darkening plain he saw bonfires burning and he was envious of the light and heat. The temperature had dropped as night descended. There were matches in the front pocket of the waders, he knew, but what would he light? Maybe just one leg of the sheep like a torch. He sat shivering in his T-shirt and waders, listening to the murmur of voices, which was sometimes punctuated by shouts and screams – an eruption of unseen conflict. He sensed that a black moon had risen, a sphere of sleeplessness that pulled at the tides of blood – an invisible explanation for the madness welling inside.

Once in the night, his eyes sought out the source of a terrible far-off shriek. He saw a figure cloaked in fire rushing into the darkness of the prairie. He stood and watched as it suddenly dropped out of view, wondering if the burning figure was the source of his echo. The sheep was still in the dark corner, its breathing a wheezing rasp.

It occurred to him that he was in a bed. In bed with a sheep, sporting a hard-on. This realization triggered a fit of laughter that he couldn't seem to kill. He roared with guffaws and his echo followed. Just as it seemed to be dying down, it would flutter back into his chest and he would shudder in waves. His maniacal spasm must have signaled a lapse in his defenses since, during this fit, he was rushed by a number of people – men, women, and children. They swarmed the truck, climbed up over the racks. Some came bounding over the hood and onto the cab. They threw themselves down at him. He was knocked to the floor and a mob piled on top of him, crushing him under their squirming bodies. He kicked and ripped at anything he could close his hands around. He gouged at any opening his fingers found. Through the flailing limbs, he saw his sheep lifted, swept up and over the rack by a raging current of hands. He screamed until a knee smashed into his mouth. A desperate, raging strength rose in him and he kicked and squirmed until he found an opening in the thicket of limbs. He rolled off the tailgate onto the hood of the car he had hit earlier. He kept rolling until his legs dropped over the side and his feet found the ground. He growled and bulldozed his way through the people jumping down from the bed, bowling them over and stomping them as he made his way to the cab, where he grabbed the hatchet from behind the seat.

Then he was running through the maze of tightly packed cars looking for his sheep. He called out, 'Bring back that animal that is mine!'

His echo was still laughing.

He overtook a man in his path and swung at him, driving the blade of the hatchet into the man's shoulder. The man screamed, his hand going to the deep wound. Chase tugged at the tool, freeing the blade from bone, and swung again as the man tumbled to the side, scrambling to get away from his attacker. The swing caught him on the forearm, opening an angry gash. The man fell away with a groan.

He charged into the dark campsites, stepping on people who were sitting on the ground, hacking wildly at their heads and bodies, knocking down their fragile shelters as he stomped through. The sleepless yelled after him, tried to hold him back, but he plowed ahead. He brought the small ax down on the back of a woman who ducked before him, throwing her arms over her head. She yelped under the blow – like a dog's bark – as he stormed onward, hearing with satisfaction her ragged inhalation, shattered ribs gouging her lungs.

Chase imitated the sound she let out when he struck her. 'Bark, bark, bark!'

'*So funny!*' his echo said.

He charged a group that had gathered around a fire. 'The animal is mine!' he yelled. Chaos opened up before him as people panicked. He swung at the scrambling bodies, catching a man in the face, knocking his jaw askew. Teeth flew, blood in a warm spray, the handle of the hatchet getting slick. Hard to grip as he caught an elderly man in the head. The hatchet stuck in the man's skull, and when the man hit the ground, Chase kicked frantically at his head to free it.

Someone broke something over his head and he staggered, his legs wobbling under him. He could feel that there was a wound. When he touched it, he felt a strange pressure in his teeth. A delayed rush of pain exploded over him. Hands from a swarm of shouts grabbed at him from behind, but he was too slick to hold. He tore away.

The blow had robbed him of his sense of direction. He stumbled aimlessly, head ducked low and arms raised, waiting for more assaults. He kicked and swung at every nearby voice or moving form, sometimes connecting and setting off screams. But as he wandered on, the chaos quickly receded behind him. Only twenty feet farther on and it was as if nothing had happened. He saw that this was a new world. A kind of dark heaven, a world without consequence.

In the flickering light of a nearby fire, he caught the profile of his father. What was he doing here? He's supposed to be teaching in Boston. Chase approached him and said, 'I had sheep and the one that was the only one left has been taken by these people here.'

'They will send helicopters,' his father told him, 'and you'll see all this come to life, rising on ropes when that wind hits. What's that angry thing I'm seeing there?'

Chase put his hand over himself, but his father was pointing at the hatchet.

Chase held it up so he could see it better. His father frowned.

'You better hand it over to me with your own hand.'

Chase surrendered it. 'Remember what happened to Jordan with the hammer he was swinging at the slugs he was making?' he asked his father. 'That's how he lost his eye when it shattered into pieces against the concrete floor and shot like bullets right through his eyelid closing them didn't matter.'

'I could use this,' his father said, 'for the stripping of the branches so we can see the road from here when the tanks come.'

It was not his father from the front or back, only from the side. He could see that now as the man pulled away and wandered off. Chase followed him with his eyes, thinking the almost familiar will somehow lead him to the familiar. And it worked. He spotted Felicia, moving through the darkness. She turned and, seeing him over her shoulder, gestured for him to follow. He was pleased to see that she had no wounds and that, in his activities, he had not axed her.

But she disappeared behind a shaft of darkness, then was nowhere to be seen. He wandered forward, calling for her, until he found himself at the concrete heart of the rest stop, standing before the cinderblock bathroom buildings. He peered into the complete darkness of the men's room. An animal sound, one he attributed to the strangling of a sheep, seemed to emanate from inside. He yelled into hard space: 'Felicia?'

'No, just me,' his echo responded.

Chase stepped inside to find people there, standing in the darkness or huddled on the floor. The tiled floor and walls amplified their murmurs so that the space buzzed with a hive-like hum. He stepped carefully around people, men and women, he could tell. Animals somewhere, too. He thought he heard the panting of large dogs and smelled the sour odor of wet fur, though it was soon overpowered by the smell of urine, the funk of shit.

His eyes slowly adjusted, helped only a little by the feeble light coming in from the high windows over the row of sinks. He could see his vague form moving from mirror to mirror, like a man passing behind a wall of windows, as he walked down the long row of toilet stalls. The floor was wet under his rubber-booted feet. Probably piss from the pissers, he figured. Yet the stain of fluid coming from under one of the far stall doors was dark. He could see the fat line it made on the tiles, running down the gently sloping floor and into a drain.

Chase was drawn to it. He had to move forward, toward it, pulled by some strange new strand of momentum – a thin tether, yet one charged with an absence of self. He was growing distant from that core he had always felt so compelled to protect, to hold tightly together. He was aware that the dark form moving in the mirrors was no longer his responsibility. He was the opposite of all that he had been. He had been turned inside out.

He stepped over the long stain on the floor. It looked black in the light but he recognized it as blood. Listening at the door, he heard voices, sounds – maybe sex, maybe whimpering. He imagined his whole world behind the door: his family, Felicia, Jordan, his sheep, every escaped prisoner, gangbanger, or psycho killer he had imagined, every monster, human or otherwise, blood draining out of all of them. All crammed into the small space. Did he belong in there with them? He pushed against the door with his shoulder. It was latched shut.

He found himself in the next stall, sitting on the toilet in his waders. In the darkness, he remembered the matches and dug them out of the large front pocket. It took a long time to light one. His hands were shaky and he found it difficult to focus on the simple task. Eventually, one lit with a spark and a hiss and he was able to see that the walls of the stall were covered with graffiti. Pornographic boasts and invitations, sappy sentiments and proclamations of love. Filthy rhymes. Cock-and-balls etchings like some kind of ancient religious symbol. But most striking was the elaborate butterfly drawn on the wall to his left – the wall connected to the stall from which the blood drained. It had the wingspan of an owl and its wings were ornamented with eyes. The butterfly's head, from which sprang long, wiry antennae, was a dark circle. In fact it was a glory hole that someone had bored through to the neighboring stall.

As the flame crept down the match, Chase leaned forward. He peered through the small portal and was confronted, as the flame bit at his fingers, with an eye staring back at him. Startled, he tossed the match on the floor, but not before glimpsing the wide black hole of the pupil ringed with green. The eye of his echo, he knew. Glistening and open, unblinking in that instant he found it, before the match flame flitted out, leaving him again in darkness.

He felt it watching him, so he jabbed his fingers through the hole, hoping to spear it. Nothing. The eye, he sensed, was just out of reach. He slapped a hand over the hole and, with his other, worked down the waders over that engorged part of himself – that persistent spike – so that they bunched stiffly around his knees. Now he would reach the eye, and blind it. He moved into position, keeping one hand over the hole.

To hear it scream, he knew, he had to scream first.

Thirteen

It took only half a day's distance from the warehouse, walking through abandoned industrial parks and wide expanses of dry brush toward the foothills, for Biggs to conclude that he still slept, still dreamed. The insomniac had died on his own. The man was at the end of his rope already, and all the activity pushed him over the edge. The rage caused something inside him to snap. Broke his jaw throwing himself against the cage or the floor. Then blew a fuse and that was that.

And the ring? It was Maria who had given it back to him, he had always suspected. Slipped it onto his finger as a gesture of goodwill – a refund since, after all, he didn't require her services. Or maybe an exchange for his wallet, which was missing when he woke up.

He tested his syntax by saying, 'I can still sleep, and dream.'

He repeated this as he approached a cluster of abandoned cars in a parking lot. Out of habit, he peered in the windows, hoping to see a key jutting from the ignition. He could try each door, search under the seats and floor mats, check the visors and glove compartments. But he had learned that this was an unrewarding and time-consuming endeavor, especially with deliberately parked cars. Chances improved when the cars had been abandoned on the road, but because they had been ditched by sleepless drivers with the engine running, it was likely the gas had already been burned through.

He walked on, making his way to a wide avenue that extended up into the foothills, where large homes lined the ridges. Power line towers stood like skeletal sentries, positioned at receding intervals up the grade, arms burdened by the endless dead lines that sagged toward the earth.

The once impeccably landscaped lawn of the median had gone feral and was now up to Biggs's chest in places. He could see trails pressed into the grass by other walkers, maybe coyotes. Overhead, palm fronds clattered and creaked in the wind. Doves cooed. He was tempted to curl up in the grass and reclaim some of the many lost hours of sleep, since he was still in the red. To dream again, to maybe see Carolyn – to draw her out of the dark margin of his eye. But that would be reckless. After all, it seemed to him that the sleepless were now drawn to him when he slept, moths to flame.

He walked on. A short distance up the avenue, he caught sight of a billboard. It was suspended on a wide trunk of steel, sitting three stories over a used car lot – an ad for a vacation getaway. The graphic was an expansive white sand beach. The impossibly blue water sat beyond, framed by an arch of coconut tree trunks. The copy read: INSERT TOES HERE. An arrow pointed to a spot in the sand. It was a campaign he had worked on. In fact, the line was his. This was his creative legacy, this sign.

When Biggs saw that its retractable ladder was lowered, he headed toward it. He had become attuned to possible safe havens, like the cage in the warehouse or the abandoned Humvee he had inhabited for a short nap what seemed like years ago. Yes, the danger was that a safe place could easily become a trap. And he wasn't great with heights. But if he was able to pull up the ladder behind him and somehow sleep out of view – maybe on the floor of the catwalk along the sign's base, if he laid down some cardboard – the billboard's location would be worth noting.

He picked his way through the used cars. As he neared the ladder, he realized it was suspended higher than it looked from a distance. He stood under it and leapt for the first rung, grazing it with his knuckles before dropping back to the hot pavement. He looked around for something to stand on. Come on, he told himself, you can reach it. He took a few running steps and jumped. This time he caught it with one hand, then, after a wild swing, the other. He groaned and lunged for the higher rung, and the next, until he could bring his feet up onto the lowest rung. Now able to stand, he climbed up the ladder to the iron grate landing of the billboard.

He saw that the ladder could not be prevented from dropping back down. The crank lock was broken. He could, if necessary, use one of his locks to hold it up.

He was pretty high up. It looked higher than it did from the ground. Maybe four stories. He felt the altitude in his knees and wished he had Carolyn's fearlessness when it came to heights. How she insisted on checking the weather by leaning far out of their sixth story window. How she once sat in the window frame, one leg dangling over the alley far below, as she snapped pictures of a nearby fireworks show. Just seeing her perched there had given his stomach a turn.

And yes, there was the skylight. She had climbed through it at least once, maybe more, pulling herself up the frail hook pole. What had she done up there on the roof, where no one goes? She had gone up and out of view, into a blind spot. She returned to earth with her bare feet blackened by tar. Of course he was reminded that there was another time, a longer stretch of time, that she had once disappeared into. A more significant blind spot – a cave of darkness that had once held her for six weeks. Even now, standing in the shadow of his sign with the foothills of her family home in sight, his mind tried to peer into the opaque fog of that lost chapter.

She had barricaded herself there in her childhood bedroom over a year ago. She wanted isolation, she had explained, to get fully immersed in a new project. Biggs had reluctantly endorsed this abrupt residency, having witnessed her mounting distress at being unproductive for weeks. It was a block, she insisted, attempting to explain her sleepless nights and mood swings. She just needed some space to work through it. The literal space she had in mind was the studio she had fashioned in her walk-in closet during high school, when she made stop-motion cartoons with repurposed Barbie dolls and hacked action figures.

She had asked him not to visit her, and she never showed him the work she had done there. When she returned to the city, she refused to discuss her time away. She seemed drained of her desire to create. He was perplexed by her sudden lack of drive, and by the unceasing agitation that lay just under the surface. She had long suffered bouts of insomnia – a pioneer of sleeplessness whose struggles reached new heights over a year ago, when she returned from her father's house. What had happened there? What did she find in that darkness – tumbling in that void – that seemed to hang like a dark veil in front of her face?

He believed it was possible that he'd find her there now. Maybe whatever it was could somehow be their salvation now that the world had been turned inside out.

He took his bearings, sighting his path onward from the mountain ridges. He looked over his shoulder at the blue wall of motionless and silent ocean – the massive decal of colored dots smoothed over the backboard. Maybe, when he found her, this is where they would come. Away from the cave. They could live out their days on this narrow metal ledge, the two of them, sheltered by one of his bright ideas. Beachfront property, he thought. It was a peaceful scene, a dream vacation. An empty, two-dimensional dream he had authored. Nothing like the turbulent dream sea that had brought them together, but real in its own way.

As he stood there looking at the vast arrangement of tiled rooftops, a sleepless policeman passed underneath with no awareness of his presence. Carolyn was right, Biggs observed. No one ever looks up.

He reached the house by late afternoon. It loomed above him, a sprawling, modern compound that Carolyn's father had designed himself – an institutional-looking building with broad windows and glass bricks, a flat roof with cantilevered eaves. The front door was wide open. A bad sign, Biggs thought.

There were people in the house, but they were not Carolyn's family. They were most likely neighborhood people who had just wandered in, confused. Biggs observed how they seemed baffled by the position of the walls, the location of doors, the height of the ceiling. The carpeting confounded them, as did late afternoon views out the window and the elegant mahogany furniture. They murmured to themselves as they picked through closets or stared at family photos, trying to situate their own dim histories – memories now distorted by the forces of exhaustion and hallucination – into the storyline that surrounded them. They were insomniacs under the impression that they were home, yet home had somehow disowned them.

Biggs was ignored as he moved among them, employing their shuffle, their twitching mouth and eyes. He counted at least fourteen people in the sprawling house. They were in various states of dress – men, women, some college-aged kids, a small child peeling off wallpaper in the dining room. They, and others before them, had toppled the furniture and flipped the beds. The hallway smelled strongly of urine. The family's possessions were now a chaotic tumble that crunched underfoot. He found the flat surfaces of his father-in-law's office brittle with the obsidian fragments of the man's fabled vinyl record collection. The ground was littered with papers. Biggs kicked at them – business records, tax filings, ancient spreadsheets, letters.

He moved on to the far wing, toward Carolyn's room, where he too had lived one summer. The walls of the corridor were hung with family pictures. Some had been knocked to the ground by the heavy swipe of an insomniac's arm or the drag of a shoulder. Others were askew. A large picture of her mother served as a centerpiece. He remembered it from the memorial service. There were pictures of Carolyn and her sister, Mary, as children, wearing stiff dresses, socks bunched at their thin ankles.

He stopped before a picture from his wedding. He and Carolyn smiling into the camera. Behind them, a glimpse of the meadow. Nearby, he knew, just outside the frame to their left, was a long table where all their family and friends had sat for both the short ceremony and the all-night dinner party that followed. There was a series of smaller images taken that day as well. Carolyn lifting her dress and running barefoot through the grass, chased by children. Carolyn standing on his feet, his chin resting on her head. A shot of him, knee-deep in a pond in his wedding suit, holding Carolyn in his arms over the water. The whiteness of her dress like a cloud reflected on the pond's surface.

It struck him, standing in her house and staring at these pictures, that he didn't think he could live without her. He needed to find her. Nothing else made sense. He tore himself away from the images and continued down the hallway toward the bedrooms. The rooms had been preserved for the daughters, should the world send them running home. Carolyn had done exactly that over a year ago, so why not now?

He pushed the door to her room wide open. She would be there, he hoped, reading in her bed. The Carolyn he knew from years ago flashing that mischievous smile at being discovered. Mysteriously recovered and reaching out to him, erasing the images in his head, burned there the last time he saw her – a snarling, red-eyed insomniac tied to a chair – and even those from just before, when she moved with a weary yet beautiful sadness.

He took in the ransacked space – her clothes, papers, books cluttering the floor, the bed. The collage that each life produces, arranged by the artless hands of sleepless strangers. Light sliced through the vertical slats of the blinds, striping the otherwise dim room. No Carolyn.

'Well,' he said with a sigh, 'of course not.'

He could hear glass breaking somewhere in the house, followed by the toppling of something heavy. People moving about. It was desperate to come all the way out here. But he had had no choice, he told himself. He entered the room, stepping on books that littered the floor. What else did he have to go on? She had vanished without a trace. This was the only place she would have gone, if she had the presence of mind to steer in a specific direction.

The disappointment, though not unexpected, washed coldly through him. He knocked aside the clutter on the bed and sat down heavily. They had made love in this bed many times, early in their relationship. Silently, so her father wouldn't hear. It was the summer she came home to help with her mother's hospice. Biggs had joined her, since wasn't that what The Dream suggested?

With a sweep of his arm he brushed all the remaining items off the bed and lay down, face pressed into her pillow. The sweet odor of her was faintly held there. He recalled her skin, the goose bumps that appeared when he touched her. The hunger of her mouth when she forgot herself: the light electric scrape of her teeth, the erotic shock of her tongue. She was like that about everything. Either intense to the point of hurting herself, or overly self-conscious and constrained. There was no middle ground with her, and he loved this about her, once he got used to it. How many times had she refused to talk to him on the phone, saying 'I can't talk now,' then hanging up? It took him several years to learn not to take this personally, to understand that her mind was just savagely engaged in something else.

He turned and, lying on his back, stared up at the ceiling. This is it. The exhaustion of his very limited ideas. Two places on the planet where she would most likely be, and yet she wasn't. He felt the frightening range of maybes open up beneath him, the vast expanse of anywhere. He pressed both hands against his eyes, blocking out all light, holding everything in. Creating a vault of darkness. This, he thought, is where she lives now. Here but hidden.

As he removed his hands and his eyes adjusted, he saw a dark flutter again in the far right corner of his eye. He turned his head – half expecting to find someone standing there – and found himself staring at the door of Carolyn's walk-in closet.

Biggs stood and stepped over the debris on the floor, then slowly pulled open the door to her makeshift studio. He squinted as he peered into the small, dark space. Could she be there, blending into the black backdrop? He needed more light. He went to the sliding glass window and opened the vertical blinds with a tug on the beaded chain. Late afternoon light pushed into the room and seeped faintly into the closet. Her dream chamber, he remembered her jokingly calling it.

The room had been outfitted for stop-motion shooting.

Carolyn had mounted lights on the ceiling and draped the walls with black. A drafting table, which served as the production stage, sat against the far wall behind a cluster of tripods, portable dolly tracks, and light stands. He knew how the backdrop could be quickly switched from black, for puppetry, to a green screen for chroma-key work, depending on the film or scene, or the look she was after. The camera could be suspended over the table on a jib, shooting directly down, for flatwork, drawings. It was a scaled-down version of her studio at home, but fully functional on its own.

The room even came equipped with a computer – a laptop that she used to edit the files, set on a small desk. The desk was lined with metallic external hard drives. Filled, he knew, with projects dating back to her earliest attempts at filmmaking.

Biggs sat down at the desk and opened the laptop. He pressed the power button and, to his astonishment, the machine stirred. He heard the whine of the drive. The monitor lit up. First blue, then gray as the machine cycled through the start-up. Then he found himself staring at her cluttered desktop – the file icons nearly concealing the desktop image – and it was something like being in her presence. The files were mostly video clips, but he could also see documents for grants and scripts.

The disarray said something about Carolyn's chaotic process. No time to organize things. Not with her breakneck pacing and laser-guided focus when she was in the zone. It occurred to Biggs that her last project, the one she came here to work on, was probably one of these files on the desktop. He swiped his finger along the touchpad and, with a point-and-click, rearranged the icons by date. The most recent file was indeed a video. A file named *Missed*.

He doubled-clicked the icon.

At first, he wasn't sure what he was seeing. The image was

very grainy, an array of black-and-white pixels. The camera eased back, revealing the full image, and Biggs understood that he was looking at an ultrasound of a womb, a snapshot. The camera locked in and focused, with the small, amphibian-like shape held in the center of the frame – a tiny blur of prehuman creature floating in the dark oval of uterus, anchored by the umbilical tether. The picture was slowly rotated, but the contents remained motionless until an aquatic sound faded up. There was a ripple of movement as the ocean sound – now the pounding of waves – peaked, then gave way to the two-step beat of a heart. The pixels swam, clenching and loosening. A flutter appeared in the torso area of the tiny embryo, a hand-drawn pulsing of concentric lines, and the large eye moved faintly under the translucent lid. The stillness undone.

The life, Biggs understood, restored by Carolyn's invisible hand.

He watched the animated heart beating for nearly five minutes, expecting a cut, a new scene to start. But nothing of the sort happened. The rhythm continued, the beat played on, until, about seven minutes in, the screen went blank. The battery had finally expired. He tried a few times to reboot but there wasn't enough juice to get past the start-up, then it stopped responding altogether. That was it. A vault of memories – a kind of mind – forever closed.

Unless there was a spare battery around.

He searched the closet, then raked through the clutter of the bedroom floor with his feet. What was that little film about? There had to be more to it. It couldn't just be that single shot – the animated embryo, heart pulsing in a flurry of static. Maybe it was just a looping sequence that she nested in some other scene.

Biggs didn't yet wonder where she got the image – the scanned ultrasound. She was always appropriating images from all kinds of sources. It didn't occur to him that the image was actually a snapshot of her womb until, in his search for a battery, he came across a plastic jar of pills – brown-tinted bottle, white childproof top. Not placebos this time. The prescription details, under her name, were taped to the side. Painkillers: codeine. Take one capsule every four to six hours until pain subsides. Prescribed just over a year ago, when she had retreated to this room for her six-week remove from the city.

From him.

He thought he understood the meaning of the film. It was a kind of wish fulfillment exercise – the authoring of an alternative ending. She had done it before. Here, in this room, where they stayed together as her mother was dying and produced a computer-animated remake of The Dream. She insisted it was therapeutic. That it was a creative way of coping. It was also something they could do together, since he was the dreamer of The Dream. They had been together for only a few months at that point. 'It will make us tighter,' she had suggested.

'How can it bring us together when all I'm doing is telling you the same dream over and over?' he once asked, frustrated with her need to hear him tell it for what seemed like the hundredth time.

'You learn a lot about a person when you make stuff together,' she said.

The repetition seemed to work. The Dream's place in the world transferred from his head to the shared space of reality. The telling of it, he observed, became its own thing: a script of sorts, scrawled by her hand on a yellow pad, then typed neatly on the laptop. It was a real thing, birthed from his head. Yet she insisted that he storyboard out the flow as well. While she was sitting at her mother's side with her father and sister, he was in her room, struggling with his limited drawing skills to recall the angles, the positioning of the characters – the *blocking*, as she called it.

She would return to the room emotionally drained, hollowed out by watching her mother suffer through her final stages. Let's go out, he would offer. Get some air, though he really meant perspective. He wanted her to see that the world rolled on. As foretold, she seemed to be purposely drowning herself in grief. He was here, he had to point out, to help her from slipping too far into it. The Dream, he reminded her.

But something had shifted in her. The remaking of The Dream, not his guiding presence in her life, seemed to be her salvation. He pointed this out and she smiled wearily. 'Don't you see they are the same thing?'

In her exhausted state, she refused sleep, insisting on making progress with the film. She studied his sketches and re-created them, using stand-in avatars in a 3-D environment on her computer, which she said would look more realistic than a stop-motion approach with dolls. She showed him how the program's virtual cameras could be positioned anywhere along the x, y, and z axes. And how, though The Dream was witnessed from his perspective, the film would show him in the scenes. 'Otherwise, if it's shot entirely from your POV,' she explained, 'it will be harder for us to understand your role in the action.'

'Okay. But that's not how it looked in my head,' he said cautiously.

'It's a re-creation, not a replica.'

'The difference is pretty subtle.'

'Maybe in the words, but not in the thing.'

The next step was shooting the reference videos. Biggs liked this step because they had to do it together. It wasn't something she could leave him to do alone while she sat in a tormented state down the hallway, holding her mother's hand. She pushed all the furniture to one side of her room and hung a green screen from ceiling to floor. 'It's a magic window,' she said, allowing just a flash of whimsy. 'Stand in front of it and we can go anywhere.'

She insisted that they be naked for these shoots. 'We have to see how the muscles move,' she said. Not a problem for him. Their bodies were well acquainted at this point. They had been voraciously intimate from the start. Her sexual needs seemed to stand apart from everything else happening in her life, he had initially observed. He finally realized, as they came to endure her mother's decline, that her hunger for release had everything to do with her growing sadness and anxiety.

But the reference videos weren't a kind of foreplay, he soon realized. They were short clips that would inform how she moved the 3-D models in each of the scenes. Carolyn positioned his body or the tripod with the same professional coolness. In this mode, she did not seem to see his body as the flesh-and-blood incarnation of her lover, but rather as a life-sized puppet for her to control. She asked him to repeat his movements over and over as she stood back watching the monitor. Her directions were precise: 'Now walk forward as if you are seeing me in the waves. Now raise your arms, cup your hands in front of your mouth, and call to me. Now run in place like you ran to the water. Wait, start that over,' she directed. 'Remember, you're hitting the waves about five steps in, so you want to show a reaction to it. It's cold water, remember? It's like ice.'

She pressed on, sometimes glazing over, zoning out, at the computer. Or wiping away tears as she adjusted the lights, her hands in oversized heat-retardant gloves. She would join him in bed when he couldn't put off sleep any longer. They would make love – fiercely, but silent. He would try to keep her there for the night. 'Give yourself a break, baby,' he would say, embracing her.

But she would shake her head and gently push away. 'I need to keep working,' she would say, leaving the bed. 'She's so close.'

He realized she was trying to complete the film before her mother passed. Why? To show it to her? Would she even know what she was seeing? It seemed to Biggs that she was already too far gone. She was unconscious most of the time, and when awake, delirious. Hallucinating wildly, even confusing Carolyn with her own mother.

'Everything gets mixed together as you go,' she observed. 'The past and present, dreams and memories.'

It seemed to him that Carolyn's opportunity to share the film with her mother had long passed. Of course, he would never say this to Carolyn. Let her do what she has to do, he told himself. Everyone copes a different way.

They were still in school then. Still two semesters away from master's degrees, less than a year from being married. As summer ended and Carolyn's mother held on into fall, Biggs had to leave Carolyn and return to campus. She remained, continuing to spend her days at her mother's side and her nights at her computer, doing the time-consuming work of animating the virtual models. She no longer needed him in the process. All that was left was the grind of production.

It was only two weeks into the semester when the day of her mother's passing arrived. He returned and found Carolyn coping better than he had imagined. He had braced for a total collapse. Instead, she was exhausted and, yes, slow and pale with sadness, but also strong for her father and sister, taking the lead in organizing the funeral and wake. 'What can I do?' he asked.

'Just be here,' she whispered, hugging him tight.

The night before the funeral, she led him into her room, where she had hung a screen above the bed. 'Lie down,' she insisted, 'and look up.' The projector was propped between them, shooting straight overhead. He watched her version of his dream flash on the ceiling. He understood that he was supposed to be redreaming The Dream. It played out as they had scripted it, very much like The Dream, but different in that he could see himself in it, as she said he would.

Yes, there was the rowboat tossing in the waves. Yes, there was the body wrapped in white, rising and falling, and the girl fighting the crash of the waves. There he was, running out to her, pulling her by the hair toward shore, holding her.

He looked over at her, but she indicated with a nod of her head to keep watching.

The story continued.

It went beyond what they had scripted, what he had dreamed. He watched as the girl broke away and charged back into the water. His figure stands helpless, watching her go. The girl swims out past the waves and climbs into the boat, curls down next to the body and continues to tightly embrace it as the boat disappears beyond the horizon and the screen goes black.

'I don't understand,' he said as they lay in the dark.

She was quiet for several moments. 'That version has to be in the world too,' she eventually said.

He asked, 'Are you going to show it at the funeral?'

'No,' she said, turning to him. 'No one else will ever see it. Just us. Really, it's only important that you see it, since you are the one who dreamed it. I made it for you.'

She claimed, soon after, that she had erased it and purged all the files from her drives. 'What matters is how it lives on in your head,' she had explained.

He had to concede, years later, that he sometimes didn't know if he was recalling The Dream or the re-creation. She clapped her hands lightly when he told her this, then kissed him on top of his head.

Fourteen

The car passed through dark washland, skirting the occasional dead warehouse complex and looted strip mall. The front of the car was dented in, the hood slightly crumpled, from when she had crashed through the gate.

Felicia glanced at the clock, her face blue-lit by the dash. It was getting late.

The moon was full, so she could see the dim outline of the mountains towering over the flatness of the wide valley. My mountains, she thought. The familiar ridges served as a measuring stick. If she imagined a line extending down from one distinct notch, she knew it would bisect her childhood home. Humans are messed up inside and out, but the landscape is still true.

When she was a little girl, she believed the peak with the flat top was a dormant volcano. When would it wake up, she had often wondered, and send a thick soup of lava into this maze of tract homes?

Dogs trotted across the road ahead and she sighted them, using a speck on the windshield as crosshairs, like playing one of Chase's video games. When she drove over snakes, they felt like thick ropes of wet clay under the tires. The dull sensation made her cringe.

Again she checked the clock. I'm running out of time.

If it was accurate, then she had only about ten minutes before her sleep shift started. We'll see if the implant's even going to work out here, she thought. I don't know why it wouldn't. It's not a transmitter. The stimulator controls the schedule.

She took a hand off the wheel and felt for the pulse generator near her armpit – a hard, raised disk under the skin. She was convinced she could feel the wire running under her skin, up her neck and into her skull, where it connected to the electrode embedded in her brain. Not just the wire, but also the signal as it traveled through it – a warm buzz telling her brain to switch modes.

At the center, Lee had said, 'That sensation is just our imagination, like a phantom limb.' He said he sometimes thought he felt it too, but he didn't let himself believe it.

'I can't control what I believe,' Felicia said. She often found herself uttering this little mantra these days.

Another glance at the clock. A decision. She was definitely not going to make it home tonight, not taking these dark surface streets. Time to pull over.

She turned down a dirt fire road, a rocky passage through the chaparral. But she was going too fast and the car began bouncing around, the wheel pulling as the rocks and rutted lanes bullied her course. To compensate, she jerked hard to the right. The car dropped into a hidden ravine, slamming hard. She yelped as the air bag exploded before her. The engine stalled with a whine and the cape of dust moved past her, drifting like a ghost into the beams of her headlights and onward.

A stillness rose around her, though her heart was thrashing as if it wanted to be let out. The car was severely listing to the right. She was hanging in her seat, unhurt, her necklace reaching for the passenger door.

Then she felt a purr along her neck and slumped against her seatbelt, asleep.

Her shift had started.

She woke up at seven A.M., the world at a tilt. Her driver's-side window faced up at the pale sky, cut into strips by power lines. It was a dreamless sleep that Lee had given them, but it succeeded in resting the body and allowing for the nightly restoration of the mind, the conversion of experience into memory.

Gravity had pulled at her all night so that she was hanging over the passenger seat but held in place by the seatbelt. The airbag was semideflated before her.

She was slipping out from under the strap when the light changed. Something moved above her, blocking the sun. She turned and was jolted by what she saw. Out the window, looking down at her.

Eyes.

She released a short scream before clamping her hand over her mouth.

A set of massive cartoon eyes in the window. A kind of monster. A giant owl head on a human body.

'Jesus!'

Just a stupid costume, she could now see. One of those school mascots, or something escaped from an amusement park. Who is this creep?

The person inside was small. Dirty shirt and ripped jeans. Skinny, scabby arms pulling at the door.

It opened like a hatch and the owl person reached in, held out a hand. A small voice muffled inside the mask asked, 'Can you get out?'

Felicia could tell that it was a girl in there.

She climbed out, avoiding the filthy hand, then reached back into the car for her backpack. It held a change of clothes, power bars, some ramen. It was all that she had brought, thinking she would be out in the field for no more than two days.

The owl stood back and stared as Felicia surveyed the damage. The car was almost on its side in the ditch that ran along the dirt road – a deep, flood-cut trench, toothy with boulders. She looked at the mountains – crisply visible, since the epidemic had done wonders for air quality – and concluded that she was probably ten miles from her parents' house. Fifteen at the most.

She was surrounded by sage, all of it going brittle and brown as the California fall advanced. The shadows were long, bugs only starting to buzz. The sad call of meadowlarks fluted from the brush.

In the near distance, she saw a row of houses, a cul-de-sac reaching out into the scrubland. A massive loop of concrete overpass loomed above the neighborhood. Its distended shadow looked like an overlay of dark river.

This girl with the owl head scratched at her elbow and continued to stare – at least that was what the frozen-open eyes communicated.

'I like your hair,' she said.

Felicia's hand went to her head. Short as a skinhead, she thought. It was just starting to grow back after it was shaved – when the implant was inserted. Porter had said he could just shave the site of the incision, but she insisted that he cut all of it so it would come back the same. The doctors both appreciated the gesture. A vote of confidence in their ability to get it right.

'I like your mask,' she told the girl. The anger at being startled was now faded, replaced by curiosity. The eyes were weirding her out, though. She leaned in, trying to see through the mesh, but it was dark in there.

'Did you crash?' the girl asked.

'Yep.'

'So did I,' she said. 'Up there.' She pointed to the overpass in the distance.

'There's like fifty cars up there, filled with dead people,' she told Felicia. 'It's super gross but that's a good place to find dogs.'

Felicia looked at the overpass wondering about the dogs comment when she was struck with a realization. This kid was talking just fine, not staggering around. None of that sleepless shambling that they do.

The girl must have been thinking the same thing because she said, 'You can sleep. I can totally tell. People around here will want to kill you.'

Now they kicked through the furrows of dust, the owl-headed girl leading the way. The dead vines were like little rotting alien arms, curled and blackened as if by flames.

The vineyards had died long before the crisis, and developers had folded the groves up along the dotted lines and laid out neighborhoods of origami houses. It had been the fastest-growing community in the world during the eighties.

Felicia liked this skinny miracle girl who was now her guide.

Her name was Lila.

'Lila, hold up,' she said.

When she gave her a power bar, the girl tore at the wrapper, her hands shaking. She lifted her mask high enough to get her hand under it. The bar was gone in seconds.

Felicia gave her another one.

'I should save this,' the girl said.

'Go ahead and eat it,' Felicia told her, patting the backpack. 'We have more.' She wanted the girl to stick with her. Maybe this will keep her close, she thought. 'What's in your pack?' she asked the girl. 'Any food?'

'No, just noisy things.'

Felicia didn't know what to make of this, but the girl had moved on down the trail that cut through dried mustard stalk.

'I need a car,' she called after her. 'Know where I can get one?'

'Probably,' Lila said with a shrug. 'When we get to those houses.'

There was a wall of homes ahead of them. The first of what seemed like thousands of rows covering the valley floor and spreading up into the foothills. Just houses and supermarket strip malls, schools, and churches. She recalled a term that was sometimes used to describe such places. Bedroom community.

'Let's see what's in the garage,' Lila said, heading toward the closest house.

There was a naked man standing in the front yard, kicking a mound of trash on the lawn. Felicia held back. The girl sensed her fear, turned and beckoned.

'Don't worry,' she said. 'They're not dangerous unless they catch you sleeping.'

She was right. The man glanced in their direction but turned away muttering to himself. Felicia could see that the front yard was filled with junk. Everything from inside the house had migrated to the dead lawn. Furniture, bunches of DVDs and video games scattered everywhere, plates and pans, hangers, tangles of clothes.

Felicia followed Lila around the side of the house and saw that every house was the same, the front yards cluttered with middle-class detritus.

'What a mess, right?' Lila said.

'Why?' Felicia asked, bending down to pick up a framed picture of a family. Smiling like they're safe forever.

'Okay,' Lila said, 'what happens is this. I've seen it so I know.

Sleepless people get lost and they just walk into any house thinking it's their house. Then they start looking for stuff that they remember having and they end up tearing the whole house up looking for it, throwing all the things they don't recognize out the windows and doors. Then they look through that stuff again when they come outside and it gets even more messed up. They're so clueless it's unbelievable.'

'Wow, you've been paying attention,' Felicia said, thinking, Lee has to meet this kid. 'How long have you been out here?'

'I don't know. Feels like forever, but probably, what, a month?'

'You must be a pretty tough kid to live out here that long.'

The girl shrugged.

Felicia asked if she would take off the mask.

The kid seemed to freeze, looking back at her with those massive fake eyes.

'You can't tell,' she said, 'but I'm shaking my head.'

There was a car in the garage – an SUV. Felicia thought it would be perfect, if there was a key. They waded through the clutter of trashed belongings that surrounded the vehicle and Felicia got behind the wheel. She was hoping a solution would present itself.

'Hot-wire it,' Lila said.

'I don't know how to do that, do you?'

'No. I know HTML though. And a little CSS.'

They checked under the seats and behind the sun visors. Felicia emptied the glove compartment as Lila looked on, snatching up a flashlight and stuffing it in her pack.

'Yay,' she said. 'Light.'

'Good idea.'

'I used to sleep in the car,' Lila said. 'When it first started happening to my parents. I'd lock myself in there and it was safe. For a while.'

'Where are your parents?'

'Out in the desert.'

Felicia waited for more, but the mask was silent and she was reluctant to prod. That could wait for the right moment.

They entered the house in search of the car keys. Light flooded in the window, revealing the cluttered floors. Couch ripped open, TV facedown in the debris. Glass crunched under every step. Holes had been kicked in the walls.

This could be my house, she thought. She had been carrying around the image of home as she had left it. Meticulous, the way her mother liked it, needed it to be. Both parents sitting on the couch in front of the TV, or out on the patio, tending to something on the grill. Even the bizarre picture Chase had painted – the walls of the house filled with bees that produce a sleep-inducing drone – was better than what she was seeing now. And that was just a hallucination, she reminded herself.

'If we had the Internet,' Lila said, 'we could look up how to hot-wire a car. We could look up anything.'

'Not anything,' Felicia said.

There's so much they couldn't tell us, she thought. Still can't tell us. The answers aren't out there. At the center, all Kitov and his team of geniuses could do is come up with a sad workaround. Hot-wiring our heads, since they can't find the keys.

The smell came in stinging little hints at first, then got over-whelming as they approached the interstate on foot. Felicia pulled her shirt up over her mouth.

'Where is it coming from?'

'It's a dead thing,' Lila said.

They started across an overpass where the sunken freeway cut through the developments, embedded four stories down.

Halfway across, Felicia looked east and west. Not a car was moving on the eight lanes of grooved concrete.

The smell rising up around her was like a physical presence. She retched and ran to the railing, intending to vomit over the side. That was when she saw them. Piled across the lanes below, a barricade of bodies. A broken tangle of limbs and torsos, heads at the heart of dried eruptions. She staggered to the other side: more.

Suicides. Even at the center they had seen it begin. Annika throwing herself off the bluff onto the rocks below. That was a sure thing. This didn't seem high enough and spoke to the desperation of the dead below.

Blocks up she saw another overpass and the dark low pile beneath it. Barricades of bodies all the way into the city.

Lila was running to the far end, crossing over, her pack jangling loudly. Felicia watched as she tore off the owl mask and vomited onto the sidewalk. She saw the side of the girl's face, her long hair, before she herself was doubled over, the contents of her stomach splashing over her dusty shoes.

By the time she reached Lila, the girl was wearing the mask again.

As evening approached, Felicia started to regret wasting so much time looking for car keys in abandoned homes. She recognized that they still had a few miles to go, that they wouldn't make it before downtime hit unless they ran.

'Where's a safe place to spend the night?' she asked Lila.

'In a house,' the owl-head said, 'since there's two of us. Someone can keep watch.'

They had seen about a dozen living people all day, most of them just shambling along. Some had called out to them, or headed their way, but most just looked past them. Eyes blinking, mumbling. Seeing visions only the sleepless see.

'People actually seem pretty harmless out here,' Felicia said.

'They wouldn't be if they caught us sleeping. They would seriously try to kill us.' Lila said she had seen it happen to a girl who was found sleeping in a tree house, killed by a bunch of kids looking for firewood.

'They hit her with hammers and axes,' she said, 'and rocks. Even when she fell out of the tree and was dead on the ground I bet they kept doing it. I don't know really because I ran away but I bet. They go bonkers when they see sleepers.'

She was quiet a long time. Felicia wanted to see her face, to know what was going on in that dark globe. She watched her – small shoulders and skinny arms, pants sagging in the seat – as they crossed the vast parking lot of a supermarket.

They peered in through the glassless windows. It was now just a dark cave, picked clean by looters. Rows of empty shelves disappearing in the black space. Someone was sniffling somewhere in the darkness and they moved away from it. They went into an abandoned ice cream store.

'I'll take a triple,' Felicia said to the invisible worker. This was where she and Chase had spent a lot of her waitress money. Memories of those early days flashed through her. The two of them on her scooter, his arms around her.

'I'll take a banana split!' Lila yelled.

They sat at the table and ate power bars instead. Lila got up and went around the counter. She turned on the faucet and water rushed into the stainless steel sink. 'See?' she said. 'There's still water here. We ran out at home so we had to scoop it from the aqueduct. It was so completely vile.'

They drank out of a plastic pitcher and sat looking out the window in silence.

'I think this was hers,' Lila said.

'This what?'

'This,' she said, pointing to the mask. She explained how

she hid out in a girl's room, wore some of her clothes. Found the mask in her closet. She was a cheerleader, Lila said. 'I could tell we wouldn't have been friends. But we could both sleep so maybe we would have found each other, like you found me.'

Felicia was confused. 'Wait. Who are we talking about again?'

'The girl,' Lila said. 'The one they killed.'

They decided to find a house and try to lock themselves in it.

In a quiet cul-de-sac, they picked one that had a For Sale sign, the thin post hammered into the lawn. The uncut grass reached up for the sign, promising to eventually conceal it. Most of the windows along the front of the house were still intact. As with many of the other houses, dying orange trees stood in the front yard, which was littered with clothes, papers, and a weave of scattered belongings. There were For Sale signs all up and down the street.

Inside, they checked everywhere for sleepless people hiding in closets and showers. The task made them jittery. Lila took Felicia's hand and squeezed it as they slowly pressed forward. They jumped at everything, especially upon glimpsing a long coat hanging from a hook on a door. They screamed, then laughed nervously.

Then Lila tore it off the hook and threw it to the ground. She kicked it around the room, saying, 'Wake up! Come on, up and at 'em! Rise and shine!'

Now they really laughed, collapsing to the carpeted floor.

Lila took a string of empty cans from her backpack and pulled it tight at the top of the stairs. She strung up an elaborate web of trip wires all the way down the stairs, hanging the bells, cans, and jangly ornaments she had collected for her pack of noisy things, as she called it. She did this with professional efficiency, admiring her work before retreating to the room, where she hung a wind chime on the doorknob as a final precaution.

'That's what I do now,' she said.

As the darkness set in outside, they were camped out in the master bedroom behind the locked door. They lounged on mattresses that they had to drag up from the bottom of the stairs, where someone had tossed them. A Santa Ana was brewing outside and occasional gusts caused the house to shudder.

Felicia told Lila to sleep while she kept watch.

'Why don't we both sleep?' she asked. 'I think we're safe in here.'

Felicia said, 'I can only sleep at certain times. From exactly ten to seven, actually.'

'What?' Lila asked, like it was the most ridiculous thing she had ever heard. 'Why?'

'Well, I have an implant that makes me get to sleep.'

'An implant?'

She explained how it worked.

'There's no way to wake me up, once I'm under. It's not like normal sleep.'

'Whoa,' Lila said. 'Do a lot of people have those?'

'Just about twenty of us. We're all people who worked at a sleep research center at the university. We fixed ourselves. Lee did, anyway, with Porter. I was the first to volunteer.'

No reason to tell her about the disaster with Kitov, she figured.

'Everyone should get one,' the girl said.

Felicia agreed. 'That's why I came out here,' she explained. 'To take my family to the center, if they're still here.'

The mask stared at her for a long silence.

'Will you take me?' Lila finally asked.

'Of course.'

'Is there food?'

'Hope you like pasta,' Felicia said, smiling at the thought of all the pasta she had eaten at the center. The security team had found what appeared to a hundred years' worth of the stuff in the university's emergency stores.

'Cool,' Lila said. 'Pasta's awesome.'

'Then you'll like the center,' Felicia said. 'It's down in San Diego, overlooking the ocean. It's practically a resort.'

She winced. That was laying it on pretty thick.

The girl was quiet for a long time and Felicia thought maybe she had fallen asleep, until she asked, 'So do you have a boyfriend?'

Felicia lay back and stared up at the ceiling. 'I did,' she said.

'What was his name?'

'Chase.'

'I like that name. What happened to him?'

'I don't know. We broke up just before all this started.'

'Why did you break up?'

'We had issues.'

'What kind of issues?'

Felicia paused, not sure she wanted to get into all this, especially with a kid. 'It just wasn't working out,' she finally said.

'Were you sad?'

'Yes. It was awful. We knew each other since we were kids. Even younger than you are right now.'

'Where is he now? Chase.'

'I don't know,' Felicia said. 'The last I heard from him was a voice mail, saying he and our friend Jordan were going away on a road trip, and that he would be back in time for my birthday. That was before we knew what was happening,' she added, going silent as her thoughts raced on.

Lila was silent too. Felicia sat up and studied her. The girl was sitting on the mattress, leaning against the wall. Her mask pushed forward, and those big eyes staring at her feet. 'Are you asleep?' she said quietly.

'No,' a small voice said from inside the mask.

'Go ahead. It's safe.'

'I believe you,' the girl said.

She decided to leave the girl alone, give her some space. Maybe she's thinking too much. Maybe she thinks I'm going to attack her.

'I'll be quiet,' she said.

For a while, she watched the girl's foot move. It was wagging slowly. From behind the mask, she said, 'I will never go home. I don't want to see it.'

'See what?'

'Them,' the girl said.

'Your parents?'

'Yeah, but dead.'

'How do you know that?'

'They told me in a letter,' Lila said flatly. 'They said they were going to do it.'

'I'm so sorry,' Felicia said.

The girl said nothing, but her silence seemed to send a message. Her silence and the big still eyes of the mask. Yours will be dead too, they seemed to say.

In the morning, at exactly seven o'clock, Felicia awoke to find herself alone in the room. She blinked and rubbed her eyes. All the furniture they had used to barricade the door had been pushed aside. Felicia went to the door and saw that it was still locked, the wind chime still in place.

She must have gone out, locking the door behind her, Felicia thought. But why would she do that?

The girl's backpack, she noticed, was gone.

She opened the door and called out for her. The house was quiet.

Felicia dressed and went downstairs, walking right into the trip wires Lila had set up the night before. The cans clanked and rattled like dull bells. She picked her way through them and entered the garage, squeezing between the cars parked there.

Oh no no no, she said, looking up and down the street. Why would she leave?

Then she was running down the street, calling out. The houses stared out at her, blank, empty. No sign of the girl.

Felicia returned to the garage of the house and waited, peering out at the street. Maybe she'll come back, she thought. Maybe she went to find us something other than power bars to eat for breakfast. But the fact that she took her backpack said otherwise.

She stared out at the street, or watched flies zigzagging in the air, passing through dust-filled shafts of light. The sun moved over the houses, pushing shadows across the cluttered yards.

A few men passed by, stumbling along and talking to themselves. She ducked low, watching them for any hints. It was clear they were lost, disoriented by their sleepless state. She could smell them though they were thirty feet away.

I can't wait all day, she thought, but I will wait as long as I can.

Later, a woman came down the street and looked directly at the house.

Felicia put her age somewhere in the midthirties. She had a dirty face under a ratty tangle of hair and a slipper on one foot. Her simple flower-print dress was torn. She was wearing it backward.

The woman lingered in front of the house for a minute or

so, staring up at it as if trying to remember something. Her mouth was moving. She was either chewing something or silently reciting some endless conversation.

Felicia let her wander off. But when the woman came by again, only minutes later, she decided to try to talk to her. She was kicking at a crack in the sidewalk when Felicia stepped out of the shadowy garage. When the woman saw her, she froze and stared with exhausted eyes.

As Felicia approached, the woman appeared to recognize her, but was then immediately devastated to realize that she didn't. She wavered on her feet and Felicia went to her side and held her up, gagging at the sharp tang of urine.

'Have you seen a girl?' Felicia asked. 'About this high? Wearing an owl mask?'

The woman just stared, her eyes moving over Felicia's face. She was searching for something, her mouth frozen open. She said, 'Dreams got so upsetting to him because he had to watch every one of them and they were so ugly and evil that no more sleeping and dreaming was allowed to happen in our heads.'

This was a new one to Felicia. Lee would be interested in hearing it, but what about Lila? It was clear this woman was too far gone to help. Felicia lowered her to the curb as the woman's face continued to flash between joy and despair. There was something electric about it, as if the different motor cells of her brain were being shocked with a probe, causing her face to open and close like a fist. Felicia could see the muscles working spastically under the skin as she backed away.

Two hours later, she decided she had to move on.

Felicia turned the corner and looked down the street of her childhood. She was having doubts about actually entering her house. It was easy to imagine how she would find them, after what she had seen yesterday.

Did she really need specifics to haunt her? Dreamless sleep was a blessing, she had already learned. No dreams, no nightmares.

She stopped and sat under a parkway tree, setting the backpack on the curb. The neighborhood was silent. No barking dogs, she observed. No hammering from construction sites, or airplanes flying over. No rumble of school buses. This kind of sunny September day would still bring the splash of neighbors doing cannonballs into their pool, the referee's whistle from the soccer field. The pulse of bass from a car going by, the whine of the gardener's blower.

What had happened was this, she realized: the world had been turned inside out. That was the only way to describe it. That was the result of a world without sleep. All outside things were now inside. Everything else that we kept in our heads, in our hearts, has flooded out into the open air.

But what about Lila? If she was still sleeping, there must be others. Maybe, and maybe was enough.

My mother, father. Maybe my sister. Maybe my brother. Maybe the walls filled with honey.

She said it out loud, 'Maybe is enough.'

The house sat low in the shade of elms, the debris of their lives on display before it. Family pictures were strewn about the wild lawn, a garden of memories to pass through.

Felicia stood at the base of the driveway looking up at the shattered windows. The front door was partly open. She felt it like a wound. The darkness it revealed seemed impenetrable. Her body was trembling, teeth chattering. She decided she couldn't do it, couldn't take that first step up the driveway, and turned back. But the maybe was there to move her forward, until she was standing at the darkened doorway.

She stood there for a long time. The door and the space

beyond were familiar, but filtered through all that had happened since she last stood there. At that remove, they felt like props for a dream she had once had – a dream of an entire lifetime now mostly forgotten. Familiar things, like the doorknob that they all touched but didn't see or feel, now had an otherworldly aura. Their unique truth had resurfaced, wiping out for a moment the generic memories. She felt as though she was visiting this place for the first time, though she was also aware that she was intimately familiar with it.

Still, she couldn't reach out to it now. She couldn't even nudge the door wider with her foot because of the terror that now had her by the throat. She closed her eyes and listened at the opening. Then she called out hoarsely, 'Hello? Mom? Dad? You there?'

Nothing came back.

'Hello? It's me!'

Nothing.

That's all I can do, she thought. She remained in the doorway for several minutes, just to be sure. Nothing changed.

She was backing away when she heard the voice. A low murmur. Coming from inside. Someone talking.

'Hello? Who's there?'

The murmuring continued.

She was pulled forward by the possibility. She passed quickly through the living room, then the kitchen, stepping over the shards of dishes, the racks from the oven like the walls of a cage. In the dining room the table was on its side. A chain led out the shattered back door and she could see that it was locked around one of the patio pillars. The chain they once used to keep their dog, Zeto, tethered to the tree and out of the pool. She pulled on it and there was resistance, a tug like a fish on a line. She dropped it as if shocked, but followed the chain down the hall.

It led into the first bedroom, where she found that it was bolted around Chase's ankle.

Chase was delusional, talking to the wall. When he saw Felicia, he redirected the stream of garbled words in her direction. At first she thought he was speaking another language. He seemed to recognize her behind his exhausted eyes, but his reaction was subdued, as though she had just stepped out of the room for a moment and returned.

He was lying on a mattress, shirtless, his torso badly scratched and scarred as if he had crawled through a thicket of thorns. Some of the scratches were scabbed over, but others were fresh. Felicia could see that he had lost a great deal of weight, ribs and abs showing like furrows, face hollowed and gaunt. His filthy boxer shorts hung loosely at his hips. He's starving, she thought.

She threw herself at him, said his name. She kissed his neck, his face, as he looked beyond her, mumbling. She couldn't make out what he was saying. Something about it growing in not out. Something about a head stuffed with hair.

Is he talking about my haircut, she wondered?

'Sit up, come on,' she told him. She pulled his arms and he rose, still talking over her shoulder. 'I knocked up night,' he seemed to say past her ear.

He looked at her, unsmiling. 'Say that again,' she asked, but he didn't respond.

The emaciated state of his face, his body, scared her. She grabbed the backpack and pulled out a fistful of power bars. 'Chase,' she said. 'Come on, eat these.'

She tore one open and held it out. His body did the rest, sending out his hand for it, cramming it into his mouth. He was chewing, but already tearing open another. He must need water, she thought.

In the kitchen she tested the tap. Water streamed out. She filled a pot with it and brought it to Chase. He drank, but not with the same fervor that he ate. The chain, Felicia noted, was long enough for him reach the sinks, the toilet too. How did he get chained up, she wondered. Did her family do it? She looked at how it had been secured to his ankle. There was a screw pushed through the loop of links and bolted tight. She tried to undo it with her fingers but it didn't budge. She needed tools.

'Did you do this?' she asked him. 'How did you do it, Chase? Listen, how?'

The old Acura was in the garage. No sign of her father's car. They drove away in it, she told herself. She had already searched the entire house. There was no sign of them. Off to somewhere safe, she insisted. Maybe to find me, as they had once discussed during one of their final phone calls. She speculated that they must have left before Chase arrived. He tried to make sure he wouldn't wander off as his condition worsened, and made use of Zeto's chain.

She thought, They are together, at some kind of sanctuary. The whole thing hasn't touched them. They left this car for me.

She had carried a key for it since she was sixteen. She had learned to drive behind the wheel of this car, her father coaching her through three-point turns and parallel parking. He had always kept a small tool kit rolled up in a towel and stashed in the trunk, and she used it – the pliers and wrench – to get the chain off Chase's leg. She led him to the passenger seat and strapped him in.

The car had a full tank of gas, but she noted that the clock was broken. Stuck at 8:33. Right twice a day.

She pulled out of the garage slowly and parked on the incline of the driveway. It was stupid, she knew, but she got out and pulled the garage door shut. Her mom had always hated leaving the garage door wide open like that. Anyone could walk in, she used to say.

Then they were driving through her old neighborhood and Chase said something like, 'Cards were switched is what he said at the top of the world but who did that to what cards on the top side of clouds?'

'Chase? What cards?' she asked. 'Did you say cards?'

He turned to her and mumbled, 'It's dreams all the time now so nothing is nothing anymore.'

She told him they were on their way to get help. At the center, they would take care of him and he would be good as new. She explained everything about the implant in her head, even showed him the generator bulge under her skin. 'There's a wire,' she said, 'going from the generator to the implant in my brain. I know it sounds weird, Chase, but it works. They'll give you your own implant.'

They had talked about implants before. He had pretended to joke, and when she laughed, he was hurt that she seemed to think it was such a stupid idea. He thought it could save them. She remembered his anger, saying he would be able to fuck her whenever she wanted to be fucked. That's what she wanted, right? Seething, punching walls and doors. Not angry at her. At his own body.

'You don't need an implant or pills or any of that, Chase,' she had told him then. 'You just need to be honest with yourself.'

'Then why am I always dreaming it? Why am I fucking you every night in my dreams if it's not you that I want?'

'Stop saying "fucking,"' was all she could say.

Later that week, he had attacked her. She had felt him behind her, dreaming one of those dreams. She took him inside, thinking it could work like the mechanics of a key. Hoping, by fitting together in that most simple way, he could unlock her and let out the possibilities she had already stored away.

She was able to kick him away when he became violent. His head hit the wall and he realized what he was doing. He quickly gathered up his clothes and fled. They didn't see each other much after that, until she met with him to tell him it was over, even though it crushed him.

Both of us, she thought.

Felicia knew she couldn't take the freeway. Bodies of jumpers were there, piled in the shadows of the overpasses.

They passed through the cluttered surface streets, sometimes swerving onto sidewalks, over lawns, as they moved through the mess. She decided she wanted to look for Lila one last time.

She pulled up to the house where they had stayed the night. The gate groaned as she passed through and entered the house for a quick search. Still no sign of the kid. She called for her up and down the street and, back behind the wheel, she dared to honk the horn. This excited Chase, who shouted, 'The sheep will not come back!'

When a couple of men appeared at the end of the street, staggering toward them, Felicia drove slowly in their direction. The sun was going down and she reluctantly turned on her headlights, begrudgingly acknowledging that time was running out. Only a couple more hours until the implant put her under. The men watched her glide past and she scanned them in return, searching for any sign of Lila. They were pretty far gone, twitching faces, murmuring mouths. They peered in, maybe astonished to see the lucid look in her eyes, the steadiness of her hands. Frowning now, so Felicia kept going, thinking there was nothing more to do. She told Chase this with a sudden sob. It hit like a sneeze. She wiped back the tears and drove on.

She told Chase about Lila as she worked her way slowly out of the labyrinth of obstructed roads and tangled housing developments. Progress was slow. She wished the clock in the car worked, but guessed that she had only another hour before downtime hit. She eventually found her way to a highway through the chaparral. Here Felicia could actually pick up some speed, rushing along under the low ceiling of stars.

Then, in the headlights, she saw what appeared to be a building in the road. As she closed on it, she saw that it was a bus, spilled on its side, blocking both lanes.

She tried to ease around it, but there was not enough shoulder. They'd have to turn around, backtrack to an intersection several miles back. She knew now that she needed to pull over. It was because I waited so long for Lila, she knew.

The car sat at the end of a street for a neighborhood that was never built. There were only the roads and wooden stakes in the dirt, marking off imaginary homes.

She had decided that she would stay in the car with Chase. In the backseat, rather than out in the weeds. She recalled the soft thump of snakes on the road from the night before, the roaming packs of dogs.

Chase didn't resist the chain.

Felicia looped it around his hands and then around his body and the car seat. She kept pulling it tight, taking up the slack, as he talked into her hair, breathing indecipherable words onto her neck. It was a long chain. She wrapped it around his waist and the car seat a few times. She looped it around his thighs, and as she did this she noticed that he had become aroused.

Felicia looked up at him and saw that he was there, present, his eyes sad and heavy, his face contorted, pained, and she held him, kissing his forehead. 'We just need to get through tonight,' she told him. 'Tomorrow I'll take you to people who can help.'

He tried to raise his arms – to hold her, she thought – but they were chained down. He thrashed.

'Chase! Don't. Just sit still.'

His face started flashing through emotions, like the woman she saw earlier on the street, as he strained against the chains.

She couldn't watch it. It was like his face was flashing every moment of his life.

Felicia fled to the backseat, her hands shaking. It must be close to ten, she thought. She sat directly behind him, talking to him. Trying to soothe him.

The car shuddered as he rocked side to side. He shouted nonsense and groaned. It was like a child's tantrum, or seizure.

The chain bit into the back of the seat.

Felicia covered her ears, clamped her eyes. His rage seemed to peak. She glanced up and noticed that in her struggle to secure him, she must have knocked the rearview mirror askew. Should she straighten it? She couldn't have him seeing her sleep. He would kill himself trying to get to her.

But she could hit downtime any minute now. Any second, even.

So she sat wondering, eyes darting to the mirror, to the broken clock.

Damn it.

She jumped up and squeezed between the front seats, reaching for the mirror.

Then nothing.

Fifteen

They used glass bricks that were stacked by the pool to shatter the sliding door. Shards exploded inward. The sound alone threw Biggs from the bed as the blinds slats swung and twirled wildly and morning light flashed around the room. They came charging in, howling with rage: mostly children, a couple of adults. Some kind of roving pack. They must have seen him through the blinds, which he had opened to let in the evening light and then neglected to close. Maybe summoned by his snores, they had peered through the glass and spotted him crashed out on the bed – a sleeper.

There were already four in the room, and more pushing in from outside, by the time he had gotten to his feet. Their screams were piercing as they entered the small, hard space. They stumbled over the books and clutter, some falling to their hands and knees. Small kids, maybe five, seven years old. One looked like a toddler. They were followed by two men, eyes wide with a kind of warped astonishment. A woman in a hospital gown too. All animated by an unnatural fury.

Dazed, disoriented by the pills he had taken, Biggs lifted the mattress as a barrier. They kept coming, red-eyed and shrieking. They had seen him sleeping – due to his drug-induced carelessness – and they would not be deterred. He threw the mattress over them, pinning some underneath and giving him the few seconds he needed to make it to the door. Others stomped over the mattress and those underneath it, reaching for him.

His only escape option was to push through them, plow past the shattered sliding door, and run toward the pool, groggy from painkillers. As he neared it, the howling pack came rushing after him. He ran along the tiled deck, putting the pool between them. One or two children toppled into the dark water.

Others came around the pool, trying to cut him off at the far end, but he beat them by a few steps. He scooped up a metal deck chair and swung it behind him, letting it fly at the oncoming adults. He made it to the gate and kicked it open. It swung wide, wobbling on its hinges, then slammed into the vine-covered wall, smashing hibiscus blooms. He charged down the side yard, running along the oleander hedgerow and out onto the street. His movement was automated, instinctual. Pure flight.

He had his locks in his cargo pants pockets. They were banging hard against his legs as he ran. Something else, too, a plastic rattle. The bottle of pills, he recalled, stuffed in his pocket the night before.

They were painkillers, right? He had taken a couple, to numb him to a terrible notion. An idea that had gotten into his head that he could not shake.

Oh, Carolyn. What?

There were a couple of ways to interpret the clues, but both scenarios made him feel very far from knowing her. She had, it seemed, for a few weeks at least, carried life inside her. But it had ended, either by her choice or naturally. And she had said nothing to him about it. Not a word. She had escaped to the cave of her childhood room, had attempted to heal there, or at least to paint over the damage.

The drugs caused him to carelessly fall asleep. There, in the exposed bed, an inciting diorama behind the glass doors. Now the remaining pills rattled with every stride as he gradually outpaced his pursuers.

The sound, a dry muted clatter like fragments of bone, followed him as he scrambled up the ladder onto the billboard. The sea loomed flat and frozen behind him. His tagline hung overhead: INSERT TOES HERE.

This was it, finally. Trapped in the open.

He pulled the ladder up and paced the catwalk as the sleepless straggled in below, urged forward by a grotesque mutation of resentment. They looked up at him, some of them reaching into the air. They screamed and it set off more screaming in the distance, like car alarms triggering one another. Others appeared and moved toward the group, passing through the car lot maze in winding routes.

Maybe if he somehow sat out of view, they would eventually wander off. Some already had – a man in a blue jumpsuit, a naked woman, and a couple of kids – but others, those maybe not as far along, displayed the same unshakable focus as the man who had cornered him in the cage. Biggs lowered himself and sat on the narrow catwalk, his back to the sign. He could see the sleepless through the grillwork and studied them vacantly, blinking down at them. The drugs were still in his system. Soon, as the adrenaline rush passed, grogginess settled in.

He was thinking: Maybe there was someone else. Maybe it wasn't mine.

His mind shuffled through the possibilities. She had few friends, male or female, since she worked at home and for the most part alone. There were a couple of assistants for projects with decent grants, but they were college girls. He worried about her being so isolated. But she said she preferred it, after being drawn into the Whitneys' lives and suffering through the heartache the situation ultimately brought her.

'I'm talking about meeting people our age,' he told her. 'People with similar interests.'

'Hang out with filmmakers? I don't know about that.' She had expressed before that artists should work away from the influence of others, and study only the work of the dead. At the time, he was grateful that she didn't judge him for his profession's total engagement with the here and now, and how it shamelessly fed off itself. Still, he thought she could use some time away from her work, out with others. Once, in bed, he suggested a book club. Maybe some kind of volunteer work.

'Baby,' she said, 'you seem to be forgetting that I have someone to talk to, and I don't really need anyone else.' She pressed in close, squeezed his wrist. She did that every now and then, without comment. Did she think he couldn't tell that she was checking his pulse? Like her sniff test, when she inhaled deeply while kissing his cheek, these were little tests she ran to check . . . what? If he was actually there at all?

No, he really couldn't imagine that she had had some kind of affair. She was too cautious about entanglements, too resistant to make room for other people's stories in her own narrative. She had allowed him in, and had made space for the plot point of a child – their child – on their arc. Though more recently, she seemed to have abandoned it. They hadn't surrendered completely, however. They still enjoyed the occasional erotic outburst. One of those sweaty encounters could have sparked into a tiny flame. But what had happened to snuff it? And why had she said nothing of it?

He couldn't think this through with the shrieks from below. '*Shut the fuck up!*' he yelled.

This only triggered a deafening response. He saw that there

were more now, a gathering at the foot of the billboard. Their rage seemed to infect him as he dug into his pocket for one of the locks and whipped it at the sleepless people below. It struck a man near the collarbone, bringing a new color of anguish into the cacophony.

Biggs pulled another lock from his pocket. I'll kill one of these fuckers and the rest will take off, he thought.

He targeted a man standing a bit taller than the others and fastballed the lock in his direction. The lock somehow managed to miss everyone below and clattered against the pavement. 'Shit,' Biggs said.

He had one more lock and, sighting up his target, let it fly. The lock struck the man in the face, but he did not go down. He howled, hands over his face, slamming into those around him. But soon he resumed screaming up at Biggs from behind a badly broken nose. Biggs dug in his pocket again and extracted the only remaining item. He sat and studied the prescription label on the tubelike bottle. He recognized the address of the pharmacy, since it was only one number off from the address of their first apartment.

The idea did not come to him immediately. It crept up, over a couple of sleepless days and nights trapped on the billboard. It was like a pill, rather than a pea, felt through a stack of mattresses. A vague discomfort at first, and then like a jagged boulder pressing at his spine. He used every trick he had acquired to stay awake – pulling out his hair, slapping himself, twisting his flesh. He could trigger a surge of adrenaline by leaning far out over the edge of the catwalk, tipping slowly forward until he caught himself.

If he were to fall asleep here, in full view of the cluster of insomniacs below, he feared it would only reset their single-minded determination to tear him apart. Though some had wandered off, the two men and the kids who had originally seen him would not abandon rage. They pissed and shit where they stood, hoarsely screaming up at him. They would not forget. They knew he had sleep inside him. They wanted to pull it from him and smear it over the pavement with their own waste.

A day passed, then a cold night, morning drizzle. His pursuers remained below, focused on his every move, and the idea grew in persistence. The next afternoon was blazingly hot. There was nowhere to hide on the platform. The shadows of the palm trees on the beach behind him offered no relief from the sun, nor did the flat field of blue dots that read as water below. He took no comfort from the tagline that had once won his firm a much-needed account. He could see his arms reddening from sunburn, and the heat made him lightheaded. Or maybe it was the lack of food and water. Other than a peppermint that he found deep in a thigh pocket, he had nothing to eat or drink.

As this standoff wore on, his mind increasingly wandered. He found himself attempting to recall the conflicts in front of the clinic next door. The lines of protesters who had sometimes locked wrists and blocked the entrance, who were righteous and defiant during their arrest and carted off in the police van. The women attempting to pass through were from every walk of life, every age and race. Sometimes boyfriends or husbands or fathers would be at their side, or out in front, pushing their way through like linebackers. But most of the time the women were alone or with other women. He tried to imagine Carolyn arriving by herself. Maybe there were no protesters, or maybe just that one woman, the one who showed up with a sign and did a single pass on the sidewalk. She and Carolyn exchanging a knowing look. Carolyn stepping past her as the woman lowered her sign. But why? What excuse did she have? What hardship? Wasn't it all that she had wanted? Wasn't it she who had once said she could never do it? That she didn't blame or judge those who did, because she did not know their story, their reality, but she, within hers, would never do it. He recalled then, with startling clarity, one comment of hers, made late in the night – almost an utterance from her dreams. As always, he had been sleeping at her side as the machinery of her mind churned into the night. She must have nudged him before speaking. He surfaced long enough to take in the line like a gulp of consciousness. She said, 'What could maybe be unbearable is knowing that something was dreaming inside you.'

He waited another day, staring out over the endless echo of rooftops as his thoughts darkened and despair settled in. The mountains beyond like gnarled and kinked muscle. He ignored the ragged people below waiting to kill him. He had tuned them out as his grasp of the world became increasingly loose. The dark blur in the corner of his eye remained, he realized. It was Carolyn, hiding there. 'Come out,' he urged her. 'You owe me an explanation. We need to talk.' But it was only the tip of a black shroud that blew inward. It wrapped around his mind and soaked up his memories. It weighed down his head so that his chin cut into his chest. He saw that there was no way out of this. The idea, reinforced by the decimated world around him, by the fad of extinction and the sheer unpopularity of carrying on, filled the few hopeful spaces inside him with a dense blackness. When it came to erasing herself from her worlds, she had always embraced the tedium of it. There was something of duty in her resigned approach to removal. He suddenly understood that now.

An hour before sunrise on his third night, his body wilted and his mind scrambled, he ate all the pills in the bottle.

*   *   *

Later he would tell them, 'I had taken the pills and I was just waiting, lying faceup on the billboard landing. I could hear them below, screaming up at me. There was no other way out. I thought I saw a bird land on the top of the billboard, but when the shape of it dropped down over me I saw that it was her. I said, I'm almost there, and she said, You can't. She turned me on my side and put her fingers in my throat. They tasted like clay. Everything inside me came up, except the dreams yet to be dreamed. The pills fell in clots through the metal grille. She positioned me, curling me up, my face staring at the beach scene on the billboard. Then she seemed to drop away, and one by one I heard the shrieking from the sleepless people go silent.'

Because he was the dreamer, they did not know if what he was telling them was a dream or not.

When they asked, Dr Lee would say, 'It doesn't matter.'

Sixteen

She wasn't sleeping, though it must have been past midnight. This was unlike her. Lila was a sleeper – a natural sleeper.

Don't freak out, she told herself. I mean, being up this late isn't the usual, but it's probably just because today wasn't the usual.

Today she had met another sleeper, the first she had encountered in weeks. A pretty college girl with cropped hair: Felicia, now sleeping at her feet in the dark room. From where she sat in her owl mask, Lila could see the moon through the high window, floating beyond the branches of an olive tree. It was just a sickle of light, hanging in the sky among a wild spray of stars. All that cosmic luminance, traveling for millions of years, amounted to nothing more than a pale patch on the carpet.

Lila clicked on the flashlight they had found earlier and studied her new companion, who was lying on her back, hands lightly clasped over her flat stomach, ankles crossed. She had conked out exactly at ten o'clock, just like she promised she would. It wasn't natural the way it happened, Lila had observed. There was no drifting off, no yawning or heavy eyelids slowly drooping. One minute she was lying on the mattress watching Lila rub her feet together, and the next she was asleep. Like a thing switched off. Eyes closed, mouth slightly open, looking even prettier than when she was awake.

'You won't be able to wake me once I'm out,' Felicia had told her. She explained how the implant worked as they ate their power bars and night filled the room, wind gusting outside. She described how she would stay like that no matter what, even if the house was burning down or someone was slapping her face with a dead fish, until exactly seven o'clock in the morning, when she would wake all of a sudden and maybe jump up, gasping as if she had been held under water.

'Sometimes it's like that,' she had told Lila. 'Just warning you.'

Lila couldn't help trying to wake her, to see if all this was true. First she tickled Felicia's feet. Nothing happened and it was kind of creepy, like tickling a dead person. So Lila stepped up her efforts and pinched Felicia on her bare thigh. When there was no response, Lila remembered that the best place to pinch someone is on the back of the arms, especially toward the top. That's where that total idiot Dylan used to pinch her during class, so that she would scream right in the middle of a quiz. But it did nothing for Felicia, who remained firmly unconscious.

Lila picked up her arm, lifting it high, then dropped it, and the arm actually bounced on the mattress: boing boing. She did it again, then picked up Felicia's hand and cradled it in hers. It was warm and clean. They had both washed up before bed. Lila studied it under her light. It was the cleanest hand Lila had seen in a long time. No dirt under the nails and such soft palms. Her lifeline was long. When Lila curled it up into a fist to produce love lines, she could see that Felicia would have one true love.

Lila opened Felicia's hand and lightly tickled the palm, watching Felicia's smooth eyelids for any sign. 'Tickle tickle tickle,' she said softly. Nothing.

She held the hand in her lap and suddenly very strongly wanted to feel it against her face, but to do that she would have to take off her mask. This gave her pause. She had been wearing the owl's head for almost a month now, only removing it when she was alone, maybe when sleeping in the dark tunnels of the flood control channels, but sometimes keeping it on even then, thinking there could be rats that would try to nest in her hair or eat her tongue.

She slowly lifted the mask off her head, vowing not to fall asleep before putting it back on, just in case. It was always hot in the mask and feeling cooler air on her face was one of Lila's few remaining pleasures. It was like standing by the doors of a mall in the desert. With the mask on the floor at her side, she combed the sweat-damp hair off her forehead, tucking her long bangs behind her ears. The wound on her scalp had mostly healed but she now avoided touching the area out of habit.

She scooped up Felicia's hand as if it were a small pet, a kitten maybe, and brought it to her face. She put her cheek against the back of it, then turned it over and rested her chin in the warm palm. This, the light touch of another, caused a wave of warmth inside. Her throat tightened with emotion. Lila buried her face in the open palm, inhaling deeply, and closed her eyes as she moved the hand against her cheek, then bowed her head as she used it to stroke her hair. She felt it as a caress even though she was acting as the gesture's puppeteer. She performed a tenderness that she had assumed no longer existed in the world. Her chin quivered and her eyes stung so she squeezed them tightly shut. 'No tears now,' she told herself.

She brought Felicia's hand to her lips and kissed, pressing hard. The last person to kiss her had been her mother, desperately begging for Lila's forgiveness. Both of them a mess, their tears mixed together as her mother covered her face with kisses. The memory stabbed at Lila, triggering charged images: her mother and father chaining themselves to the piano, her father grabbing for her under the car, spitting threats. She pressed her lips harder into Felicia's hand and tried to think back to earlier times, when they had no clue about what was coming.

The memories scrolled before her eyes. Lying in the backseat of the car as they traveled into the mountains, the sun signaling to her through the trees. The three of them in bed on Saturday morning, listening to her father's stories about all the weird stuff he saw during his residency – the man who thought his own hand wanted to kill him; the boy who couldn't feel pain. Now, sitting in the darkness, she imitated the way her mother whispered at cats. She listened, hoping to hear her mother playing the piano downstairs or her father singing in the shower. In the morning, they would go to the coffee place in the bookstore, where they would read entire books and she would steal sips of espresso and chai lattes from her dad's blue cup and gnaw on biscotti. They would have lunch in the diner, playing old songs on the jukebox.

These scenes had the power to both comfort and sadden her. It all depended on her state of mind. At the moment she was feeling hopeful, so the memories brightened her. Felicia, appearing out of nowhere, had brought that hope. Felicia could sleep, more or less, and there were others who could do it too. There was some kind of hospital – a center, she called it – where they lived at a university overlooking the ocean. All of them with implants that put them to sleep at night and woke them in the mornings.

Felicia had promised to take her there.

As soon as she found her own parents she could take them to the center, too. That was Felicia's goal.

Lila looked at her new companion with pity. Even though she was probably five years younger than Felicia, she felt smarter about what was out here in these dark, hollow houses. Felicia, she knew, would only find bad things in her parents' home or nothing at all. Her own home was waiting in the desert with horrors inside. She would never go there, never open that door again. But sometimes, when her mood was darkened by hunger and fear, she couldn't help imagining it. They would be in bed, she believed. Her mother and her father. They would look like they were sleeping – sleeping! But they wouldn't be jolting to life at seven in the morning or any hour to come. They had fixed themselves forever.

She curled up against Felicia and hugged her warm body. She told her, 'It'll be okay. I mean, look at me. I'm fine. It hasn't stopped me and it won't stop you, I can tell. Everyone is an orphan now.'

As she reached around Felicia to pull her even closer, she felt something hard near Felicia's armpit. The hint of machine. She drew back. Slowly her hand returned to the spot. She pressed at the area, determining that the thing there – like a battery cover on a toy animal – was about two inches in diameter. She wanted to see it but didn't think she should. It would mean opening Felicia's shirt.

Fifteen minutes ticked by as they lay side by side in the dark, Lila's curiosity growing. It's not a big deal, she decided. They were practically family, even though they had only known each other for a day – sisters in sleep.

She sat up abruptly, aiming the light as she undid the buttons and peeled back Felicia's shirt. Then she moved to Felicia's other side. She aimed the light at the place where the pulse generator sat under Felicia's skin. There was nothing much to see. Just a raised area, as though a disk had been slid under there. She reached out and felt it, her fingers circling the ridge along the device's edge. Then she pressed her palm over it. She was sure she felt a very faint vibration, an almost feathery buzz.

She returned Felicia's body to its original pose and retreated to her own mattress by the wall. She studied the scene, shining the light around the room. Everything looked right except for the giant owl head sitting on the ground, eyes staring back at her. Eyes always open. She crawled to the edge of her mattress and leaned over Felicia's legs to grab it. Like a deep-sea diver suiting up for a submersion, she lowered the mask over her head. The mesh texture of the eyeholes came down between her and the world, breaking it up into a mosaic of tiles.

She snapped off the light and lay back, the smell of her own sweat and mildew crowding in as she looked on, waiting for sleep.

She was tired. But sleep stayed away.

An hour later, her mind churned inside the globe of fake feathers, trying to understand why she was still awake. When she shut her eyes, she saw a rapid pulsing against her eyelids. A dizzying strobe that beat faster than her heart and seemed to be fueled by some incessant whirring, like the blades of a fan spinning before a shaft of sunlight. She found it more comfortable to keep her eyes open. She watched the moon sail slowly across the frame of window and began marking off its progress against the rooftops of neighboring houses. The olive tree branches wavered in the wind that had arrived from the high desert – a Santa Ana. She sighted up the thin trunk, declaring it the finish line. By the time the moon crosses it, I'll be deep asleep.

When it did, and she was still staring into the darkness, she moved on to the next landmark: a darkened lamppost.

She tried to put herself in a receptive state, tamping down her worries by telling herself that she was just excited. She had been found, rescued! That's what has gotten her so hyper. Just quiet down inside and it will happen like it always happens. A drowsiness creeping in, then flashes of images, little scenes that are like bursts of speed down a runway, trying to lift off the ground. Just let that happen. Think about something on purpose until the thinking continues on its own. She thought about flying a kite.

Hey, she realized, it's working. I'm not thinking about sleep.

Then, of course, she was.

Daring a glance out the window, she could see that the moon had passed the lamppost. Oh, man. This isn't good.

She sat up and felt the first jolt of panic, a terror freeze. Why? Why would it happen now? It wasn't because she had broken her routine or abandoned a good sleeping place. This was the most comfortable setting she had chosen for sleep in weeks. It was a bedroom, after all. A place for sleeping. So much better for slumber than the drainage tunnel, webbed in with trip wires. She was actually lying on a mattress, not cardboard or a pile of dead people's clothes. So what was the problem?

Maybe it was the power bars. Some of them were energy bars. Or maybe it was just eating so much. Usually she was hungry at night. Maybe her body just wasn't used to *not* feeling hungry. Maybe it was that, or maybe it was the mattress, since she wasn't used to such a soft place to sleep, but maybe it was the power bars. Who knows what they put in them to give you energy. She recalled her mother saying, as they first started hearing about the crisis, that it was all those energy drinks and energy bars and energy pills people were taking. 'Everyone is so goddamn energized,' she had said, and they all laughed, because no one thought that everything would happen the way it did.

She lay awake trying to control her thinking, focusing on her surroundings as she searched for a clue, still certain that sleep would eventually come. She thought, Maybe I should try to make myself throw up those power bars. But maybe it was too late, and maybe it wasn't them anyway. Maybe it was the air in the room. It was pretty stuffy. She was hot in the mask, so maybe she should take it off. But it would be strange at this point not to sleep with the mask on. She had gotten so used to it. Maybe it was the season changing, from summer to fall. Maybe it was the air in the room. Maybe it was the excitement about finding Felicia. Maybe it was just having a new friend. A friend, period. Someone like a sister. Maybe I'm asleep now, she thought.

She heard the tinkling of a wind chime.

Not the one she had hung on the doorknob as an alarm, but farther away, turning in the wind. A clear, sparkling sound. Metal chimes, not glass, not bamboo. Lately, she had started collecting them for her bag of noisy things. She sat up, listening to the chimes as they sang out in the darkness, coaxed into raucous arias by sudden gusts.

She needed it, she decided. If they were going to walk out of here, maybe all the way to the coast, they would need all the bells and whistles they could find. Outside, the wind was building in strength, pushing against the house, causing it to creak. The shingles clattered on the roof. She heard the chimes again. They sounded close, but the wind was playing tricks with distance. It carried the sound forward, then drew it back. The chimes were in the neighborhood, she was certain. She would just go grab them and come right back. Maybe getting out, getting some air, would help with the sleeping too.

Minutes later, she was picking through the elaborate array of trip wires she had woven across the staircase earlier. The twine, pulled tight and weighted with bells and empty cans, formed an ornamented cat's cradle that even she, with her careful movements and knowledge of the pattern, couldn't negotiate without triggering a rattle of empties. It's not like Felicia would be bothered by it, dead to the world up in the room with the wind shaking the window glass. But that's no reason to tear it down and then have to redo it all when she came back, she figured.

The wind was roaming the neighborhood, shaking the trees and herding the loose trash down the street, pinning papers against fences and garage doors. It came in blasts, tugging at the owl mask on her head. It seemed determined to expose her. She held the mask down with one hand, the other clasping the flashlight. Through the mesh she could see the moon, now much lower in the sky. There were no clouds and the stars blazed. They hung low in the smogless sky. Close enough, Lila thought, to be blown out like birthday candles. This was the wind that had inspired area founders to plant rows of eucalyptus trees along the edge of their citrus groves – windbreaks to protect the crop. This was the wind that had knocked her ailing grandmother down one Christmas as she exited her old Cadillac, unsteady from the chemo, like a kite in her big coat. The wind tried to carry her away.

She studied the dark street for movement without turning on her light. The many For Sale signs swayed and turned in the wind. Storms of litter blew through, making it hard to see. People wandered the streets at all hours now, no longer following the pattern dictated by the sun and the moon and the turning of the earth. Yet other than those objects – trees, bushes, loose debris – animated by the wind, there was no sign of life up and down the street. She moved into it, twisting her entire body left to right in order to see out the mesh openings in the mask. The chimes rang out when the wind rushed through, allowing her to slowly zero in on the sound.

Trash churned around her, sticking to her mask, as the wind led her down the street and through the yards of two back-to-back houses, so that she emerged on the neighboring street. The houses were identical to those on the street she had just left – a mix of single- and two-story ranch-style homes. Steep driveways and two-car garages. Once-landscaped yards now cluttered with junk, the gutters bone dry.

The wind hit a lull so she had to stand in the street and wait, not sure which direction to go. When it picked up again, the chimes rang sharply to her right, like sparks of sound. She went to it and found herself in someone's backyard, staring up at a second floor balcony. She could make out the general shape and movement of the chimes, which had been suspended from the corner. They shivered and danced as the wind rose and fell.

But something dark – two black forms – swayed next to the source of the sound. She heard the creak of the balcony railing as the shapes were slowly turned by the wind. A sweep of the light revealed what she already sensed. Bodies. One, a man. The other appeared to be a large dog. Hanging side by side as the chimes spun and stirred in their faces – producing a sound they must have carried into death as they kicked and jerked from the choke-chain collars that had cinched shut their windpipes.

Lila looked up at them. She had seen many bodies over the last month, but she had yet to become desensitized. The sight of the dead triggered a strange reaction in her: a coppery taste in her mouth. It made her resist swallowing, and the saliva accumulated in her mouth. She had to raise the mask, wiping her mouth with the back of her hand after sloppily spitting. The fear triggered by the sight above her was of the cold and sickly variety, like a large slug boring through her chest. She choked back the nausea produced by its slow undulations.

Still, she wanted those chimes.

She would have to go through the house to get them. The sliding glass door that opened to the patio was closed, but not locked. She slid it open and peered into the dark space. The void held patches of darkness. She clicked on the flashlight and put her hand over it, not wanting to signal her position should anyone be around. Her palm was illuminated, a ring of red flesh, until she pulled her hand away, allowing the light to stab forward and paint the scene.

Furniture piled up, an exercise bike on its side, a birdcage with a dead parrot inside. She noted a path through the clutter and put her hand back over the light. The wind shook the dark shelter around her.

In this way, she moved through the house, slowly navigating the carpeted stairs with flashes of light, passing down the hallway of bedrooms to the door at the end. There she entered the master bedroom, with its narrow balcony.

At the sliding door, she was hit with a blast of air. It blew through the gaping opening with a rumbling fury. The curtains whipped around, snapping at her. She dipped her head and stepped out, leading with the mask like a helmet. A heavy wrought iron table was pinned against the railing. The leashes had been cinched to its legs, so that it served as an anchor. The railing groaned as the wind swung the bodies hanging beyond view. Lila avoided looking down at them. She reached down through the railing on the side of the balcony, feeling the air for the chimes. But she retracted her hand, suddenly overwhelmed by the feeling that someone, or something, would grab hold of it.

The wind blew and the chimes rang below her.

She shook off the thought. Nothing's going to happen! Just grab it and get out of here. Again, she reached through. She pushed into the railing so that the mask pressed up against her face as her hand felt at the air. It fluttered in space as if waving to someone below, until her fingers hooked the line and she was able to bring up the chimes, landing them like a fish pulled from the water. They went silent against the slat floor.

She quickly retraced her steps through the house, chimes held tightly in one hand, flashlight in the other. Once outside, she crouched at the edge of the backyard, again looking for human movement. The wind surged in a massive gust. She heard the snap of tree limbs and the clatter of tiles torn free. Dirt blasted up from the ground, but it was screened by the mesh before her eyes. She stood and walked the length of the side yard, holding the mask down, then passed through the yard of the house to the rear. Toppled trash bins slowed her progress. She made her way to the street, where she studied the row of identical structures, looking for the house where she had left Felicia. She strained to make sense of the scene, which had been sifted by the wind. The FOR SALE signs were no longer standing and the loose debris had been violently rearranged.

But before she could recognize that she was still a street away – having forgotten that she had crossed two streets earlier – she heard another chime. The wind carried the sound to her from down the street. She hesitated. But why not? She still wasn't sleepy. And a night like this, with all this wind, is the best time to gather up more noisy things.

She started down the street. She kicked away papers that the wind attached to her legs and peeled them off her chest – shreds of newspaper, magazines, ads. Boxes were blown along like tumbleweeds. The feeble parkway trees bowed in the face of the explosive gale.

This time the chimes were hanging from a rafter on the front porch of a house that at first glance she believed was the very house with Felicia inside. But she would have noticed the chimes earlier. And the olive tree out front didn't seem tall enough. It wasn't even an olive tree, was it? There was no FOR SALE sign either.

Before she was even able to drag a patio chair under the

chimes and lift them off a nail, she heard another ringing out nearby.

Swimming through swirling currents of trash, she followed the sound as it drew her farther away, deeper into the maze of streets – the suburban labyrinth. She was lured by the wind into one cul-de-sac after another, one development, two, three, away from Felicia and her dreamless sleep, gathering chimes in a kind of midnight harvest.

The wind eventually stripped the mask from her head and rolled it down the street. She chased after it, the chimes she had gathered ringing out like an alarm.

By dawn, when the wind finally died down, she was wandering with her mask in her hands. She had made the decision to fill it with the wind chimes, after the wind made it impossible to keep it on her head with the chimes in her hands. It now served as a soft bucket filled with muted noise, grinding like shards of glass when she hugged it close as she walked on, looking for Felicia. The sun rose over the mountains. Her long shadow stretched out beside her, sliding over the cluttered yards. It was the second time in her entire life she had stayed awake through the night – the first being the night of the car crash, which seemed like a lifetime ago.

How had insomnia worked its way in? In her distressed state, she could only think that it had something to do with Felicia's appearance. More specifically, she kept feeling the faint phantom buzz of the pulse generator against her palm. She never should have touched it, she concluded – her mind already fogging over from lack of sleep, thoughts sticking together in unreasoned clusters. The toxic elements of the epidemic traveled in a vehicle of vibration into her system. And like the sleep directive the pulse carried through the wire in Felicia's neck, the signal had traveled deep into her brain. Only the message had gotten garbled, scrambled, and it was received as *on* instead of *off*.

And now what I've seen happen to everyone will happen to me, she recognized with a shudder. To have dodged it this long was an impossibility – succumbing was inevitable. Yet a part of her had believed she was truly immune. Somehow special. Endowed with a resistance that was possibly the product of her parents. Their blend of genes, their blood. But no.

Oh my god.

She needed to find Felicia, to return to the center with her. She needed one of those implants. It caused all this, but it could fix it too.

The streets were a scrambled mess, a picture of epic disarray. She ran through the cul-de-sacs, the chimes in the mask emitting a metallic crunch with each step. All the houses looked the same. She entered a few, convinced she was in the right place. She began to cry as her fears mounted. With her hands occupied by the mask, she had to wipe her eyes by pressing her face into her shoulder. She tried desperately to remember where Felicia's parents' house might be, but Felicia had said nothing about its location.

Her only option was to walk the streets of the developments, stepping over the fallen tree branches and shattered roof tiles, kicking aside the duff of documents and records expelled from home offices and sifted by the Santa Ana. The sun bore down. She walked past the occasional insomniac down on hands and knees combing through the littered yards – that ceaseless searching. Why fear them now? she thought. Why hide? I'm one of them. Mask or no mask, she was largely ignored as she passed through the abandoned neighborhoods. There was only a germ of relief in this.

In the early afternoon, she found herself at the edge of the neighborhood looking out over an undeveloped expanse. Even the tawny chaparral was now speckled and dotted with wind-blown trash as far as she could see. The scene was divided by a chain-link fence that ran from the foothills down through the entire valley. She made her way to it. The fence ran along the cracked concrete banks of an aqueduct. Peering through, she saw the dark, mossy water slowly passing through the channel. With a flash she remembered the man who had drowned trying to get at her as she floated on the tethered raft. Could this be the same aqueduct that ran past their house in the desert? Her father had said that it ran all the way to the ocean, carrying water from the Sierras to the reservoirs of the L.A. suburbs and inland valleys of farmed land, then onward to the sea.

If she followed it, would she find herself on the beach? And from there, could she find the university where the sleep center was located?

She walked along the fence until she found a gate. It was locked but the gap between the posts was wide enough for her to squeeze through. Only the mask, with its noisy cargo, could not fit. She decided to heave it over the fence, stooping over and swinging it between her legs, then catapulting it upward like a beaked basketball. It cleared the top of the fence, chimes spilling noisily out of it, then came down hard on the steeply sloped concrete bank with an explosion of sound, a chandelier crashing from the sky. The mask rolled to a stop at the bottom of the basin, where there was a bank of flat cement that dropped away abruptly to the wide channel at the bottom. There the water flowed slowly along.

She squeezed through the gap and edged her way down the slope, collecting the loose chimes as she went. They jangled as she scooped them up. The mask was in poor shape. The impact had blown out one of the eyes and a seam in the back had split. She picked it up and held it together so the chimes wouldn't spill out.

Down in the channel, she could see up the endless corridor of concrete to the north, where the mountains loomed – crisp and detailed in the wind-cleared air. To the south, the dark water ran away from her, narrowed by distance into a thin black line slicing through the valley.

Yes, it probably ran all the way to the sea. She could walk along the edge, following it down, all the way to San Diego. Scanning the ridges for the campus Felicia described. They would see her. They would hear her, jangling noisy things with her feet in the cool water. Felicia would be astonished to see her.

But another thought struck her: it could also lead her home, to her parents. It was maybe the first opportunity she had had since the crash that stranded her here to find her way back.

It made no sense to go there. They were gone, she was sure. But something tugged at her – a strong current of emotion pulled her toward home. She could show them that she was the same. That she was just like them now.

Upcurrent, about thirty yards away, she saw the dark maw of a drainage tunnel opening into the steep cement bank that blazed whitely in the sunlight. She angled up the bank, carrying the mask in her arms, and eased into the cool, dark space. It wasn't the first time she had sought refuge in a drainage tunnel. She peered into the impossibly dark hollow as she sat down, her back bending to the curved wall. What she needed was some time to stop and think.

If this was it, if she was now sleepless, the notion of going home pulled at her. That's where she would be reunited. She would wait out the heat, then start the journey.

She propped the mask behind her and lay back, resting her head on its lumpy form. The chimes clinked dully under the weight of her head. She imagined walking up to her house and hearing her mother playing the piano inside. She could hear every note of the music so clearly.

Minutes later, the music echoed on into her dreams. She had once again found her way to sleep.

Seventeen

He told them, 'She once said that no one ever looks up. I remembered that she had shinnied up the skylight pole and onto the roof. I went back to the loft to see if she was there. When I opened the door, I found her sitting at the table, fully restored, with Maria, the lullaby singer, sitting across from her. They were eating baked pigeons and a salad of nests. My wife smiled and nodded toward an empty chair. Sit down, she said. There is enough. I sat and they put food in front of me. I held a bird's body in the palm of my hand and it pulsed like a heart.'

His audience listened with their usual indifference. Distracted. Studying their hands or staring out the window as seagulls floated, held in place by the wind blasting up the bluff from the ocean. Some stared off at an abandoned aircraft carrier, sitting out in the blue expanse. It drifted in the current like a skyscraper on its side. Some looked bored enough to doze off. But of course they couldn't do that. Not until exactly ten at night, when the switch was flipped in their dreamless heads.

After the recital, when the survivors had shuffled off to their chores, he approached Dr Lee. He said, 'I need a car and some guys. I want to check if she's there.'

'It was only a dream,' Lee said.

Biggs laughed. For Lee to say this. He who had built a cathedral to dreams. Lately, Lee was only sometimes Lee.

He told him, 'Once I woke up and her feet were dangling from the ceiling, black with roof tar. I had forgotten all about that.'

'We can't put you or the guys at risk,' Lee said.

'Just give me Morales.'

Lee shook his head. 'The city is a long way away.'

He told them that it wasn't his child. That's why she had expelled it from her body. She had explained everything. She had been attacked by a creature that was half man, half bear. Only, she explained, the bear was the outside half and the man was the inside half. The creature had lured her into an underground laboratory where it was conducting experiments. She watched as it put the dream of a cat into a chicken. The chicken fell forward, dead. Then it put the dream of an eel into a hamster. The outcome was the same for the hamster, though it stood up on its hind legs before dropping. The only way for an animal dream to live inside a human, it explained, was to grow an entire dreaming animal inside a human. The dream needed the animal container as a kind of filter of flesh. The beast held her down and put the animal inside her womb with a few quick thrusts. As soon as she was able, she cast it out, along with its tiny bladder of toxic dreams.

Only Morales, the security muscle, spoke to him at first. Biggs had encountered him one night smoking on the deck and staring out at the dark field of ocean. He was moving past the security man, seeking his own solitude, when Morales spoke without looking at him. 'So, bro, do you take requests? What I'd like to hear,' he said, 'is a seriously nasty sex dream. I'm talking quadruple X. I know you have them. Don't hold out on us, dude.'

Dr Lee approached Biggs in the lunchroom later, standing at his table as Biggs slowly turned pasta on his fork. Lee said, 'I feel like there's too much interpretation happening. Maybe too much crafting.'

'It's impossible not to,' Biggs said. 'I have to speak them, not somehow broadcast them into their minds.'

Lee sat down and Biggs winced as the chair chirped loudly against the concrete. The tabletops were blazing with light coming in through the windows.

'They're just so tightly fitted to your situation,' the researcher said. 'I'm hoping for something more universal, so that they can see something of themselves in them.'

They watched a gull just beyond the window, hanging in the air.

'Could Carolyn really be all that you dream about?'

'Maybe not,' Biggs said. 'But they are the only dreams I remember.'

Lee laid it all out again, patiently explaining the purpose of the recitals. 'You are the dreamer. What we're doing is exposing the community to the texture and fabric of the dream world. Without it they won't stay human for long. We are the only species whose dreams are interchangeable. We can live inside the dreams of others, we can breathe there. That says something about the human family, and the true smoothness of our faces, our odorless souls. You're dreaming for all of us now,' he said. 'You can't get in the way of whatever's coming through.'

So many words. This was not at all like Lee, Biggs thought. I may be dreaming right now.

* * *

Biggs volunteered for a scavenging mission. The task at hand was an equipment and supply run that would take a team outside the compound and into the nearby hospital, which they looted regularly. Most of the residents dreaded the idea of leaving the security of the center. But it was much less dangerous now, since it was rare to encounter the sleepless, yet common to stumble over a body. Other than the security team, no one would volunteer. By stepping forward before Lee followed through on his threat of randomly selecting people, Biggs hoped to win points with Lee and the community.

They passed through the desolate university campus in two vans, skirting the edge of the campus, cutting through vast parking lots, rolling past the International Studies Center, the woolly, unkempt clover playing fields, the abandoned super-computer and boxy student apartment complexes. The elephant-gray dorm towers jutted above the brittle eucalyptus fringe, and the school's famous glass library, like a crystal hive perched on concrete pilings, flashed through the trees. When they took the narrow access road along the base of the structure, they found themselves fording a lumpy moraine of books that seemed to have been deposited by the receding glacial library.

The caravan rode on, arriving at the loading docks for the hospital. They waited in the vans for the security team to check things out. Dr Porter went over the long list of things they were after and distributed surgical masks. He paired them into teams, partnering Biggs with Warren, who had been a graduate student at the lab when the crisis hit. Their assignment was to find paper for EEG printers.

'Paper?' Warren asked through his surgical mask. 'That's it?'

They followed a hand-drawn map that Porter gave them, with a final directive to use their flashlights sparingly. They passed through the lobby and up two dark flights of stairs, their lights probing feebly before them. On the fifth floor they found themselves in the intensive care unit – a series of patient rooms ringing the semicircular cluster of the nurses' station. Sunlight poured in from the skylight but seemed reluctant to venture too far into the rooms.

Biggs said, 'There's probably a supply closet around here.'

'Did you dream that?' the young man asked.

'Don't be a smart-ass,' Biggs said crisply. Then, realizing it was an earnest question, he softened his response. 'I didn't dream it, but it makes sense, right?'

Both of them were avoiding the dark patient rooms, but when they failed to find any surplus of paper, they knew they had to at least check the bedside machines. 'You start at that end, and I'll work toward you,' Biggs suggested.

Warren shuddered, then made his way across the floor. Biggs had managed two rooms, finding neither paper nor bodies, when he heard Warren come up behind him, whispering, 'Pretty sure there's someone in there.'

Biggs could see that Warren was spooked behind the mask. Warren leaned in close and said that he had seen someone moving in one of the patient rooms and thought he heard something. A moan, a whimper. Biggs started cautiously toward it.

'Why don't we just leave?' Warren asked, grabbing his arm.

'Because it could be someone,' Biggs told him.

Warren took this in, then looked up, eyes wide. 'You think maybe it's Felicia?'

'Felicia?' Biggs knew the name, knew the story. She was the student worker who had fled the compound, stealing a car, with a plan to rescue her parents. She was also the first person to volunteer for the implant, he had been told, after the principal investigator, Kitov, died in the operating chair. They all talked about her like some kind of guardian angel, still setting a place for her during meals and taping notes to the door of her room imploring her to come back. He was indebted to her as well. After all, she was the reason he had been found. When Lee had sent out security people to look for her, they found him instead. Warren's hopeful eyes, his desperate assumption, both moved Biggs and revealed possibilities. There was much to consider, but not now.

'Come on,' he whispered. 'Let's check it out. Just stay behind me.'

Warren loosened his grip and fell in behind Biggs as he crossed the floor and slowly pulled back the curtain. He snapped on his light and peered into the room. At first, yes, he thought it was a person, somehow crouched in the corner. The ground was smeared with blood. Viscera flecked the nest of blackened sheets on the bed and the smell of rot cut through his mask. The ape – a chimp, it seemed – snarled, showing long yellow fangs. Before Biggs let the curtain drop, he caught a glimpse of metal ring mounted to the animal's hairless head, posts disappearing into the skull. A crown of empty wire ports. Biggs backed away, pulling Warren, as the animal bounded through the curtain, tearing it off its rings. They retreated to the nurses' station as it fought to throw off the cloying material, then trotted past them and onward, down the corridor, its feet and hands padding against the tiles, crowned head darting left and right, ducking under shafts of light. Trailing handprints of browned blood.

He told them, 'She told me the news over the phone and I drove straight home from somewhere. I brought three roses, one for each of us. When I gave them to her they had changed into orange rinds. She showed me the ultrasound and we were astonished. Something was moving. We went to breathing classes and had regular checkups. Carolyn had morning sickness for the first three months, but no weird cravings. We did another ultrasound and we could see that it was going to be a girl. But another showed that we had a boy on the way. This kept changing every time we looked away then looked back. This person hasn't decided yet, the technician said. Carolyn ballooned and her tiny frame looked absolutely hijacked by this new bulk. Her belly gleamed and sometimes rang like a bell at night from the kicks inside. We had to induce because our doctor was going to be away on a ski trip on our delivery date and Carolyn really wanted her to do the delivery because the doctor had vowed to take special measures. We drove to the hospital without panic. They put us in a delivery room and we listened to Daniel Lanois's first album, the one with "The Maker." She tried to deal with the contractions but after a while it made no sense to go forward without the epidural. They brought in a shaved cat and gave it the epidural. At first the anesthesiologist couldn't find the right spot on the cat's spine. Then it didn't seem to work and I realized I was standing on the thin tube that carried the medicine into the cat. Carolyn started trembling violently and I ran out to get someone. They came in and made some adjustments to the cat and this stopped the trembling. When it was time, the doctor came in and told me to hold Carolyn's left leg. It was just the three of us until the baby emerged and then there were four of us in the room. When I cut the cord it seemed to me that the cord was just a strand of gelatin, incapable of carrying nutrients and waste, or messages of any kind. Yet here was a baby being drawn into Carolyn's arms as if they had already been introduced.'

The move and monitoring of his sleep that followed could not be seen as anything other than a punishment. It was a reprimand from Lee, Biggs believed, for failing to convey the dreams with sufficient purity and verisimilitude – too much plot, too much spin, really. Too much Carolyn. This was what he suspected, in spite of Lee's denials. The plan was to put him in the smart room, which was wired for dream research.

The community of survivors didn't like this idea, but their opposition was not in defense of their dreamer, Biggs. The smart room had been where Felicia lived before she made her rescue attempt. They confronted Lee about the issue at a morning meeting, after Biggs had recited yet another dream about returning home and finding Carolyn alive and well in the loft.

'We all love Felicia,' Lee said, 'and we all want her to return safely. And I'm confident she will. We're still looking for her, as you all know. Whenever we can spare the guys, they go out and they do their best to track her. One of these days, they will bring her back. I really believe that.'

Biggs heard the quiver in Lee's voice, a coating of gloss.

'Will you leave her things there?' Fran asked, voice trembling. 'Because we think it's important that she knows her place is waiting for her.'

Lee nodded reassuringly.

Lee said, 'Her things are in their true place and we wouldn't want to undo that. We just need the equipment that's in that room. There are dreams moving under the dreams we're hearing about, and we need to get down to them. To stay human, yes, but also because there may be answers there, about how we can all return to our natural state.'

They didn't understand the whole point of the dream recitals.

Lee told them, 'There is a constant pressure, a tide of animal energy. It has surged and eroded away the walls we have erected over the millennia by migrating the contents of our dreams into this world. Everything around us, the remnants of our world, was birthed in a dream, brought forth and hardened under the sun: the roads, buildings, the institutions of thought and knowledge, the urgings of the heart, the fuel of desire. Sleep is the bridge over which these fantastic constructions have been passed, piece by piece, particle by particle. You see us from a distance like ants carrying a shiny white brick of future in our thorny mandibles. Sometimes that white speck is a bone from a beast, evidence of their own elaborate infrastructure – the only hard thing about them. We carry it across the bridge too. Now that bridge has been brought down, except for one silken strand. This is what our dreamer provides – a way to carry the contents across.'

'But,' they said, 'every dream is about his wife. It has nothing to do with us.'

'That's how it may seem,' Lee said. 'But believe me, it has held us in place. Without these recitals, you, Warren, would have already grown antlers. You would be trapped inside a coat of fur.

'And, you, Fran, you would have gills and large unblinking eyes on opposite sides of your flattened face.

'And Porter, he would be brooding from under his cobra's hood.'

Morales waited for him to catch up in the corridor. He said, 'You probably thought I was joking about what I said before. But you know what, bro? You don't know what it's like. When your head doesn't work right, when it stops telling you stories. It's like there's just a hole there. You throw stuff in it and nothing comes back. You can even hear that shit hit the bottom. It's just falling forever into nothing. You don't think that will drive a person insane? I got to have something of what I had.'

Biggs heard a waver in his voice and glanced over as they walked. There, under his eye, a shining trail.

Biggs liked Morales. He was the first person from the center that Biggs had encountered. What he desires, Biggs thought, is desire.

They moved him from his bunk in the common room to Felicia's room and shaved his head. From the bed, he could see an arrangement of mementos Felicia had set up on a narrow metal desk in the corner. There was a small stack of books – mostly trade paperback novels, but also psychology and physiology textbooks fringed with sticky notes. Small brass figurines of a pig, an owl, and a squirrel sat inside a tangled ring of necklaces made from amber and polished stones. A small jar filled with tin Mexican milagros. An older couple posed in a small, ornately carved gold frame. No doubt those are her parents. The ones she went to rescue, he concluded.

He had heard some members of their little community refer to Felicia as a dreamer. One note stuck to the door said, Follow that dream. He assumed, as he looked around the smart room, which was still occupied by her possessions, that they meant it figuratively. That it was her nature to have aspirations, that she wouldn't simply settle for the circumstances she had been given.

She was pretty, he noted, studying the pictures she had stuck to her mirror. They revealed her dark Latin looks – smooth hood of black hair, red mouth, proud nose. Her bright smile and shining eyes, a kindness there, something hopeful. He was happy to study it, though his own dour image, which loomed behind her snapshots, kept distracting him. How white his exposed scalp looked. How he, without hair, seemed to have aged. He had lost nearly forty pounds when he was on the streets, and though he shoveled as much lunchroom pasta into his system as possible, he had only gained back about ten.

A skeleton is looking back at me. A dreaming skeleton.

*   *   *

There was a hood of sensors that he was to wear at night. It would measure his brain activity and, immediately after a dream ended, ring the phone at his bedside. He would wake, the dream still fresh in his mind, and write it down.

'It's like the poet who held a spoon in his hand as he drifted off,' Porter said as Warren, a tech, fitted him with the hood. 'When the spoon dropped, the sound of it ringing against the floor would wake him and he would write what he had seen.'

Biggs rubbed at the stubble on his head, felt at the hardness of his skull.

When he was alone with Lee, he asked, 'Am I a prisoner?'

'The opposite. But I can't let you go,' Lee said. 'You are an amazing gift to all of us. It would be wrong to put you in danger.'

'Don't you think going back and seeing what there is to see will bring closure? Don't you think it could clear the way for different subjects?'

'Yes, I've thought about that. I know that's what you are seeking. Matt, along those lines, I've been doing some research and I found this.'

He handed Biggs a piece of paper, a page torn from a medical journal. Biggs quickly read the description of a *delayed miscarriage* – when the fetus dies of natural causes in the womb during early stages of pregnancy. When this happens, the clipping told him, the *products of conception* must be either surgically or medically removed. Both can result in complications that cause prolonged pain and bleeding.

Biggs looked up at Dr Lee, not sure what to make of the information.

'Didn't you say she titled the film you found *Missed*?'

'Yes,' he said. 'The file anyway. I'm still not following.'

'Well, another name for a delayed miscarriage is "missed." A *missed* miscarriage.'

Biggs sat with this information.

'I don't think she did it,' Lee said. 'You see where I'm going with this, right?'

Biggs said nothing.

Lee stood. At the door, he turned back.

'Tell you what. I'll send out Morales,' he said.

He told them, 'We drove up the coast, right on the beach. On the hard sand at the edge of the water. Morales knew the streets of the city. He got us there. We went up the stairwell and kicked open the door. A cold wind pushed through. We were standing on a meadow that spread out on the top of a mountain. There were purple flowers and giant rocks jutting out of the grass. A figure stood in the distance. I called out to it, called her name. The figure was either wearing a cape or had wings. We moved toward it but couldn't close the distance. We started running but then tumbled into a hole with steep sides. We couldn't climb out. We could only shout for help and watch the sky cloud over. There was nowhere to go but into the walls of dirt.'

He told Morales, 'The room was pitch black. The couple – the man and the woman there – had no sense of time or space. They had passed through sleep into a nothingness that formed along the shape of their bodies. There was only their bodies. He felt the heat of her skin, smelled her hair, the sweet sweat of sleep. Her mouth was a soft wet circle of heat that moved over his skin.'

He couldn't continue.

A long silence passed.

Morales said, 'Bro, it's cool.' Morales squeezed his shoulder. 'It's all right, seriously. I'll take you.'

* * *

They drove up the coast on the glassy sand, but not for long. Cliffs rising out of the water stood in their way. The waves beat against them and fell away defeated, reduced to a wash of foam. They turned inland. Morales drove along an estuary, flushing a flock of snowy egrets, and onto the highway, where they began their negotiations with an array of obstructions, including bodies from overpasses.

'Lee will have my fucking balls when we get back,' Morales said.

'Maybe. But maybe this will be good for everyone.'

'I'm telling you now to not get your hopes up, my friend. The only thing out here is bad news.'

He looked at Biggs. It was clear that he wanted to say something.

'What?'

'These search missions he sends me on? They're bogus.'

'What do you mean?'

'I mean that we aren't looking for Felicia anymore. You hear what I'm saying?'

Biggs studied his face. He saw that they had found her.

'You don't want to know,' Morales said.

He drove on but after a few miles, he said, 'Someone went after the implant, dug it right out of her head. Tried to pound it into his own skull with a rock. Bashed his fucking brains out. We think it was her boyfriend.'

'How long ago was this?'

'That we found her? Weeks ago, bro. Like right after we found you. Lee's just pretending that she could still be alive. He says he's doing it for them, but I think he's doing it for himself.'

They had to stop once for Morales's three-hour sleep shift. Like all security team members, his schedule was split into shorter shifts that overlapped with the other men's. Biggs stood under a tree, waiting for downtime to end. With his eyes he followed a column of ants up the trunk, then squinted at the sun pouring through the leaves. In the distance, he saw a billboard and recalled how he woke to find himself alive, the front of his shirt soaked with vomit and the pattern of the floor grille pressed into his cheek. He remembered how, in his confusion, he thought she had been there with him. And how the ground below was littered with bodies. Like the man who cornered him in the cage, they must have ruptured with rage at seeing him unconscious.

His sleep, he noted, could kill.

After exactly three hours had passed, Morales woke with a start. Biggs watched as he looked around, then beeped the horn.

It took the entire day to reach the shattered drugstore, the small park where he had once stolen naps in the shrubbery. The building stood where he had left it.

He climbed the stairs, Morales right there behind him.

He pushed open the door.

It was like visiting home in a dream. This is because, Biggs thought, I had decided to die. I had tried to die but I lived. Everything from before should be gone, but it's here.

Here was their bed, their clothing hanging in the closets. Their books lined the shelves, a wall of stories receding into the past. He studied their pictures on the wall looking for discrepancies, changes. The great expanse between himself and his memories confused him. There was something more than time in the way. This may be me protecting myself, he thought. I wish I wouldn't do that. Just break if you're going to break.

'No one's here,' Morales said. He turned to see that Morales was holding one of Carolyn's stop-motion puppets. He had checked the studio.

'How can we get up there?' Biggs asked, pointing up to the skylight, which indeed was open. Had they left it that way? The hook pole hung down. It wouldn't support either of them, even if they were nimble enough to climb it.

They brought a stepladder out from the studio and put it on the dining table, which they pulled under the opening in the ceiling. Biggs went up, pushing the bubble window wide and pulling himself through. The sun was going down, but the heat still rose from the tar. He sat in the opening as she once had, his feet dangling. Below him, Morales waited for him to report what he was seeing, but he said nothing.

There were her footprints in the dust. There was no way to know if they had been pressed there a year ago, when she first went up, or recently – if that is, in fact, how she had found her way out. He put his hand in one of the prints, aligned his fingers with her toes. His palm came away blackened by dust. He slowly stood and took in the surroundings – the elevator housing, vents, and stovepipes. A low brick wall crowned the roof. He looked beyond it, holding his hand against the low sun, and scanned buildings, the city flaring with sunlight and, far away, the low ridge of the hills to the west.

The footprints marked a path along the circumference of the rooftop. She had walked along the edge numerous times, the footprints overlapping and obscuring the form of her feet. He walked alongside the prints and, feeling very certain that he was being watched, glanced back at the skylight opening, expecting to see Morales's head jutting through. But no, he was still below.

At the far end of the roof, there was a shed. Yes, she had investigated it herself. Her footprints disappeared into the doorway. Biggs approached it and peered in, dreading what he might find there. Stacked against the walls were buckets of tar, rolls of tarpaper. The shed's roof angled upward and beams formed a narrow shelf. He was startled to see a large owl there looking down at him. Its eyes gleamed as it calmly observed him, saw all of him, he felt, every vision that had passed through his head. For a moment he braced himself, expecting the bird to fly at his head. But instead it leapt over him and, with two silent wing beats, drifted over the side of the building. Biggs accepted an unspoken invitation. He stood on a bucket and saw the eggs there, sitting among the loose twigs and dried bits of fur and bone.

By the time he returned to the loft, Morales was eating the food they had brought along from the center – pasta sandwiches and raw squash from the graduate housing gardens. He helped him down from the ladder and put a sandwich in his hand.

Biggs wondered if Morales had heard his ragged sobs, the primal groan. If he had, he would probably be under the assumption that Biggs had found Carolyn, or all that remained of her. But the outpouring Biggs had finally felt, as if the membrane holding back a flood of anguish had finally given way, didn't require evidence that Carolyn was gone. He suddenly felt it.

Morales didn't ask what Biggs had found, or not found. Instead, he said, 'You've told us so much about her, you know, the dreams of her. But I got to admit that I wasn't sure she was real.' He nodded at a framed picture – the wedding picture of Biggs holding Carolyn over the water as he stood in the lake. 'Hey, now I kind of feel like I'm standing in one of your dreams.'

'This place is everywhere she should be but isn't,' Biggs said, looking around.

'She moved,' Morales said, chewing thoughtfully. 'She's got a new place inside you now. Must be even more crowded than here. Dude, I had closets bigger than this place. I bet you paid a fortune for it too, right? City suckers.'

Biggs knew his face was blackened with dust from his hands. It didn't matter, he thought, if he wore that blackness forever.

Morales agreed that it was a good idea to stay the night. Biggs said he would sleep in the studio so Morales could keep watch in the main room, after his three-hour shift on the sofa. 'Maybe I'll read some of these books,' Morales said.

Biggs dragged the mattress into the studio, just as he and Carolyn had done a few years ago. He pulled her black, light-proof curtains over the door and window and found himself in total darkness. The scent of her was still there, in the blankets, on the pillow. Faintly, faintly there. He waited to feel her sniffing at his cheek.

'Is it me?' he would ask.

He fell asleep and dreamed about something else entirely.

Acknowledgements

I offer my gratitude and appreciation to the many people who were helpful in producing this book. I thank my parents for making books part of my childhood, and my brother and sister for a lifetime of support. Thanks to the many friends and fellow writers who read and commented on these pages, notably Laurel Goldman and her Chapel Hill workshop, Steven Gamboa, Ryan Griffith, Mona Awad, David Baeumler, Matt Salesses and the late John Harrelson.

Thanks also to the Millay Colony for the Arts and the Writers' Room of Boston for providing much needed space and time.

I am forever indebted to journal editors who published my stories over the years. I'd especially like to recognize Whitney Pastorek, Andrew Tonkovich, Hal Jaffe, M.T. Anderson, David Milofsky, Adam and Jennifer Pieroni, Libby Hodges, Jeff Parker, Cheston Knapp, Nathaniel Rich and Christopher Cox.

My talented editors, Zachary Wagman and Parisa Ebrahimi, have my deepest respect and appreciation for their smart and soulful suggestions. And I owe the world and more to my agent, Claudia Ballard, who is a remarkably gifted shaper of story and a fearless believer that hard work will be rewarded.

Above all, I dedicate this book in infinite gratitude to Anya Belkina and Sophie Calhoun, who endured my excessive sleep requirements and inspired the plots of my most hopeful dreams.

HOGARTH
LONDON · NEW YORK

In 1917 Virginia and Leonard Woolf started The Hogarth Press from their Richmond home, Hogarth House, armed only with a hand-press and a determination to publish the newest, most inspiring writing. They went on to publish some of the twentieth century's most significant writers, joining forces with Chatto & Windus in 1946.

Inspired by their example, Hogarth is a new home for a new generation of literary talent; an adventurous fiction imprint with an accent on the pleasures of storytelling and a keen awareness of the world. Hogarth is a partnership between Chatto & Windus in the UK and Crown in the US, and our novels are published from London and New York.